Over THE Limit

K. BROMBERG

Praise for

K. BROMBERG

"K. Bromberg always delivers intelligently written, emotionally intense, sensual romance . . ."

—*USA Today*

"K. Bromberg makes you believe in the power of true love."

—#1 *New York Times* bestselling author Audrey Carlan

"Always an absolute must-read."

—*New York Times* bestselling author Helena Hunting

"An irresistibly hot romance that stays with you long after you finish the book."

—#1 *New York Times* bestselling author Jennifer L. Armentrout

"Bromberg is a master at turning up the heat!"

—*New York Times* bestselling author Katy Evans

"Supercharged heat and full of heart. Bromberg aces it from the first page to the last."

—*New York Times* bestselling author Kylie Scott

Also Written by
K. BROMBERG

Driven Series
Driven
Fueled
Crashed
Raced
Aced

Driven Novels
Slow Burn
Sweet Ache
Hard Beat
Down Shift

The Player Duet
The Player
The Catch

Everyday Heroes
Cuffed
Combust
Cockpit
Control (Novella)

Wicked Ways
Resist
Reveal

Standalone
Faking It
Then You Happened
Flirting with 40
UnRaveled (Novella)
Sweet Cheeks
Sweet Rivalry (Novella)
Sweet Regret
What If (Part of Two More Days Anthology)

The Play Hard Series
Hard to Handle
Hard to Hold
Hard to Score
Hard to Lose
Hard to Love

The S.I.N. Series
Last Resort
On One Condition
Final Proposal

The Redemption Series
Until You

The Full Throttle Series
Off the Grid
On the Edge

Holiday Novellas
The Package
The Detour
Forever More

Published by JKB Publishing, LLC
ISBN: 978-1-942832-79-9

Editing by Marion Making Manuscripts
Formatting by Champagne Book Design

Printed in the United States of America

Prologue

Lachlan
Ten Years Ago

"**L**ACHLAN!"

Fuck.

Awesome timing, Dad.

But when I turn to face my dad, there's a smile on my lips, because even though I'd much rather be making out with Olivia—*much rather*—I won't be a dick to my dad.

"Yeah, Dad?"

"You're late."

I glance over my shoulder to where Olivia was. Thank fuck she's no longer there, evidence hidden. "I'm not." I shrug it off and hope to sell the lie. Is fifteen minutes really considered late? In his book, maybe. In mine? I'm on time. "I was just . . ."

"Just what? Being a teenager? Just making out with a girl? Just what, Lach?" He angles his head to the side and gives me that look. The one that says he's calling me on my bullshit. I don't have time for this, which is clear as I sight my crew in the distance, looking our way.

I sigh loudly. "Just yes to all the above," I finally say.

He nods. "The team comes first, mate. *Always.* Your crew. Your team-mates when you get one. Your sponsors."

"Yeah, yeah."

"You want to be nonchalant about it? There are a hundred more drivers qualified to take your spot. Who'd kill to have it. The drivers who fail are the ones who forget that all these people are there for them and the success of the team."

"Got it. I understand."

"Could've fooled me. I raised you better than that. To respect every person out here. Besides, you've worked so hard for this—to finally get where you are. You're so goddamn close you can basically taste it."

"I was just having a little fun. You're making a way bigger deal than there needs to be."

"Are you going to risk throwing it all away for a girl? You can get laid on your own time." He throws a thumb over his shoulder. "Not on theirs."

"Jesus." I cough the word out. It's true. I was copping a feel because Olivia has the best tits *ever*—not like I've felt many yet—but Christ, my dad talking about getting laid? That's the last thing I want to hear.

"What?" He crosses his arms over his chest. "You want to be a man? Be in charge of your own schedule and your responsibilities, then I'll speak to you and treat you like one."

"Dad." I huff.

"No. Let me finish." He shifts on his feet. "As a man, you'll have many choices in life. Ones that will further your career. Ones that will build relationships. Ones that will . . . let's say, satisfy your urges."

Whatever. I roll my eyes.

"Don't worry. I know you know all about the birds and the bees. I'm sure by the color of your cheeks and your undone zipper, that you might have just been learning a bit more."

Oh. My. Fucking. God. There is no way to casually zip up your pants. Not anytime. Especially not right after your dad just called you on it and the reason why he did. Or that he's fucking right on all accounts.

The high from Olivia's hand being down my pants vanishes. Gone like I wish I could be from this conversation.

How the fuck do I not look guilty with my zipper down?

"But what you don't truly fathom, Lach, is the consequences of your actions."

"My team is waiting."

"*Exactly.* Your team is waiting." He lifts his eyebrows. Great. *Judge me.* I meet him stare for stare. *Come on, Dad.* "Just like they've *been* waiting while you chose to flirt, *among other things*, with Olivia, who's no doubt hiding until I leave. I'm sure she's charming and has many favorable attributes but making them wait while you mess around isn't acceptable."

"Can this conversation be over now?" I ask.

He holds a finger up. "Every one of those people in yellow uniforms by your car are here for you. Sure, they're earning an income, but it's a choice they make. A choice to help further your career while choosing to miss time with their families, to overlook things they need to do for themselves, and all to help you realize and chase your dream of making it to the top. Kyle just had a son and he's here with you—*for you*—instead of with his newborn. *You*, Lachlan, will always come first in your racing career, but all those men and women over there, come a close damn second and you need to never forget that."

"I hear you, Dad."

"Your teammate, your crew members, your staff—they are just as important as you. They are your team, and they deserve just as much respect because your talent is nothing without them helping you utilize it."

And the guilt trip is working. I swallow over the lump in my throat. "I know."

"There will be many Olivias in your lifetime, mate, many women to get lost in, but there will only be one Formula 1. And the day you wonder which one comes first, is the day you should probably consider hanging it all up."

I disagree with him. I've seen drivers have wives, have girlfriends, and it doesn't fuck up their game. But I don't argue. I'm in no damn place to do anything other than say, "Yes," because he's right about everything else.

He reaches out and squeezes my shoulder. "Hard work and dedication aren't always fun, but I know the time and work you've put in and how badly you want this. Your mum and I will do everything in our power to support you in this as we always have, but you also have to be the man that people want to support."

"I *do* want it. I *am* that guy," I say as guilt eats at the edges of my resolve. As inconspicuously as I can, I zip up my fly.

"You sure?" He looks at me with an earnestness like never before. He looks at me man-to-man and it makes something constrict in my chest. *This is what I've wanted for as long as I can remember.*

"I am." *Formula 1 is the ultimate goal.*

"Okay." Another squeeze to my shoulder before he pats me on the back. "What have I always said to you?"

I repeat the words I've heard from day one in this hamster wheel. Words I know I'm lucky enough to hear and that are rare in this world of pushy fathers who try to live vicariously through their own sons' successes. "That this is supposed to be fun. That the minute it's not, it's okay to decide to try something else and walk away if I want. That this sport doesn't define who I am. I do."

He nods, a proud smile ghosting his lips. "And I mean that. I always have and I always will."

"I know you do."

But while I can parrot his words, this sport does define me. It has since the first time I got behind the wheel of a kart. Since that first rush of adrenaline as I crossed a finish line and saw that checkered flag. Since that first time I stood at the Australian Grand Prix and felt the rumble in my chest and heard the distinct whine of a Formula 1 engine.

There has never been another option for me.

A driver is who I am.

Making the elite twenty-driver squad in Formula 1 is my goal.

Lachlan Evans. World Champion.

Like always, my dad is right. *This has to be my complete focus.*

I want to win.

I. Will. Win.

I'll accept no other option.

Chapter One

Blair

THE MUSIC BEATS A VICIOUS TEMPO AND A CHEST-VIBRATING BASS. People are everywhere. The doorways. Standing on their tiptoes lining the walls. Twisting their lips as they wait impatiently, trying to move toward the bar area in a surge that seems to happen every ten minutes or so.

They're all hoping what this party advertised to be true—that it's the hangout spot for Formula 1 drivers when the race comes to town. A little promotion before race week swings into full gear. If you were lucky enough to score a ticket, you might just get to rub elbows and perhaps take some pictures for your social media to prove you were "hanging" with them.

And after several hours of sitting here, it's definitely living up to expectations.

An hour commitment was all the evening's sponsor had asked of the drivers. We're on three hours now, and I'm more than over the noise, the chaos of the event, and everything else that comes with it. This girl can only handle so much fake, and it's here in droves tonight.

The old stone mansion where the party is being held is on the outskirts of Barcelona. And when I step outside for some fresh air, I'm surrounded by manicured lawns and extensive landscaping. Gorgeous in the daylight but a tad intimidating in the dark if it weren't for the strings of overhead lights adding a softness that chases most of the shadows away.

I run my hands over the evenly cut hedges and enjoy the smell of the gardenias. I focus on anything and everything around me but feel like I don't actually see it.

"Sick of the chaos too?" a gravelly, Australian accent says through the darkness.

I jump. Maybe even yelp. What I do know is that I put a hand to my heart and bite back the curse that's present on my tongue. "Jesus," I finally say as my pulse pounds in my ears and adrenaline races through my veins.

"Sorry. Didn't mean to scare you."

I take a few more steps and Lachlan Evans comes into view. The shadows carve lines on his face, but it's one I know. The dark head of hair with a slight wave to it. The sun-kissed skin. The light green eyes. The full lips. The pensive stare.

It's a face I've studied numerous times from afar. Curious about what he's thinking, where his intensity comes from, and how exactly he fits in this world when he seems so very different than the other nineteen drivers who inhabit it.

My heart may be decelerating but my nerves are still charged. "Didn't your mother ever teach you not to sneak up on girls?"

"My mum taught me a lot of things about women." He flashes me the grin he's known for. "But it seems as if you were the one sneaking up on me." He points to the set of steps he's currently sitting on. "I was here first."

"Semantics," I mutter through my smile as I rest my ass on the short retaining wall opposite him. In the times I've interacted with him, there's always been something about him that puts me at ease and right now is no different.

We're about thirty feet away from the entrance to the party. Headlights of arriving partygoers sweep over us, as yet another car drops their occupants off. Someone laughs and I turn to look their way, but when I look back, Lachlan's studying gaze hasn't wavered.

"Want one?" he asks and holds out a hard candy, its wrapper making crinkling noises.

"No, thanks." I pause. "Candy from strangers? That's a little cliché, don't you think?" I tease.

"Except I'm not a stranger and what's wrong with peppermint?"

"Peppermint?"

"Yep. Peppermint." He nods unapologetically and pops one in his mouth. Its unmistakable scent immediately permeates the air.

"Nothing's wrong with it . . . I don't think."

He smiles. It's genuine and makes the lines at the corners of his eyes crease and the ridge of his nose scrunch. It makes him look boyish yet surprisingly manly too.

"So, are you?" he asks after a beat.

"Am I what?" I ask. There's a chill to the air, and I'm starting to regret my choice not to bring a jacket.

"Sick of the chaos?"

"Yes. Maybe." I glance back toward him and then something hits me. "*Too*. You asked if I'm sick of the chaos *too*." I narrow my eyes at him. I've yet to meet a Formula 1 driver who shies away from the limelight. "You're telling me you are?"

His nod is slow as he brings the bottle of beer I didn't notice in his hand to his lips. "Perhaps."

I snort. "Oh, c'mon. You guys live for this shit. The screaming fans. The nonstop advances from gorgeous women—*and men*. The cameras following your every move." But the minute the words are out of my mouth, they feel less certain than they sound.

In that moment, I realize that in all my time interacting with Apex Racing—and the drivers in general—he's the least enamored with . . . or maybe even desperate for the attention.

"At times, yes. At others? Not so much."

"And this is one of those times?"

He looks to the left at yet another car arriving and then back to me. His shrug is as ambiguous as his answer. "Mmm."

I immediately want to know what the sound means, but it's not my place to ask, so I settle for a topic that's less intrusive. "Big week ahead."

"Race week is always a big week," he says.

"Do you think the crew has all the . . . issues, kinks, whatever it's called worked out?"

"Kinks?" He lifts a lone eyebrow and fights a smirk as the mint clicks against his teeth. "Is that why you accosted me out here in the moonlight? To talk about kinks?"

"Funny."

He sets his bottle on the concrete step beside him as we let the comment settle between us.

I tilt my head and study Lachlan Evans, Apex Racing's understated teammate. Understated? That's not exactly the right word since he's just as talented as Rossi . . . but he does it with less panache. With more of a quiet confidence, I don't think I've ever really stopped to contemplate until now.

He angles his head to mimic me as we openly study each other through the darkness. Assessing. Wondering.

"The cars?" I ask to interrupt the sudden awkwardness. "Do you think the race engineers—"

"More racing? C'mon, now." He chuckles. "Is that what you really want to talk about?"

"It's my life." I shrug and then backpedal when I realize how ridiculous that sounds talking to a driver. "I mean not like yours or the others, of course, but it creates the avenue for me to do what I do."

"And . . . do you like what you do, Blair Carmichael?" he asks, his voice sounding like honey running over sandpaper. Something about my name on his lips, and the intensity in which he looks at me, has chills chasing up my spine.

I run my hands up and down my opposing arms. "I do. Very much so. I love the sport, the community that has been built around it . . . and using F1 and its popularity to bring happiness to those in the community is very fulfilling."

Community Outreach Ambassador. It's a longwinded title but one that I love and wear with immense pride.

"It is. I can understand that." He purses his lips and nods. "I can imagine, knowing that you've introduced kids to the sport from all walks of life is a pretty cool feeling."

"It is. Especially ones who might not ever have gotten the chance otherwise." I shrug. "Then again, I wouldn't have the chance to if there weren't drivers like you who make the sport attractive."

He laughs. "The sport would be attractive whether I was in it or not. I'm not that much of an egomaniac to think otherwise."

"That's not what I—"

"I'm just teasing you." He pauses a beat when a couple walks between us. "You don't tire of the constant travel or the fact that we're always *on?*"

"My spotlight is vastly different than yours. I have to be *on* so to speak for an event or a quick interview, but other than that, no one pays much mind to who I am."

"Surely you get your fair share of attention? Good, bad, and ugly?"

"When you're a permanent fixture, you become background noise that nobody notices much."

"I think you underestimate yourself," he murmurs in a way that has me crossing my arms over my chest.

It's not delivered as a pickup line like so many other men would. It's more a statement of fact that I assume is said to make me feel better.

Uncertain how to respond, I motion to our surroundings and revisit his original question. "And yet I'm out here right now, aren't I?"

"True. I wasn't sure if that was because of the people inside or the person you came with," he says.

"Maybe all of the above," I admit.

He shrugs. "For the record, if the choice was to be out here with you or in there with *them* . . . the answer's a no-brainer."

"Oh." I blink, his answer surprising me.

"Sorry. That came off wrong." He holds his hands up and chuckles. "It's just . . . sometimes people pick the wrong things to focus on. It's been a running theme as of late between me and my teammate."

"Seems to be a common thread these days," I muse. *Isn't that part of the reason I'm out here right now?*

"You sure you don't want one?" He holds out a mint, the candy again crinkling between his fingers.

"I'm sure. Thank you, though."

He chews the inside of his cheek. "So an American who works in F1. How'd that come about?"

"An army brat who moved a lot throughout Europe from base to base until we ended up on one in Italy. Our house was near a track, and we'd spend weekends there. It was an inexpensive way to have a family outing at the time. It was there that I met the right people at the right time." I shrug. "That type of thing."

"Probably a little bit of luck and some hustle on your part."

"True." I nod, thinking of how hard it was for the once shy version of me to get those introductions to put me on the course of where I am today.

"I lost you for a second. Where'd you go?" he asks.

"Nowhere." My smile is fleeting and bittersweet as I think of so many firsts that were had at that track. "There's just a lot of history there. Behind it. How my life progressed." *How it's still happening.*

"Why'd you say it like that?"

"No reason." I clear my throat and glance back to the entrance and the party still going on inside its doors. "Just history, but one that was well worth it. I love my job."

He studies me for a beat, and I fear he can see way too much. But the curiosity etched in the lines of his face vanishes when he smiles. "It's a damn cool one."

"Says an F1 driver who has the best job in the world." I roll my eyes at how funny his comment sounds but more than appreciative of it. "What about you? You started in karts. Was it always your ambition to be an F1 driver?"

"Isn't it all of ours?" he asks.

"I'd think, but I don't know."

"I'm sure you can google every interview I've ever given on the subject," he says and then lowers his voice and leans toward me. "Or are you after my deep, dark secrets?"

"How did you know that's what I was after? I'm looking for the good gossip," I say, chuckling. I do know some of Lachlan's rise to F1, as I do of all the drivers, but we've never chatted like this. It's fun, and even though I've witnessed his personality from afar, it's so much better up close and personal.

"The good gossip, huh?"

"Yep. Tell me something no one knows about you."

"You mean besides my addiction to peppermint?"

"Yes. Besides that."

"That's a hard one," he muses as he leans back on his elbows, his lips pursed in thought. "I have a vast knowledge of random animal facts."

"What?" I bark out a laugh. That was not what I was expecting.

"Yep," he says with a definitive nod. "I was determined to be a vet when I was growing up, so I learned everything I could about animals. The stranger the fact, the better, because that meant I'd be able to solve even the hardest cases."

"A veterinarian, huh?"

"The Formula 1 thing is just a fallback job."

"Something to fill the time."

"Yep." His smile crawls slowly across his lips. There's a boyish charm to it that I hadn't noticed before tonight. "Just filling time until I get up the courage to chase those dreams of mine."

"If I told you I didn't believe you, would you tell me one of those random facts?"

"You want an animal fact?"

"I do. I want to see how vast this knowledge of yours is."

"Let's see." He furrows his brows as he thinks. "A hummingbird is the only bird who can fly backwards."

I chortle. He really *was* telling the truth. "Okay. Fine. But how is that random fact going to help you save the day?"

His face lights up. "I was a kid. For all I knew, that fact could have saved the world. I'm a work in progress, Blair." He winks. "I only get better with time."

His words settle between us as we stare at each other, our soft smiles remaining in place like we shared the silliest of secrets when we really didn't at all.

"What about you?" he finally asks, breaking the comfortable silence. "What were you going to do to save the world someday?"

The random memory hits me out of nowhere and pulls my smile wider. "I was going to learn to fly."

"As in be a pilot?"

"No, as in me. *Just me.* I was going to learn how to flap my arms and fly like how I could in my dreams." Normally I'd blush at the peculiarity of my confession, but oddly he doesn't make me feel ridiculous.

"You get to fly in your dreams? That's awesome."

"Not anymore. Only when I was a kid . . . hence, that was a wish of mine."

"Okay. That's a solid take. Did you have a destination in mind or . . ." The smile returns, playing at the corners of his mouth. "Or you just wanted to fly around the neighborhood?"

"Hey, don't knock how I planned to save the world."

He holds his hands up. "I'm not knocking shit. Just know if you needed to fly backwards for some reason, I was probably the person who'd be able to figure out how to fix that for you . . . so the way I look at it, this conversation was fate."

Before I can say anything, my phone alerts a text.

Emilio: I'm about to pull up to the entrance.

I see the sweep of headlights just as I finish reading the text. "I—uh—my ride is here," I say and stand up, confused over why I'm not as eager to leave anymore.

I like Lachlan Evans. I mean, I've always liked him—he's pleasant and great with people—but this conversation made me realize he's funny and charming and . . . so much more than the intense driver who shares a team with Rossi.

He rises to his feet. "Let me walk you to the car."

"No. That's not necessary—"

"Humor me," he says and places his hand very briefly on the small of my back to usher me in front of him.

"Thank you but—" I stop and turn around. My unexpected action causes Lachlan to run into me. We're chest to chest.

His cologne.

The peppermint on his breath.

The heat of his solid body against mine.

It's a split second of time before we jolt apart with startled gasps and apologies on our lips.

"I'm making sure you get in safely," he states, his eyes flickering away before moving back to my eyes.

Did that shock him like it did me?

His stoicism is as unreadable as his silence, but he motions for me to keep walking. I take one step backward before turning to move toward the driveway.

It might only take a few seconds to get to the turnaround, but I've never been more aware of someone behind me in my life. The fall of his footsteps. The accidental brush of his arm against mine.

"Ah, it's Emilio," he says as we approach, recognizing one of the Apex crew members in the driver's seat. Lachlan opens the rear passenger door, and then he bends over so they can chat briefly before he steps out of the way for me to get in. We stare at each other for a beat in that small space. His voice lowers. "Thank you for the conversation, Blair."

"Thank you for keeping me company." I nod and then slide into the passenger seat.

He holds out a peppermint candy. "A small token of appreciation for your time. To remember me by." He winks and I roll my eyes.

How on earth is this man still single?

"As if I could forget the backward-flying hummingbird." I smile and take it. Just before he shuts the door, I say, "Lachlan?"

"Hmm?"

"To see the northern lights dance across the sky."

His eyes narrow. "What?"

"Where I wanted to fly," I say and then shut the door. It's the strangest thing. I haven't thought about that in years. *Why now? What made me think of that now?*

Our eyes meet through the closed window, a ghost of a smile on his face as he nods.

"You good, Blair?" Emilio asks from the front seat, my eyes still on Lachlan's.

"I am. Thank you for picking me up."

"Not a problem at all," he says as he puts the car in gear and pulls away from the curb.

I know Lachlan Evans.

Everyone does. I've seen him in the garage—it's hard not to when we literally travel to the same cities month after month during the season—and I've interacted with him for work. We *know* each other but don't *know* each other.

Yet as we drive away, I find myself looking back at the shadowy figure in the night, standing there, staring after the car.

And I think about him, hummingbirds, crinkly peppermints, and northern lights long after I should.

There's something about Lachlan that struck me differently tonight—his unabashed honesty. *His quiet charm.* His subtle humor. How strange that we've never really chatted before.

I focus on his shadow until it blends as one with the night.

Although, I guess the fact that I've been dating his teammate could be the reason for that.

Chapter Two

Lachlan

"**Y**OU WANT TO EXPLAIN WHY YOU'RE THRASHING AROUND HERE like a bull in a china cabinet?" I ask, not bothering to even glance at Rossi where he keeps picking up shit and then tossing it back down unceremoniously.

This is my garage, not his. My space, not his.

And yet in clear Rossi fashion, he's making it his. By his continuous sighs and gravelly grumbles, he's clearly in need of attention. Or a sounding board. Or possibly even a punching bag.

All of which I don't care to be right now.

It's fucking annoying. Especially when I'm trying to run every damn inch of the track through my head. Where to let up, when to brake, which stretch I can accelerate, and what chicanes will be the most cumbersome.

And the person with whom I'm currently vying for my job—my greatest distraction.

"I'm not," Rossi mutters.

"You are."

"I have every right to be."

Ah, yes. There's the Rossi I expect. All about him. All the time.

I turn to look at my teammate. He's staring at me behind dark sunglasses and the brim of a baseball hat with a scowl on his lips. His race suit is unzipped and tied at the waist, and his black Nomex shirt is pulled up at the sleeves much like mine. He's wearing his *fuck this* attitude in his posture.

"And why's that?" I ask as I lean back in my chair, mental practice session clearly over, while we kill time before our Team Apex meeting.

"In case you hadn't noticed during testing today or fuck—our last half dozen races—we're having power issues. My fucking car has no guts to it. Yours can't keep up like it should. In every damn race, we're not where we should be, and I'm getting pretty sick of it."

"That's racing," I say, not wanting to fuel his fire, even though he has a valid fucking point. One I've talked privately with my crew and our team principal about.

"That's racing?" he scoffs and tucks his sunglasses in the collar of his shirt without looking around to see who might overhear him and his harsh words for our team.

"You can't tell me you're not worried about it. They've already filled one of our seats for next season. So that means we're fighting for the other spot with a contract renewal. If we can't race, then we don't place . . . if we don't place, then—"

"Then educated people in the sport understand *the why* behind it. That we can only do what we can do with a subpar car."

"You mean a *shit* car."

"It doesn't diminish our skill, though."

"It does and it has. We are not a fourth-place team, Evans, and yet that's where we're fucking sitting, and if we're not careful, we'll be sixth or seventh in the next two races."

"I have faith in the team. The engineers. They'll figure the problem out," I say, knowing I've had my own doubts during the past few months over whether they'll be able to figure shit out and stop the bleeding.

"If we're not careful, this team is going to fall to shit, and then we'll both end up groveling for that open seat at Gravitas when that's the last fucking place I want to end up."

"What's so wrong with Gravitas?" I ask of a rival team. One that is typically beneath us on the Constructors' ranking. Moving there is like a step down and yet . . . the sun shines on a dog's arse some days.

His Adam's apple bobs. "There's history there. And Apex is better. Has always been better. *Needs* to be fucking better."

"I'm sure the crew will get everything sorted."

"Do you ever have anything negative to say? Ever?" Rossi gripes like a child.

"All the time. Except only about things I can change. It's no use bitching about things other people know way more about," I say as Rossi picks up one of my gloves and then throws it back down on the console in front of him.

His groan fills the small space.

Fuck. This is when I wished he cared more about whether he had more friends on the grid.

"You want to tell me what's really bugging you?" I ask, because it has to be more than just this. Both of us will land somewhere. One here at Apex. One somewhere else.

The options are dwindling though, so a good season is needed for both of us. A good season that neither of us is getting.

"Nothing. Everything. *Fuck.*" He sighs the last word out, and a part of me doesn't even want to ask what that means. I have a feeling I know.

The man's not one for small talk, but those three words pretty much sum up every guy's feeling when it comes to women.

"Sounds about right." I go for the noncommittal answer.

"She's pissed at me."

"Probably has good reason to be," I say, not wanting specifics, but I know who he's talking about. Admittedly, a small, petty part of me wants to know why.

"It's not like I care. I mean, she'll get over it."

"Or she won't," I deadpan. *And you should care.*

He stops and puts his hands on his hips and just glares at me. "What's that supposed to mean?"

"It means *how bad did you fuck up?*"

The muscle in his jaw pulses as I glance over his shoulder at our team beginning to congregate out front of the garage area. It has to be getting close to meeting time.

"I don't fuck up, Evans." He chuckles and shrugs. "And even if I did, she always comes back. I'm always fucking golden when it comes to her."

I bristle. "We are talking about Blair, right?"

There's the slightest pause in his response that has my irritation firing. We better be fucking talking about Blair because while Rossi is Rossi—a player, a guy who talks a good game, a man you don't want on your bad side—I didn't take him to be a cheater. Then again . . . he *is* Rossi. Far from an angel.

His smirk is as sarcastic as his tone. "What do you think?"

"That sounds fucking convincing." I snort. He doesn't deserve her.

What the hell are you talking about? You barely even know her.

And yet the woman has been living rent-free in my head since our talk of hummingbirds and the northern lights. Nothing happened. Not a fucking thing, but hell if I can't forget her shy smile, the hint of her perfume, the feel of her body pressed briefly against mine, the sway of her hips, or her perfectly kissable lips.

"What the fuck ever. I don't need your approval for what I do or don't do. Just like I don't need hers." He lifts his hat and runs a hand through his hair. "All these people thinking they can tell me what I can and can't do. Fuck that and fuck them," he mutters more to himself than anyone, before looking back at me. "With Blair, we have our lines in the sand and . . . history. She lets me be who I am and I let her . . . you know."

There's that word again—*history.*

"No. I don't know. From what I see, she has a pretty good head on her shoulders. Perhaps you're scared of what might happen if she were to start to use it when it comes to you."

The comment is out before I can stop it and garners the reaction one would expect from him.

"What the fuck does that mean? What's it to you?" Anger peppers his voice as he squares his shoulders and takes a step toward me.

"It's nothing to me," I say.

"Stay out of my business, Evans. That's all you need to—"

"Don't bring it up then."

"Oh. Sorry," a female voice says at the edge of the garage. Her footsteps falter. "I didn't mean to interrupt . . ."

I look to my left and see Blair. Her gray eyes are wide, and her lips are parted as she looks from me to Rossi and then back. The automatic smile you'd expect a girlfriend to give her boyfriend when they see each other is more hesitant than anything.

But when she meets my eyes, the damn thing lights up her face.

Fuck.

It's not like she hasn't smiled at me before or during our mandatory participation in her F1 outreach events, but this just feels . . . different.

Like when an old friend, who you've been waiting to see, says hi.

Like when a woman you haven't stopped thinking about finally acknowledges you.

"Lachlan," she says in her signature rasp.

My name is a greeting and a question all at the same time. Our gazes hold longer than normal, and I have to force myself to look away. Just like I have to tell myself to ignore the way everything about her sets everything fucking ablaze in me.

Because it shouldn't. Can't.

She's Rossi's.

Not mine.

But fuck . . . man.

Her throaty voice is as seductive as her smile. As are the full curves of her body. As is her personality.

"Hey," Rossi says and thankfully interrupts thoughts I shouldn't be having.

"Hey." Her attention shifts to him as she walks farther into the garage. "How was testing?"

"Shit." Rossi sighs and shakes his head as she steps up beside him. "But that's par for the course, isn't it?"

"You looked pretty good out there to me," she says and tucks a piece of auburn hair that's fallen from her messy bun behind her ear.

I study her much like I did the other night. Maybe even more so. She's average in height with a full figure that begs for hands to be run over every single curve. Her lips are full, and her cheeks hold a natural pink on the apples of them. Her lashes are thick, highlighting expressive eyes. And lately, I've wanted those eyes to look toward me instead of Rossi.

You know this woman, Lach. You've interacted with her for several years now. On the track. At her outreach events. In the paddock. You've spoken to her casually many times. You know her.

So why does it feel like I actually see her all of a sudden?

"Right?" Those storm-cloud eyes turn my way, her eyebrows lifting with them.

"I'm sorry." My smile is as automatic. "What did I miss?"

"Lach's busy trying to figure out ways he can sugarcoat our shit luck," Rossi says but doesn't quite pull off the lightheartedness he tries to infuse it with.

Blair shrugs Rossi's hand off her shoulder and rolls her eyes. "Just like you're always trying to stir shit up, hmm?"

"Always," he says and winks.

"The masquerade ball. That's what I was talking about. I asked if I could count on you to be there."

"Yep. Why wouldn't I be there?"

"I knew I could count on you." She winks and chuckles as she takes a step back.

"What? You can't count on me?" Rossi asks jokingly.

"Nope. Never," she teases but there's a raw hint of something in her answer—a subtle strain of tension. *That's what I saw last Saturday night too.*

And of course, Rossi smirks like no harm, no foul.

His attitude toward her irks the fuck out of me. *And even if I did, she always comes back.* I grit my teeth as his words replay in my mind.

She's not disposable.

Far fucking from it.

Yet that's how he treats her.

Or maybe I'm just fucking crazy and overthinking shit that is none of my damn business.

If she weren't happy, she wouldn't be with him. *Right?*

"Talk to you later," she says to Rossi and pulls me from my thoughts.

"Maybe. I have plans. We'll see," Rossi says. Blair winces before taking a step back without looking my way. Almost as if she's embarrassed that I was witness to this exchange.

Definitely strain between the two of them. I'm not crazy.

We both stare at where she just was, no doubt wondering completely different things.

I wait a beat and then look at my teammate. "Really?"

"Really, what?" he asks, shoulders square, arrogance in full effect.

"I don't know what crawled up your arse, mate, but I'd make it go away if I were you."

"This is where you mind your own business," Rossi says.

"Then don't ask me for advice." I shrug.

He lifts a lone eyebrow, his stare challenging me for a beat before he actually speaks. "Stay away from my girl, Evans."

"Wasn't thinking about going near her." And it's the truth. I wasn't.

"Huh."

Our eyes meet and hold. Tension fills the space between us.

"I'd like to assume the two of you are discussing how to bring this team together rather than tear it apart, ya?"

The German accent fills the garage as we both look up to see our team principal, Johann Wagner, standing at its edge, his arms folded over his chest, and his eyebrows raised. He's a no-nonsense man of few words, and one whose expressions usually say it all.

Right now, it's saying he can sense something's amiss, and that's the last thing he wants or needs amid an already trying season.

"Correct," Rossi and I say in unison.

"Just shooting the shit," I say as I stand and grab my hat.

"Chatting the day away." It's impossible to miss Rossi's sarcasm.

"Are we ready for the meeting?" I ask.

"We are," Johann says as I skirt around Rossi and head toward where the entire team—my crew and Rossi's crew—have congregated. It's a sea of blue composed of people I trust implicitly.

"It's race week, everybody," Johann says to an enthusiastic cheer of everyone around us. "Testing was good but not great. Our power issue seems to persist, but we're in the midst of making some more adjustments on the powertrain."

The meeting runs on. Housekeeping items and goals for the upcoming race. Nothing that I haven't already talked about with Johann or know about, but it's important that I be here. That they see me here. That they know I care about every aspect of this team.

But just like the past few days, my mind wanders. To things it shouldn't be thinking of. To someone it shouldn't be wondering about.

It's not like I looked her up on purpose.

Not like I scrolled through her social media to see what pictures I'd find. The majority of her posts are of trips she's taken, friends she's dining with, trips home to her family, or events she's helped organize for her job. And maybe a few sporadic ones of her and Rossi—albeit from a long time ago, guessing by the race suit Rossi was wearing in them and the braces on her teeth.

Not like I looked *them* up. Strangely, given how long they've known each other, when it comes to Rossi's pages, there's barely any mention of Blair.

And none of this information is pertinent to the meeting going on all around me. The talk of team goals. Of pit stop target times. Of race day protocol.

None of it.

And neither is my glance out of the garage down pit row to where Blair is talking with another team of racers. Her curves. Her utter confidence. Her goddamn beauty.

Yeah, I'm definitely looking at her.

Damn. When's the last time shit like that happened to me?

Um . . . never.

Team.

Teammate.

Crew.

The holy trinity in my world. The three things I've been taught to give the utmost respect. Acting on my attraction would fuck that all up. And Rossi's right, it is a contract renewal year. The last thing I want to do is cause a scene, other than a podium finish.

Besides, I'm attracted to a lot of women. Being attracted and acting on it are not one and the same.

"Scintillating content today, huh?" Rossi mutters as he rests an elbow on my shoulder like we're best buds.

I shift away from him as irritation hits.

Irritation? Or is it *resentment?*

I can feel the weight of his stare while I return my focus to Johann. On what matters. On where my focus needs to be.

To compete with the man beside you for a spot but to have to be his right-hand man and vice versa out on the track.

It's like dating your enemy in some screwed up way.

"So that's where we're at," Johann says. "We need a podium. We need consistency. And the two of you"—he points to Rossi and then me—"need to start working together to get us there."

"And we need engines that work," Rossi says. Every head in the garage turns to look at him.

"He's right." I back him up even though this clearly isn't the way I would have opted to go about this ongoing complaint. "Our skills only get us so far."

Johann's expression is impassive. "We all feel the pressure. Believe me. And we're doing the best we can to remedy the situation. We think we have a few more things dialed in after testing today. But I don't think I need to remind anyone that the driver lineup for next season is still in flux as does Apex's continued sponsorship of the team." He smacks his hands together and rubs them as if to reinforce that we made our point, but his was made too. "We are a team. Us. You. The two of you together. I don't need to state how important that is to anyone in this garage."

Drive to survive. Place to continue to race. Work together toward the goal.

The underlying threat still rings loudly when I walk out of the garage a short time later. The momentum Apex had toward the end of last season never carried over to this one. New engine and car regulations have left all the teams scrambling to make adjustments, but for some reason, Team Apex is struggling more than most.

It's been a maddening first quarter of the season. Blown engines, loss of power, and our cars underperforming in general. There's only so much lemonade you can make with rotting lemons.

But Johann is right. So right that when I look up to find Rossi talking and laughing with Blair across the paddock, irritation once again fires.

He treats her like shit. How have I never noticed that before? If a woman like that was mine—

What the fuck is wrong with you, Evans?

It's not like she hasn't been on the circuit forever. Her job makes her presence at each track a constant. My position as one of only twenty drivers means our interactions are a foregone requirement. She's not a stranger to me.

Not by any means.

But after this past weekend, after talking to her outside the party, it's like she's fucking everywhere I look.

I can't unsee her.

I can't unthink her.

And one thought is on repeat as I walk toward the team paddock suite, as I prepare for my telemetric review, and it's that Rossi is wrong.

Sure his social media is curated by his PR team, but one thing's for fucking sure: if she were mine? Everybody would fucking know it.

Chapter Three

Blair

I FLIRTED.

I flirted when I don't normally flirt, and I liked how it made me feel.

Does that make me a bad person? Or does it make me human?

Human.

It has to.

There's no harm with a little innocent flirting. There's no harm when you do it to see if your boyfriend notices. *News flash.* He didn't. And maybe he didn't because he's the king of flirting himself. The prince of being oblivious.

Especially when it comes to me, it seems.

And yes, this is beginning to sting more than it used to. Or maybe I'm just realizing I deserve more. Better. That what I thought was equal is far fucking from it.

It's Skylar's fault.

I smile at the thought of my best friend and everything I saw when I visited her last month.

The longing glances across the room her new husband would give her. The subtle touches they shared without even realizing it. The laughter between them—God, there wasn't a tense moment in that house.

And yes, they were in front of me so I'm sure they were on their best behavior, but you can't fake the looks you give when you think no one is watching.

I left there sad. I started making comparisons I shouldn't be making.

But I deserve that too. All of it. And it's becoming obvious—and has been for some time but maybe I just didn't want to see it—that Rossi isn't the man giving that level of affection and attention to me.

Is that why Lachlan's kindness the other night affected me more than it should have? Is that why I flirted with him today?

An engine rumbles somewhere on the track. Somewhere beyond the wall of the garages I can see from my window in Formula 1's own hospitality suite in the paddock.

Its sound is comforting to me. A soundtrack to my every day and to the job that I love.

And fittingly enough, I'm looking at the Apex garage as I think.

But if the flirting were harmless, Blair, then why are you sitting at your desk staring at graphics for the upcoming event and zeroing in on Lachlan's image?

Because he was gruff.

Because he acted like the moment outside the party never happened.

Because when he met your eyes earlier in the garage it made your tummy feel weird when it shouldn't have.

But there's no denying that it did.

And because since then, you keep replaying the moment in your mind. The look between us that lasted a little too long. The bob of his Adam's apple when his gaze flickered down to my lips. My desire to look back at him even after I forced myself to look the other way.

"Carmichael?" I look up and my boss, Paolo, is standing in the doorway of my portable office. "Have a minute?"

"Yes. Of course."

He motions for me to follow him. I rise from my desk while fighting that sinking feeling in my stomach that anyone being unexpectedly summoned by their boss can understand.

Within moments, I'm seated in the conference room before him with his clasped hands and stoic expression. That feeling of dread only grows heavier as my mind races a million miles an hour over the events of the past few weeks.

Did I mess something up? Is it my turn to be let go because of this whole department's overhaul?

"Is everything okay?" I finally ask when Paolo continues to study the papers in front of him instead of me.

He looks up, his smile guarded and placating.

My chest constricts.

"As you know, the department has been under some restructuring as of late. Duties have shifted. Then shifted again. Co-workers have been reallocated to other facets of the F1 animal that we are." Nice speak for *people have been let go.* "And we'll most likely continue to be in a state of disarray for a while as budget reallocations take place and needs are reviewed." Nice speak for *and more people will be let go.*

"Paolo, you're killing me here. What does that have to do with me?" I wipe my palms on my pants.

"You've been patient with us, and I want you to know that hasn't gone unnoticed."

I nod, uncertain what to say.

"How long have you worked for us?"

My pulse pounds in my ears. "For F1 as a whole or this department?" I ask. I spent five years in basic administration with the entity doing every benign, meaningless duty before Paolo hired me.

"This department."

I eye him. He knows the answer to this, but I respond nonetheless. "Four years."

"That long, huh?" He nods slowly.

"Yes." If he takes any longer to explain why he's asking me these questions, I'm going to chew a hole through my bottom lip.

"Then I think it's only fair for you to be given the chance to really prove yourself."

Proving myself could mean a lot of different things.

"As in?"

"As in I think it's time your name is the one listed beside the event name."

"What?" I try to remain cool and casual, but the single syllable comes out in a pseudo-shriek. *Is he saying what I think he's saying?* "Are you serious?"

His grin grows wider. "In fact, I am. You've put in a lot of hard work and long hours to prove your capabilities. You've done more than your fair share of crap work and paying your dues. It's for that reason and so many more that I couldn't be more thrilled to give you a chance at being an event coordinator."

Oh. My. God. Every emotion known to man chases one after another through my system.

"I—I don't even know what to say."

His chuckle rumbles around the room. "Don't say anything yet." He holds up a hand. "There are a few caveats."

"Like . . ." *Why does everything have a catch?*

"Like, it's an interim position. Lisa has opted to take a job with one of the motorsports teams," he explains, checking each item off on his finger. Her departure comes as a surprise as jobs with Formula 1—the overarching company who owns the trademark to the sport—are extremely desirable and hard to land, but a job with a team is highly coveted too.

"What do you mean Lisa is leaving?" I ask. "She hasn't said a word."

"I asked her to keep her departure under wraps until I announced her replacement."

"Are you telling me that the masquerade ball is mine?" This just keeps getting better.

"I am. If you want it. But that means—"

"That means I have about three months to pull the whole thing off." And the other shoe drops, but it does nothing to dull the excitement that I'm getting a chance to choreograph one of the most coveted projects in our department. I've waited for the chance at any project and to know it's the ball? *Holy shit.*

"Correct. But I have complete faith in you and the fact that you can step in seamlessly and pull it together properly."

"Not a problem. Lisa is meticulous in all she does." Talk about having to fill some big shoes. *Gulp.*

"She is. But she also kept a lot of it in her head. And in this interim where she's one foot out the door, it seems things might not be as up to speed as we'd anticipated or believed them to be."

"So I'm stepping into a powder keg is what you're telling me?" I tease, trying to act nonchalant while mentally jumping up and down.

"Most likely. There's never a better time to see how well someone was or wasn't doing their job until they leave, right?"

I open my mouth to make a sarcastic remark but stop myself. I can do this. I might be picking up the pieces of someone else's puzzle, but this is the chance I've been waiting for. This is the next rung on the ladder I'd given myself to climb. "Sure. Yes. I'll figure it out. Whatever it takes, I'll get it done."

"I know you will." He glances at his clasped hands and then back up at me. "I believe you earned this chance, Blair. Knock this out of the park, and I can see many more opportunities arise for you."

"I will. I'll make sure the transition is smooth. I'll—I . . ." A swell of emotion hits me. "Thank you for the opportunity, Paolo."

"You're welcome. I love the enthusiasm but just know I had to fight like hell for you on this. Your work speaks for itself, but it's never been looked upon favorably by the higher-ups that you date a driver."

"I've never made it an issue or tried to use it to my advantage," I state.

"You're right. You haven't and it hasn't, but there are many who will use it against you. Say he's the reason you got the job. That we hired you because we know you'd get more participation from the drivers due to your connection. Or there is the other aspect that . . . *you know*."

"That I'm a track tramp trying to use the position to cozy up to the racers and hop from one to another." I roll my eyes but by the way he shifts in his seat, it's clear that my words make him uncomfortable.

He holds his hands up. "Your words. Not mine."

"I know. Sorry for being blunt. It's just—"

"Like I said, I don't have a problem with it, especially with how low-key you have kept your relationship. You've never used it for your gain, but I need it to stay a nonissue if I'm going to give you this chance. The more eyes on you, then the more eyes on us and what could seem like fraternization of a sort."

"I completely understand."

"Good." He slides the thin folder in front of him across the table. "This is everything I have on the event thus far. The rest is on a shared drive that I've given you access to. The details have been emailed to you."

"Okay." I open the folder, and while the first page holds nothing interesting, a rush of excitement races down my spine. "I'll get to work on it right away."

"I know you will." He pushes his chair back and stands as I leaf through the papers. "Blair?"

"Hmm?" I look up to meet his eyes.

"Kick some ass on this, will you?"

My grin is automatic. "Is there any other option?"

"That's what I like to hear."

Endless thoughts of what I need to check on or see if it's even done yet race through my mind on the way back to my office. It's not like this is my first rodeo. My name may not have been the lead for previous events, but I sure as shit did a ton of the grunt work and scheduling to make other ones happen.

When I reach my office, I shut my door so that no one can see my celebratory boogie dance and fist pump. My cheeks hurt from grinning and once I let it all sink in, the first person I call is Rossi.

But it rings. And rings.

The whine of engines on the track is the only explanation I need as to why he's probably not answering, but it doesn't make me feel any less deflated.

So I end the call and move on to the next equally important person.

"Sweetheart! How wonderful to hear your voice," my mom says over a calamity of noise in the background before speaking to someone. "Yes, Cali. I'll be right there."

"Hi. How are things?"

"Good. Crazy." She laughs with that uniquely tinkly sound of hers. "Cali is currently watering the flowers, but I have no doubt the hose will be turned on everyone else shortly. Angel is baking something—or trying to—but by the amount of flour all over the floor, I'm not sure how well that's working. The twins are . . . who knows where the twins are, but I'm sure they'll come back filthy and happy. Everyone else is accounted for but not here."

"So, the usual." I laugh and a pang of homesickness hits me unexpectedly. I'm usually happy that I'm out of the chaos of having ten brothers and sisters—five biological and five adopted—but every once in a while, I miss it. The mess that comes with belly giggles. The synchronized chaos that you simply become accustomed to. A house where there's always someone home. A kitchen that might be a little messy but that always has your favorite items. "And Dad?"

"Good. There's a local soccer team that lost its coach—"

"We lived in Italy long enough for you to know to call it football."

"I know. I know." I can practically see her swatting her hand at me to say she knows. "I keep telling him we don't need another darn thing on our plate but . . ."

"But Dad can never say no to kids in need."

"Exactly. We're the fortunate ones so why not spread that good fortune, right?"

"What about his deployment?" I ask, knowing there were rumblings he might be sent somewhere.

"That's on hold for the time being. All that fuss and stress and now it looks like he gets to stay here longer." She tsks. "Bradly. Oh my God, son. Mud. On your shoes. In my house."

The baritone laugh of my brother in the background makes me smile. "Always wreaking havoc."

"Always," she says. "What about you, Blair? How are you? Tell me how my world traveler is doing. You sounded excited when I picked up. Catch me up."

"I was. I am. You know I've been working toward—"

"Rosco. No!" she yells at our big, clumsy mutt of a dog. "I'm sorry. Continue."

"Well, I was finally given the chance to—"

Something shatters. It's loud and overpowers me. "Rachel. *Oh shit.*"

"Mom?"

"Blair, I—have to go. Talk later?"

"Sure. Yes. Is everyone okay—"

"Yes. It'll be fine. Olive juice," she says, our family's childish way of saying I love you, before hanging up abruptly.

"Olive juice," I mouth to an empty connection before lowering the phone to stare at the blank screen.

We'll talk later. I know we will, but it's perfectly okay to feel a little let down. To know when I finally get the chance to tell her about my promotion of sorts, that the newness and excitement will feel massively anticlimactic.

"Hey, Blair? Guess what?" I murmur to myself as I move to my desk, take a seat, and open the folder. "I just got a huge opportunity. A promotion. Want to celebrate?"

"Definitely," I say in a different voice. "Incredible job, honey."

And then I laugh.

Hell, if you can't laugh at yourself, then who in the hell can you laugh at?

Chapter Four

Blair

MY KNOCK IS LOUD, THE BOTTLE OF CHAMPAGNE IN MY OPPOSING hand is cold, and my need to feel connected to anyone is high.

My mom got back to me via text. It was too loud at Angel's volleyball tournament for her to talk on the phone. Telling her over text wasn't exactly how I wanted to do it, but her response was a vomit of emojis—one after another—that showed how excited she was for me.

My dad's cell pushed me to voicemail after four rings.

I texted my brother Joel to tell him, but the man never looks at it or responds and forgets to hit send.

Skylar is on a no-phones getaway with Russ—even though she snuck a peek at my text to her—and promised to celebrate properly over Zoom when their self-imposed restriction is lifted.

And that, their no-phones romantic getaway, only made me feel more alone.

Is it so bad that I want to celebrate my incredible day with someone? Something more than the *"Good job. We're celebrating this tonight,"* text Rossi sent in response to the dozen I sent him about how excited I was to get this opportunity?

That I wanted to actually celebrate?

I want to sit and let the champagne's bubbles tickle my nose as I laugh and *just be* for a little bit before the chaos of tomorrow begins again.

I knock. *Again.* But I don't hear Rossi shuffling about inside or his rumbling voice telling me to *hold my ponies.* His ridiculous attempt to sound like me—American—but forgetting that the saying is really *hold your horses.*

It's race week and his team curfew is in full effect. He should be here. I knock once more.

The door beside his hotel room opens, and a rumpled head of blond hair peeks out. It's one of his crew members. "Hey, Blair. Rossi's out. You didn't hear it from me, but I think he's still at the club. Luxe, *I think.*"

Luxe? Yep. That's one of his favorites.

So much for celebrating. Well, *with me* at least.

"Thanks." I offer a pathetic smile. "I appreciate it. Sorry if I woke you."

"No problem."

His door clicks shut and I'm left alone with a bottle of bubbly that no longer sounds appealing and disappointment heavy in my heart.

Fact of the matter is I could be the clingy girlfriend and show up at the club. But that's not me. That's not us. We're not stuck together at the hip. We live our lives just like we always have, and so the fact that he completely forgot to say anything to me hurts. *A lot.*

It reminds me of Saturday night when I felt cast aside. When I'd wanted to leave the party, but he'd seemed incredulous.

Rossi's gorgeous face falls and his eyes widen. "I—um . . . you want to go?" he asks like I'm crazy.

"It's been a long week of prep." And I don't feel like yelling above the music to talk anymore. I shouldn't have to explain myself to my boyfriend with everyone around us listening.

"But this is fun. I'm having fun. Aren't you?" His hand slides to my lower back and he pulls me against him in a rare show of what he'd consider affection, something he normally reserves for in private.

"Yes. Sure. But we had plans." Just like we always do before race week. Or rather more like—like we used to before race week.

His smile falters and eyes narrow. "C'mon, Blair. Don't get like that. It's not that big of a deal if we skip it this once."

"Uh-huh." More like this would be the third race in a row. Not the first time. And by his sigh of exasperation, I know he knows it but would never admit it.

"Look. I don't want to go yet. It's been stressful and this is . . . exactly what I need."

This. This meaning the adoration and attention. The people hanging on his every word and thinking that whatever it is, it's the greatest thing ever uttered.

In classic Rossi fashion, if he's not getting it on the track, this is what he craves.

It's never what I need, but I've learned that my needs never come first. Rarely matter. I nod. "Got it." I hook a thumb over my shoulder and try to shake the disappointment that hits harder than I expected.

I shouldn't be hurt. I know plans change. Hell, they always change in this crazy, travel-heavy life we live.

Maybe Rossi and I are on a downward swing. It wouldn't be the first time we hit a bump and needed a break. Hell, while our relationship has been full of them over the years, our friendship beyond that has never wavered. Knowing that doesn't make it any easier to swallow . . . or accept.

Russ mouthing *I love you* across the patio to Skylar floats through my mind. My dad turning off my mom's alarm clock without her knowing so that she can sleep in to express his love and gratitude for her does too.

Different loves. Little ways to show it.

With a sag of my shoulders, I set the bottle down against Rossi's door—maybe it will jog his memory about the text he sent when he returns—and head back to my room. But sleep eludes me. No matter how long I stare at the ceiling or run checklists in my head over what I need to do, the clock on the hotel nightstand doesn't seem to move any quicker.

Midnight.

A whole nine minutes have transpired since the last time I looked at it, and I have nothing to show for it. Not a minute of added sleep. Not a second more of clarity. Not a life-changing epiphany. Not a knock on the door from Rossi after returning and realizing he screwed up.

Instead, I've acquired an astute knowledge of how the shadows move across the ceiling of my hotel room while pondering why footsteps in hotel hallways sound so much louder at night.

Restless and stir-crazy—knowing it's a combination of the day I've had, Rossi's broken promise, and being on the road—I take a page out of my old playbook. I head downstairs to read for a bit somewhere other than the suffocating confines of my hotel room.

Chapter Five

Lachlan

I SMELL HER BEFORE I SEE HER.

The subtle floral scent she wears is a hint in the air.

It's like everything about her has imprinted in my damn mind in a few short days, and now I can't get her out of my head.

Either that or I'm going fucking crazy.

I'll go with the latter theory rather than prove myself wrong. I don't look behind me. I don't check and see if one Blair Carmichael with the mesmerizing eyes and arresting smile is sitting anywhere in the bar behind me.

Because it doesn't matter whether she is or whether she isn't. All that matters is that she's a no-go zone for me—beyond the track limit. A term my brain should more than understand.

But hell if my beer holds my attention like it did moments ago.

Shit. I sigh and run a hand through my hair. I had my reasons for coming down to the bar. Disappointment in my season so far. Stress over not knowing where I'm going to land next year—or God forbid, if I'll land somewhere at all. It's been weighing on me. The constant pressure of the unknown takes its toll.

A cold glass of beer and the soft chords of the piano being played in the lobby—both a way to help me get to sleep a little easier tonight.

And yet now I can't stop wondering if she is or isn't here. Is she with Rossi? Are they snuggled up together sharing a drink and some quiet time?

The thought sits like a boulder in the pit of my stomach when I know damn well a week ago, I wouldn't have given it a second thought.

But now I know she wanted to fly.

Now I know she purses her lips when she's thinking of how to answer me.

Now I know those eyes of hers ask questions and express emotions she doesn't think anyone else can read.

I swirl the glass of beer in my hand, determined that once I finish it, I'll head up to my room and out of here.

She's with Rossi.

Stop thinking about her.

She's off-limits.

Stop wondering if there weren't a Rossi in her life what could be . . .

Because he is.

And that's the cold, hard truth of it.

Turn around to see it, Lach. Them together. Laughing. Talking. And maybe in this quiet bar, where Rossi isn't being swarmed by adoring fans, maybe they'll be cuddling close. Sharing a kiss.

When you've reminded yourself of the truth, grab your drink and go the fuck upstairs and wipe thoughts of her from your mind.

I take a sip and prepare myself for a punch to the gut. But the one I'm expecting doesn't come when I turn around.

It's a much different one. One that laces desire with want when I see the damn woman curled up in a chair in the far corner of the bar. She has printed leggings on and a pair of green slippers with a white puffy ball on top on her feet. A paperback is in her hand, and she's seriously invested in whatever story it's telling.

Fucking hell. Every muscle in my body tenses and each nerve becomes keenly aware of that rush of . . . whatever it is that courses through me.

Nope. I take a large swallow of my beer.

Not gonna happen. I push money across the bar top to pay my tab.

She's taken.

I stand up.

I'm an all or nothing type of guy and if I attempt to get to know her better, I know myself. I won't be able to stop. Or be able to let go.

And that's not a fucking option.

So I'm going to nip this shit in the bud.

It's when I turn to leave that my plans fly out the fucking window. She's standing in my way, her smile wide, and her eyes as welcoming as the luscious curves of her body.

Jesus fucking Christ.

"Hi. You're here?" She asks it like a question.

"I am." My gaze darts down to her lips and then back up.

"A driver out in the wild without his entourage. That's twice now. You sure you're really an F1 driver?" Her brow furrows but her lips twist as she fights back a smile.

I glance down and pat my chest in a mock check. "Pretty sure I am. Guess we'll see in quali on Saturday how I do."

"I'll reserve judgment until I can see your moves." She winks.

God, she's adorable.

"Noted. I'll make sure I pull out all the stops." I take a sip of my beer that I forgot I drained and earn a laugh from her when I realize it's empty.

"I'm hoping you have better moves than that," she teases.

"Definitely better than that," I say.

"May I?" she asks as she points to the empty chair beside me.

No.

Yes.

Why are you torturing me?

"Of course," I say and pull the chair out for her before taking a seat back in the one I swore I was vacating to save myself from this very situation.

She sits herself but turns to face me so that her knees bump innocently against mine. Our positioning leaves me no other option but to pay full attention to her.

"So, Mr. Evans," she says, her head angling to the side, and sets her book down beside her. "What exactly are you doing here at this late hour?"

"I could ask the same of you."

"You could. But I asked first. And schoolyard etiquette says you have to go first."

"Schoolyard etiquette also says whoever smelled it dealt it so I wouldn't exactly die on a hill when it comes to those rules."

She chuckles and her cheeks flush pink.

Did I just invoke the *fart rule?* Jesus, Lach. *Really?*

"Noted. But . . . I *did* ask first."

"True." I glance around the sparsely populated bar and then back to her. Nope. Definitely no Rossi anywhere. "This hotel has always been protective of the drivers when we're here. Added security at the doors. Key cards must be shown so only guests can come in. Access to private elevators." I shrug. "So it's nice that I can just sit here and . . . be."

"Why though?"

"Why am I sitting here?" I ask and she nods. "Because I get nervous before testing."

She laughs, but then stops herself when she realizes I'm being honest. "Seriously?"

I nod. "Yep. It doesn't matter how many hundreds of times I've been on the track or behind the wheel, I get nervous. I think it's a good thing. It means I'm not too comfortable. It means I respect the sport and what could happen to me at any given time. And damn, it's a fucking cool reminder that I get to do this every day."

Her grin widens and her eyes spark with wildfire. "It is pretty cool."

"What about you, Tinkerbell?"

"Tinkerb—" I motion toward her green slippers with the fuzzy white ball on the top. "A gift from one of my sisters." She lifts one of her feet to show them off.

"Very classy. As are your pajama pants."

She looks down at her black leggings with various dog faces all over them, lips pursed, and shrugs before meeting my eyes again. "You'll find I don't much care about what people think."

"That makes two of us."

"I learned a long time ago that listening to the outside noise tends to kill confidence, and I refuse to let anyone dull my sparkle."

Jesus. This woman. She's something else, drawing me in when I really need to step away.

"And what is your sparkle, Blair?"

"For one, I got a promotion today." Her words start out excited and then fade off, almost as if she's embarrassed that she just said that.

"Really? That's huge. Congratulations. I think." I pause. "Why are you not out celebrating?"

"There's no need to. It's not that big of a deal."

"I call bullshit. Every victory in life—no matter how big or small—deserves to be celebrated. There are no guarantees that there will be more to come."

"Agreed, but like I said, it's no—"

"I won't hear differently." I smack my hands on the bar top for emphasis. "What'll you have?"

"Nothing. Seriously. C'mon."

"A toast is in order." I motion to the bartender who moves our way. "A bottle of champagne please. Your best."

"Lachlan." My name falls like a chastised child from her lips. "You don't need to . . ."

I grab her hands to stop her protest . . . and the action stops the words on her lips all right, just like I swear it does my fucking heart.

What is this shit? This sudden buzz is like an undercurrent. My heart pounding like a kick drum. The flash of heat where our skin touches.

The hitch of her goddamn breath.

I hear it and it means she either felt that jolt of lightning strike too or she thinks I'm a fucking prick since she has a boyfriend.

My smile is cautious as I let go of her hands and turn toward where the bartender is pouring two glasses of champagne.

"Tell me about the job."

"Well, it's not exactly a promotion." She worries her hands up and down her thighs. "It's a chance to prove myself."

"Sounds like a promotion to me. Tell me more."

She studies me for a beat, and I wish I knew what those eyes were asking. "You know the masquerade ball I was asking about earlier?"

Everyone does. In fact, there are a lot of requirements of us as drivers—events we need to be seen at, parties we need to host, sponsors we need to promote—but the masquerade ball that raises funds to help disadvantaged youth participate in our sport is one that all of us enjoy. "Wait. *It's yours now?* For next year?"

"No. For this year."

"Wow. Holding your feet to the fire, huh?"

She smiles. "Yes, and without much warning but that will only allow me to prove I work great under pressure and with time constraints."

"I'm impressed." I slide a glass her way and pick up mine. "To not limiting your challenges, but to challenging your limits."

Blair clinks her glass against mine and then bursts out laughing. "You've been saving that one for a long time, haven't you?"

I grin and lift a hand. "Guilty as charged. I heard it somewhere a long time ago. Been keeping it with me for the right time and—"

"And I'm the right time." She takes a sip, her eyes on me from above the rim of her glass, and then scrunches her nose because of the bubbles tickling it.

"You are." I take a sip myself and fight the wince. I hate this shit but will drink it for her. "So now you get to pull together an event on borrowed time. How well do you handle stress?" I tease.

"I guess I'm going to find out." A slow smile crawls across her lips. "Plus . . ."

"Plus this is kind of a big deal," I say. "I'm not going to let you play this down, Tink."

Her grin widens. "I appreciate it. Thank you." She takes another sip and stares at the bubbles floating up for a second before meeting my eyes. "Tell me more about you."

"Me? Other than my love for backwards-flying hummingbirds?" I ask and she nods. "Like what?"

"Like name three things that would surprise me to find at your house."

"Not your run-of-the-mill question."

"I'm not your run-of-the-mill girl."

"So I'm learning. Three things, huh?" I stop for a minute to think. "I have plants. Ones that are actually alive."

"That's impressive. Even I can't pull that off."

"I have a whole bookshelf full of binders that hold newspaper clippings. They document my career from start to now. And the only reason I have them is because my grandmother makes them for me, and I don't have the heart to tell her it embarrasses me to look at them."

"That's adorable and admirable. And why does it embarrass you?"

"Anyone who likes to look at themselves that much has ego issues." I top up her glass of champagne as I try to think of something that makes me seem interesting. "And three? Hmm. I make my bed every day."

"You do?"

I nod. "Yep. I figure if my day goes to shit, at least I know I accomplished one thing. Well, that and as a kid it was a requirement before I could leave the house to go hang with friends."

She angles her head to the side and studies me. "Coming from a military family where the bed always had to be made, I sincerely appreciate the fact you still do it." She scrunches her nose. "There are days where I might not make it simply as a sign of rebellion for my childhood years."

I laugh. I like that about her. I smack my hands and rub them together. "Your turn."

"My turn?" She sighs loudly as her lips twist in thought. "I have a small art studio in one room."

"Art? What kind?"

"Watercolors mostly. Nothing too impressive but it's something I like to do to relax."

"What do you paint?"

"Things that make me feel good."

"So I'll be seeing one of me then?" I joke, earning me a shy smile and flushed cheeks.

Damn. She's stunning.

It's like I'm so comfortable talking to her and then she does something like the look she's giving me right now, and I'm reminded how goddamn gorgeous she is—even with her hair up, no makeup on, and Tinkerbell slippers.

"Do you have any photos of them?" I think of her social media posts and how none of them show anything of her hobby. "I want to see one."

"No. God, no." But the flush of her cheeks tells me she does.

"You're lying, but that's okay. I'll get you to show me sometime."

Our eyes meet and hold. Her lashes flutter above those brilliant eyes of hers. "We'll see about that. Number two . . . I collect bottle caps and corks."

"Bottle caps and corks?"

"Yes. In a glass vase. From places I've been. Experiences I've had. Things I want to remember."

"How do you remember which one is what memory?"

"Now you're really trying to embarrass me."

"Humor me."

"I may have each one numbered with a corresponding spreadsheet on my computer."

"You're serious, aren't you?"

"Yep."

"Organized and beautiful," I say without thought. "That's quite the combo."

"Thank you," she murmurs. "It's silly but . . . I just do it out of habit."

"No, you do it because it matters to you. Don't downplay it." I shift and my thigh presses against her knee. "I'm beginning to see a pattern of you not owning your awesomeness. It looks to me like the only person who tones down your sparkle is you."

"Whatever." She rolls her eyes.

"And three?"

"I like to read." She holds up her paperback.

"What do you like about it?"

"The escape. The stepping into someone else's shoes for a few pages. The feelings that the author evokes." She looks down at the cover and then back at me. "Next to art, books are my happy place."

"Really?"

"Mm-hmm. Some women like flowers." She shrugs. "I like books."

"What's that one about?" I ask, genuinely curious. She's hidden behind all these layers, and I want to unpeel them one by one.

"Attraction. Betrayal. Redemption. Like all good love stories are."

I twist my lips and stare at her. "True love doesn't require betrayal."

She grins. "I know, but damn it makes for some good fiction."

"I'll keep that in mind should I decide to pick up a romance."

"You do that." She laughs and gives the silliest shake to her head.

"So back to the original question. What is the third thing I'd be surprised about and don't tell me you have a library of books because clearly"—I lift my chin to her paperback—"I already know you like to read."

"I see how you are," she teases. "Tricking me into giving you four things."

"Guilty as charged." I hold my hands up.

"Hmm, three. Um, I have one of my dad's medals from his service framed on my dresser."

"I'm sure he loves that you do."

Everything about her lights up. "He's like our team principal. The one controlling the chaos."

"Now that analogy, I understand." I tap my glass against hers.

"He's the most selfless man I know. Both of my parents are really. Their theory is that if they can help someone, they will."

"A life of service in all aspects."

"Yes. And a house full of kids. Always."

"Isn't that a good thing?" I ask, curious as to why it doesn't sound like it.

"Yes. Of course it is." Her smile is genuine. "I'm the oldest though, so sometimes I feel completely disconnected from the new crew they bring in."

"New crew?"

"There are five of us who are biological, and five have been adopted. And then . . . they foster more when someone needs to be fostered. The house never has the same amount of people in it when I go home."

"I have one brother and it was chaotic growing up. You just said you had ten people or more in your house at a time." I try to wrap my head around it and fail.

Her smile is nothing but pure love. "I know. It's a tornado of love and fighting and acceptance and laughter all at the same time." She takes a sip. "It's all I've ever known though so for me it's just normal."

"That's cool for so many reasons. Your parents doing that. You kids for accepting it. The better chance at life you've given others. I mean . . . so freaking cool."

"I guess but I don't see it that way . . . it's just my family. I don't know any other way. I try to get back as often as I can, but you know how hard it is with the traveling involved in this job."

"And that bugs you, doesn't it?"

She tilts her head and studies me. Classical music plays on around us, someone enters the lobby and the doors make a whooshing sound, and yet it's her eyes that hold my attention. "It does. More than I think most days."

"That's admirable. Most people can't wait to leave home and never go back."

"Don't get me wrong, I was more than happy to leave and make my place in the world, but I still have this sense of disconnect. That sense of home."

I nod, understanding her sentiment. While my family is small in comparison—one brother, my mum, my dad—for the bulk of the year, I am in the northern hemisphere. Not an insurmountable distance but enough that I feel so fucking far from them most days. Sure, I've grown used to it, but that doesn't mean I don't miss them some days. "My family is close too. My dad gets to go to a good portion of the races, and I have to admit I always breathe a little easier—feel more at ease when he's there."

How did I not realize that until now?

"I get that. One hundred percent."

She talks a bit more about her dad and his impressive years of service.

Her family and the dozens of foster kids they've had in and out of their house. The synchronized commotion of a big family.

There is no denying the love in her voice. The admiration. The respect. This woman truly is special.

There's something about her tonight. Just like there was outside the party. She seems different when she's not around Rossi. As if she isn't holding herself back.

"So yeah, we've moved around a lot, from country to country, from base to base. Luckily, they've been stationed in Italy for a decade now."

"Was that hard? The constant moving?"

"The truth? Starting at a new school wasn't too terrible because there were so many of us, and that meant we had a built-in friend group in each other."

"That's definitely a plus."

"I mean, I'll admit there were a lot of averted stares and whispers over how many kids the Carmichaels had . . . but once they got to know us, it was fine."

"I didn't think of that aspect of it."

"But that's why I have the bottle caps and wine corks. A way to remember little details that I know I'd forget if given the chance. My keepsake box of trinkets of sorts."

Someone who stops and smells the roses and then takes a petal to remember them by.

Kind of fucking cool. Not like many people do that these days.

The woman has moved around her whole life, and yet she's been able to take something good, and found relevance, in cataloging those memories so she wouldn't forget them.

She's fascinating. Simply fascinating.

I've been all over the world time and again and have nothing to show for each visit save for another race . . . and a few trophies. There are distinct memories tied to those, but if I had to recall other specifics, no doubt they've all faded with time.

Bottle caps and wine corks. I kind of like the idea. A small token as a reminder of something time will erode from the memory.

Silence settles between us and I feel something I haven't felt in the longest time when it comes to a woman.

Panic.

Panic that she'll decide to head to bed. Panic that whatever this is will be over because as much as there can't be anything here, something still is.

I scramble for my next question. Anything to keep her talking and to maintain this feeling. "What was your favorite country you were stationed at or have lived in?"

"All of them. Is that the chickenshit way to answer you?" She laughs. "Probably Italy."

"Good choice."

"We were there the longest—my family is still there—and so I was able to meet more people and make more memories."

"Makes sense."

"That's actually where I met Rossi."

"Really?"

"Yep. I think I told you we used to frequent the local track. It was a cheap way to entertain all of us kids. There was a hotshot race car driver working his way up through the circuit who'd be there at times." She shrugs. "We met. Became friends. Then more than friends . . . and since then have kind of been together."

"Kind of?" I take a sip. "That doesn't exactly sound like . . . whatever it sounds like," I say, stopping myself from prying.

She gives another shrug and looks around the bar before coming back to meet my eyes. It's the quickest of glimpses and I know I'm probably reading into it way more than I should, but I swear to God I see something there. A moment of uncertainty that makes me think that all isn't exactly what it seems.

"That sounded bad, didn't it?" She shifts in her seat, her knee touching mine a constant reminder of how fucking close we are. "It's just . . . like I implied before, there's a lot of history between us. Between our families. He's been a constant in my life in one way or another since we met. Since we left home. Since we started our careers. And while we may have been off again and on again more times than we can count, he's just Rossi. Always there."

Always there. You hear that, Lach? Focus on that. On the truth behind it.

"And now you live in Monaco?"

"Nice. Close enough to be able to get to Monaco when I need to, and a helluva lot more practical on my salary."

"So it's by necessity then. One more question."

"I think this Q&A is a little lopsided."

"Last one. I promise."

"Okay. What?"

"Since you've traveled the world . . . if you could pick anywhere in it to live, where would you choose?"

"My answer is lame."

"No answer is lame." I top up her glass, enjoying the flush on her cheeks the alcohol has added.

"Well, more cheesy than lame."

"I'm all for cheesy. Lay it on me." I pat my chest and grin.

"The place I'd choose is wherever the people I love are. The location doesn't matter. Oh my God, that *is* cheesy." She squeals and covers her face.

"There's no need to be embarrassed." *Wouldn't I have said exactly the same thing?* I reach out to pull her hand off her face, and we both falter at the motion. My hands on her, our faces closer than they were, and her lips right fucking there. Her pulse pounds beneath my fingers where they're wrapped around her wrist. I can hear her stuttered breath. My voice softens. "I love that answer. It says a lot about you and what's important to you."

Let go, Lach.

Her shoulders rise and fall as her lips part softly.

What the fuck are you doing?

Let go.

This time I listen, but not before the damage is done. Not before I see her hands tremble slightly. Not before I know I'm not the only one affected when we touch.

"See? Now you have dirt on me. Not as salacious as you thought, now, is it?" Her chuckle is tinged with nerves.

"Dirt, huh?" I try to recover as adrenaline races through me.

Is the fact that I wanted to kiss you enough dirt?

"Yep." She swallows forcibly. "Dirt is always important. Blackmail and leverage aren't beneath me."

"Okay, so you're telling me that I better watch out and stay on your good side?"

She flashes a grin. "That's the best place to be, Evans. Trust me."

And then I fall even more under her spell.

Chapter Six

Blair

"**T**HAT'S ADORABLE."

Lachlan shrugs. "I'd call it . . . *manly*," he teases.

I adjust my legs curled up beneath me. The bar stopped serving drinks what feels like hours ago, so we moved to a small table and chair set on the far side of the lounge that borders the lobby. I'm too tired to even think about what happened earlier or how his hands on my wrist made me feel. Feel? More like evoke every damn sensation known to man.

"Lachlan, you were dressed in a blue tutu. I'd say that's a tad more adorable, cute, whatever else you want to call it, than *manly*."

"Whatever I was, I rocked that damn tutu," he says with a definitive nod of his head and a chuckle. It's low and unassuming but damn if it doesn't wreak the best kind of havoc on my nerves.

A yawn pulls at my mouth and sleep calls to the far recesses of my mind. A subtle reminder that I'm ignoring how long we've been out here, talking, getting to know each other, sharing silly stories that I honestly can't remember the last time I told someone.

But nothing puts the time lost into perspective until I look over Lachlan's shoulder and see Paolo talking to the front desk clerk.

Awareness hits me as I glance to the windows on the far side of the hotel and see daylight.

"Lach." I gasp his name out as I grab my phone. "It's six-thirty."

"No fucking way . . ." But then he looks toward the lobby and sees a crew member dressed in an Apex polo shirt and his eyes go wide. And then he throws his head back and laughs in a way that has the panic that suddenly hit me abate into curiosity.

"What?" I ask.

"I can't remember the last time I stayed up all night and just talked."

"Me neither."

"It was nice."

"More than nice," I say.

His smile softens much like his eyes do as he stands and extends a hand to me to help me stand. I stare at it for a beat, almost as if I know that taking it will start the ball rolling on something I'm afraid I won't be able to stop.

But that's a shit thought.

We've done nothing wrong here tonight other than talk and get to know each other. There was no blatant flirting, no particulars given of Rossi's and my relationship or of his own dating situation. It was just plain, old-fashioned communication. The kind where our cell phones were on do not disturb and face down on the table between us. Where I know I remembered odd things about my life and had no problem sharing them with him. Where we laughed at each other and with each other.

And even long after the warmth of the champagne wore off, there was zero expectation of anything more than talking.

I think that's why I reach out and grab his hand. Why I let him help me up from my seat. And why when we're face-to-face, a few inches apart, does a thought cross my mind that I immediately chastise myself for.

Kiss me.

It's there and I can't erase it. I'd never act on it though. Because of Rossi. Because of my job. Because . . . just because that's not who I am.

And yet it's there and I know for a fact he's thinking it too. He has to be by the way his eyes keep flickering down to my lips and then back up. By the bob of his Adam's apple and the lick of his tongue to wet his bottom lip.

"Blair," he murmurs as he takes half a step closer and reaches out to tuck my hair behind my ear. I freeze at his touch. At the way his fingers curl around the shell of my ear. The way they trail down the curve of my neck. At how his hand rests there and his thumb reaches over to brush against my bottom lip.

It's the briefest damn moment before he jolts back like I've shocked him.

Before I realize how damn much I'm affected by his touch. Or that Paolo and who knows who else could be watching us.

"I'm sorry." Lachlan shakes his head and takes another step back. "I didn't mean to do that. I'm tired. I'm—"

"It's fine. It was nothing. Just . . . tired." I struggle to get the words out around the guilt I feel and the desire simmering just beneath it.

A ghost of a lopsided smile paints his lips. "I have a confession," he murmurs like we have all the time in the world. Like members from both of our teams won't be trickling down soon and see us standing like this in the same clothes we were in last night.

"What?" I barely whisper.

"My plants? People help me take care of them. Keeping something alive is much harder than you think."

"And yet you keep yourself alive every time you go around that track."

"With the help of others."

I give the slightest of shrugs, our eyes still locked. "Both are impressive."

"Huh. I never thought of it that way."

"Change in perspective is sometimes good," I say.

That shy smile of his returns. The one that makes me think he has a secret he's not telling me. The one that keeps my feet rooted in place because I want him to tell me.

But laughter in the lobby tells me not this time.

Not now.

He holds out a peppermint to me. I smile and think of how I ate the last one and thought of him. How every time I smell peppermint I do.

Who am I kidding? I think about him even when I don't smell it.

"For you to remember me by," he murmurs, his hand out. *Like I could forget him*. It seems like there's so much more than a mint at stake when I reach out and actually take it.

But I do.

"Good night, Mr. Evans," I say and take a step back.

"Change the perspective." He reaches down and picks up my phone and paperback and hands them to me. My fingers brush over his, and it feels like the touch is so much more than that. "Good morning, Miss Carmichael."

He turns on his heel and walks out of the lounge area with me left staring after him. But my stare is short-lived when I see Rossi's tire gunner, Beto, studying me from across the lobby. He looks to where Lachlan is retreating and then back to me in my pajama pants and slippers with a puzzled look on his face.

I smile and hold my paperback up like it's an explanation as to why Lachlan and I are parting ways this early in the morning. It makes no sense, but then again, nothing seems to right now.

The elevator ride feels like it takes forever. The walk down the long hallway to my room even more. But the moment I close my door behind me and am out of sight from anyone else who might make the wrong assumption, I hold my arms out and dramatically fall backward onto my bed. My cheeks are sore from smiling and my stomach has the weirdest, fluttery feeling in it.

One I haven't felt in the longest time.

But it's nothing. I know it's not. I know they are a result of just feeling seen in general. Of being listened to. Of being heard. Of being made to feel like I'm just as important as the racing and career that owns his life.

And maybe until now, I never realized how much I didn't feel listened to. Or how much of a back seat I've taken—and allowed myself to take.

Is it so much to want to be the center of someone's world? Not the whole time . . . but at least for a little bit?

The cork.

I shove my hands in my sweatshirt pocket to touch the unique texture of the champagne cork. The one I pocketed long before the bar closed for the night. Way before I stayed up all night getting to know a man who I still want to know more about.

You took it because you knew something about it was going to be important. Because you knew you wanted to remember this night. The moments within it. And the way I mattered to a man I now considered a friend.

Or maybe I simply took it out of habit. Because I confessed my silly collection to Lachlan and on the off chance he saw me pocket it, wanted to make him feel like he was important too.

Even I don't buy my own lie.

I yawn. Clearly, my body is tired, and I should be worried about how I'm going to function the rest of the day for work—but I'm not. I'm still riding the high that Lachlan created. That we created.

You sound pathetic, Blair.

No. I don't. I sound . . . satisfied. Giddy. Alive.

More like a dog who was excited that a scrap of attention was thrown her way.

Dramatic much?

But . . . isn't that what and who I've been as of late? Waiting and wanting attention from the man I love and who I thought loved me? Waiting and wanting when I'm a woman who never waits and wants or takes that back seat? When I'm one who never thought she'd be with a man who let her do just that.

But Rossi has.

Heavy shit to think about on a tired mind that's competing with an exhilarated body.

I close my eyes and drift off for a beat. Kindness—his smile, his eyes, his questions—is what I think about when it comes to Lachlan Evans.

He asked about my paintings. Not just about them, but he wanted to see them. And then he called me on my lie about not having any pictures of them.

My grin returns as I hug my arms across my chest and replay the conversation. As I remember how I almost showed him the most private part of me because I felt the sincerity in his words.

When has Rossi ever asked that? He's been in and out of my place hundreds of times, and I can't remember the last time he said a word about my art. Not the half-finished painting sitting on my easel. Not the stacks of completed canvases leaning against the wall.

If it isn't about racing, he simply can't see it. *Which means, he rarely sees me.*

And that's not to say that Lachlan is better or would be a better boyfriend. It's just that . . . *screw it, Blair.* Why are you talking Lachlan down to make Rossi seem better? Why are you justifying and invalidating the things you deserve?

Shit.

I never expected to have these mixed emotions after a single night of conversation.

It's just the newness of it that makes me feel that way. The same way I probably felt with Rossi all those years ago.

I'm far from naïve. I know that the grass isn't always greener . . . but the grass beneath my feet isn't being watered anymore. It's being neglected. Overlooked. And maybe I just didn't realize it until recently . . . when I've taken time to compare our relationship with others. And now, compare it to spending time with a man who simply wants to be my friend and celebrate my wins.

But what does that mean, Blair?

With a sigh, I force my eyes open and stare back at the same ceiling that last night drove me downstairs.

He never texted me last night. Not when he got back to the hotel. Not when he saw the champagne bottle sitting at his door, which was still there when I passed on the way to mine. Not when he remembered that he'd promised to celebrate with me.

The temptation to knock on his door was strong, but the reality I'd have faced when he didn't answer—when I confirmed that he never returned to his room last night—was stronger.

Isn't that telling enough?

Maybe I need to take a step back and reevaluate things. Maybe we're at that phase we hit every so often that forces us to take a break.

I love Rossi.

I always will.

But right now that love feels very different than it used to. More one-sided. More platonic. More of an *in like* than an *in love*.

Change the perspective.

Maybe for my sake, that's what I should be doing.

Chapter Seven

Blair

"THANK YOU. THIS IS A DAY CARTER WILL NEVER FORGET. ONE I'LL never forget," Carter's dad says as he blinks away the tears welling in his eyes.

"Mission accomplished," I say as I release his hand and pat him gently on the back. "That's the hope with this program. Now, let's get you guys over to where the excitement is." I motion to Gina who is standing on the far side of our viewing platform. "Gina is going to take you over so you can see the podium celebration. Sound good?"

A cheer goes up from the ten children, ages eight to fourteen, and their families. The ones I've been coordinating this event with for the past few months. My last official duty—one that was important to me to complete—before I jump wholeheartedly into the masquerade ball.

"Thank you, again," another mother says in broken English as she passes by with her daughter's hand in hers and a grin on her lips.

"My pleasure."

I accept a few more thank-yous as the families follow Gina. The emcee's voice echoes over the speakers beyond as he fills time and works up the crowd waiting for the podium celebration.

A celebration that will not include an Apex driver. *Yet again.*

That makes for a fun week before heading out to the next race. Good thing I have a million things to keep me busy while Rossi no doubt broods over today.

And yet when I look up and see him finishing up his post-race interviews, my heart aches for him. For a man so skilled and natural at driving but whose team is currently in a downward slump. He's standing there, in plain sight, and yet feels so inaccessible anymore.

And not just because of the post-race process.

I'm talking about us. About his disinterest in connecting with me anymore.

What surprises me the most about it all? That I don't feel devastated by the thought. By his inaction.

He meets my eyes across the distance and gives his head the subtlest of shakes. I can see the disappointment there. The frustration. And while I know it's part of the sport, I hate that I can't do anything to fix it for him.

Paolo calls me over the radio to answer a few questions, and I welcome the distraction from my thoughts. For the next while I get lost in the ins and outs of finishing what I'm doing. Of thanking the staff who helped coordinate and corral our guests all day. Of making sure all the swag and memorabilia for our guests is ready for them to grab on the way out of the gates.

And maybe, just maybe, I cheat a few steps down toward the Apex Racing hospitality suite in the hopes of getting a couple of minutes with Rossi as he shuttles between the post-race meetings and the chaos that always ensues once the checkered flag drops.

My patience pays off when he heads my way. I rise from my seat on a retaining wall the minute I see him. There's a sympathetic smile on my lips and understanding in my voice.

I resist the urge to reach out and hug him, aware that I'm on the clock and that he's just another driver when I am. "Hey. Tough race, huh?"

He stops and the glare he gives me says it all. Disgust. Frustration. Disappointment. Helplessness. "Why are you over here?"

I shrug off the harshness of his words. "I just wanted to see if you were okay. I guess I wanted you to see a familiar face. A—"

"Like I don't have those surrounding me constantly with my team and crew?" he snaps and shifts on his feet.

Wow. Okay.

"Look. I get it. You're pissed and frustrated, but I'm not the car so let's not take it out on me, okay?"

"Always know how to dig the knife in deeper, don't you?"

"What does that mean?"

"It means I did my goddamn job out there. To a fucking T. Don't tell me I didn't."

Are we having the same conversation here? I study Rossi, the tension set in his shoulders, and decide to let it go. The comment. His anger. All of it. I chalk it up to him needing an outlet.

"No one said you didn't," I say to pacify him.

"Right. Whatever. Just forget about it. Let's go."

"What?" I bark out a laugh.

"I said let's go."

"Rossi . . ." My head spins from the whiplash. One minute he's telling me to leave him alone, the next he's demanding that I follow him? Which fricking way is up right now?

"Did you not hear me?" he demands and holds his hand out to me like I'm supposed to take it when he knows damn well I can't. This is one of those lines we don't cross. Not while working. And most definitely not on race day when the whole world is watching.

"I heard you, but I can't go with you."

"So first you're late this morning and now you can't go with me." The muscle clenches in his jaw as he stares at me.

"Late? I was there to kiss you good luck and fasten the neck of your suit. Just like I always am." Hasn't this been our thing for years? The good-luck kiss? Tapping my fingers to the sponsorship patch over his heart before zipping up his race suit the rest of the way and velcroing the neck of it? "I'm the one who risks my job by being there, but I still show up nonetheless. What are you even talking about?"

Today was different though. I was there. We went through the motions of our routine, but it was almost as if my presence was more of a nuisance than a comfort.

"So are you leaving with me or what?"

"Rossi. You're not hearing me. I can't just up and leave. I have to finish my job—the debriefing meeting, seeing my ten families out, a quick meetup for the masquerade ball—"

"Right. How could I forget? You're *Miss Important* now." He waves a hand in dismissal at me and takes a few steps back. "It can wait."

"No, it can't," I say as he starts to walk away.

He stops and stares at me. "What?"

"This is my job. *My promotion,* in case you forgot." There's a bite to my words, my anger evident.

He nods, lips tight and impatience emanating off him. "Right. I did. Congrats." His smile is forced. "So . . . now can we go?"

He doesn't get it, does he?

"No. We can't. I . . ." All I've wanted for months is for him to see me, to take time out for me, and now that he is, it's hitting different. It doesn't help that the way he's *demanding* isn't exactly welcoming. "Just like your job comes first for you, mine comes first for me."

"And what if I need to come first for you?"

"You can't pick and choose when you need me. I'm not at your beck and call. This is *my* job."

"I'm well aware." He snorts derisively. "But let's face it. We both know whose job comes first here. But sure, convince yourself into thinking that yours is more important than mine. I'll enjoy the mindfuckery you need to do to convince yourself otherwise."

"Oliver," I say in a rare use of his first name as I stare at him stunned. There is *no way* he just said that. "It's probably best if you walk away right now and don't finish whatever else you were going to say."

It's my attempt to keep the peace and hold on to my dignity while allowing him—a huge competitor—the grace to not say something he'll regret because he's upset over his finish.

"That's convenient for you, isn't it?"

"Convenient?" Once again, I feel like we're not having the same conversation.

"Forget I said anything. I have shit to do."

I watch him walk away, his square shoulders and PR handler jogging up beside him to protect him from the people milling about. But he gravitates toward them and flashes that trademark Rossi smile. One he clearly couldn't afford for me.

When *was* the last time he said something nice to me? Or even took a moment out of his busy schedule to let me know I was on his mind? I don't expect flowers or grand gestures but knowing I matter goes a long way. It holds me over for those in-between times.

Instead, I'm left with the nastiness of what he just said.

"We both know whose job comes first here. But sure, convince yourself into

thinking that yours is more important than mine. I'll enjoy the mindfuckery you need to do to convince yourself otherwise."

Is that how he really feels about me? Is that how he sees me?

In my head I perform mental gymnastics to try and justify my way around it. *Stop. Just stop. He spoke the words. He's responsible for them.*

A small pang of something hits me hard.

When will I learn?

Learn what? To stay away from him after a bad race or to stop making excuses for his shitty behavior?

Both seem pretty apropos right now.

At least next week is an off week. An off week that Rossi had asked me to stay at his place for the duration. While it's the last thing I want to do right now, maybe it's what we need. Some time with each other. To be together without the outside world dictating how our time should be spent. I can work during the day while he's doing his physical training and simulator time and then we can hang out in the evening.

Reconnect.

I shake my head. Just when I thought it was going to be a good race for Apex, for the guys, they were hit with a one-two punch. Rossi touched tires with Riggs and came out on the wrong end of it with his car in the gravel. And Lachlan pushed hard, challenging other drivers when he could, but never really had the power needed to overtake anyone. He only moved up in position when other cars crashed, finishing a disappointing twelfth place when Apex should be in the top six at all times.

Lachlan.

Yes, I paid attention to his race much like I pay attention to all the drivers' races. It's my job to know where they place and what the story of the race is—because every race does have its story. Its hero. Its villain. Its highlights. Its lowlights.

I've avoided him since Friday morning.

Almost as if I felt guilty for something when really, we didn't do anything wrong.

And yet, haven't I waited for someone—one of his crew members or one of my co-workers, both of whom who were in the same hotel—to ask questions? To say that they saw us and wonder what the hell we were doing?

Get back to work, Blair.

"We're heading back your way," Gina says over the two-way radio I have clipped to my waistband.

"I'm ready for you," I reply and head to our staging area of sorts. A small part of me is sad for our families to go home and for today to be over. The part of me that loves this job and the joy it brings others. Then there's the side of me who's ecstatic that this is my last task to finish out as an outreach coordinator and now I can jump wholeheartedly into the masquerade ball.

I get lost in those thoughts, in the possibilities they present, and then realize that my group should have been here by now. I've lifted my radio to call Gina about the same time I step outside the hospitality suite.

And I lower the radio when I take in the sight across the walkway from me. Lachlan is standing there. He has a baseball hat on to no doubt cover his sweaty and helmet-mussed hair. His arms are crossed over his chest and his smile's brighter than the sun as he engages with the kids from my group. They laugh. They ask questions. They take a group picture that Lachlan initiates.

I watch the interaction, thrilled for the kids while trying not to compare his actions with Rossi's. They're two completely different men . . . and yet the comparison is right in front of me.

Both men had shitty days. Both men fell short of their potential. Both men have to finish out their duties for the day even when I'm sure they don't want to.

The difference though? One of them completely and selfishly discounted me while the other tucked away disappointment with his finish and sacrificed his time—and gave these kids a chance of a lifetime: meeting a Formula 1 driver.

As if on cue, Lachlan looks over the heads of the crowd and sees me standing here. Our gazes lock and I swear my heart jumps into my throat. He stares for a beat longer than necessary before he gives the slightest of nods and returns his attention back to the kids in front of him.

But I remain rooted to the spot, staring, wondering why a stupid glance has my heart racing when it shouldn't. When we've made eye contact numerous times before. Why does it feel so different?

He spends a few more minutes with them, calling on kids who timidly raise their hands to ask questions, before his PR minder pulls him away. They head toward me, their chatter incessant and excitement through the roof.

He did that for them and I'm so very grateful for it.

"That was so cool of Evans to do," Gina says as the last of the families make their way out of the paddock.

"I know. Those kids got one-on-one time that they'll never forget."

"No doubt. And it looks like you're about to as well."

"What?" I ask but follow the lift of her chin to where Lachlan is standing at the edge of our hospitality suite, hands in front of him holding his baseball cap, eyes looking our way.

My smile is as automatic as my first step toward him. But then I pause. How presumptive of me that he's here to speak to me. "Um," I say to myself more than anyone as I stop in that suspended state of awkward indecision over what to do.

"Hi," Lachlan says, offering a cute little wave, and makes clear his intention that he is in fact here for me.

Why does his mussed hair make him even more attractive? And why does the fact that he took his hat off to talk to me hit me differently?

Because you come from a military family where taking off your hat is a sign of respect.

"Hi. What are you doing here?" I ask and then say what I really mean to say. "Thank you so much for talking to everyone earlier. You really made their day. It was super cool of you to take the time after a tough race."

"Not a problem." He shrugs. "If it weren't for a driver taking the time like that, I probably wouldn't be standing here."

"Really?"

"Really." He glances around and then back to me. "Thanks for letting me hang with them for a few minutes. It was a good reminder to me of where I came from and how even during tough seasons like this one, I'm damn lucky to get to do what I do for a living."

I angle my head to the side and study him. "You know you're not normal, right?"

"Perfect. Normal is boring." The grin he flashes is all-consuming.

"Can I help you? Did you need anything from me?" I ask.

His chuckle is low and rumbles over my skin. The quick shake of his head says he's not going to voice the innuendo his laugh might infer. The same inference that I hate that I like hearing. "Nope. I don't need anything. Just a simple thank-you for the reminder earlier that I have an awesome job."

"I didn't do anything." I hold my hands up. "See you at the next race then?"

His expression falls. "You're not going to Sterling Ridge?" he asks about Apex's private track where they test and tweak the cars.

I'm confused and I think my expression reflects just that. "Why would I be going to Sterling?"

"Oh. I'm sorry. I just assumed that you were—"

"Assumed?"

"That you'd be going with Rossi."

I hold both of my hands up. "Lachlan. What are you talking about?"

"The Apex team bonding planned for next week," he says as I stare at him with wide eyes. "The owner thought we needed a reset so we're all going there for the week. It'll give us time at the track. Time with our teams. And more importantly, he wanted our families there so we can have them around us. Just a breather to try and right this ship before it sinks." He glances over his shoulder and then back to me with a furrowed brow. "Should I assume by the look on your face that I just fucked up and that Rossi didn't tell you about any of this?"

"He probably just forgot to tell me in the chaos of race day." *Much like he forgot to celebrate my promotion with me.* The thought still leaves a bitter taste in my mouth.

"Sure," he says, "but we were told about it on Monday. Not today."

Monday? What the hell? So this was pre-promotion, pre-bad race finish, pre . . . everything of the week. And yet Rossi still didn't tell me.

Is it wrong to assume he hadn't planned to spend next week with me by choice? That he agreed to hanging out in that half-listened way men do but never really want to? What else am I left to assume because it's clear that it didn't even ping on his radar that his trip to Sterling would mean we wouldn't have time together.

What the hell is going on, because I feel like I'm two steps behind?

"Got it." My smile is strained.

"Hey, I'm sorry. I didn't mean to cause any problems between the two of you. I figured you knew."

"You didn't. It's fine." I wave a hand. "I have so much work to do, it's probably a blessing."

He angles his head to the side and studies me in a way that says he sees right through my bluff. It's in the way his eyes hold mine and the softening of his expression. "You sure?"

"Positive."

"Okay." He nods and hooks a thumb over his shoulder. "I need to get to our debrief."

"I'm sure that will be a fun one," I say sarcastically to add some levity.

"Ha. A real party. No doubt I'll be wishing I had become a vet in about thirty minutes." He takes a few steps backward and rocks on his heels. "I'll see you around then."

"Next race."

"Next race," he says with another nod before turning to walk the other way.

There's an ease to him that makes me want to keep talking with him. "Lachlan?"

"Yeah?" A crooked smile crawls across his lips as he looks over his shoulder.

"Who are you taking to Sterling with you?"

Our eyes meet for a beat before he answers solemnly. "No one."

With that he turns on his heel and strides away toward the Apex building farther down the paddock.

Chapter Eight

Blair

"YOU LOOK STRESSED."

My smile is automatic. Chills chase over my body, and I look up from my desk—and the various notepads with to-do lists on them—to see Lachlan standing in my doorway.

Twelve days. That's how long it's been since I saw him last and nope, the time hasn't seemed to do a damn thing on dampening my visceral reaction to him.

I'm an idiot to think that it would.

"Hi. Why are you . . . what are you doing here?" I ask as my surprise gives way to gratitude.

He's the last person I expected to see in my office. I've been lost in the details for hours. Details that when I took this job, I naively underestimated would take me away from the sights and sounds of the track—the ones that I love wholeheartedly. And yet here I am on the Friday of race week and not once have I had the chance to make the short distance from my portable office, across the walkway, to the garages to see any of the testing live.

I can hear it—that's inescapable—but I haven't seen it.

"Well, I hate to break it to you, but I do kind of have some business on the track over there," he teases as his grin warms my office.

"You do?"

"I do."

"Oh. Right. You're raking the gravel again."

He chuckles. "How'd you know? Being on the gravel crew is a very important position. Nice and smooth. No tire ruts from those dipshit drivers who can't keep their cars on the track."

"You'd think it would be a simple task. The keeping the car on the track part." It's hard to keep a straight face, but this banter, which we seem to fall into so easily—just feels so natural.

"You'd think, but for those pretentious pretty boys out there, they're so busy looking at themselves in the mirrors, they miss the curves in the track." He winks and I laugh.

"And ruin your damn gravel."

"And ruin my damn gravel," he repeats, our smiles wide and eyes locked as we pause in silence for a moment.

And then, strangely, nerves hit me. It's in the twist of my stomach and the jitter of my hands as I suddenly feel the need to straighten my desk, stand up, and take a drink.

"So, Lachlan, what brings you here . . . to the bane of most drivers' existences?" I ask because any trip to my office means I'm asking them to participate in something more than they already are required to. Most avoid me.

"I figured you were knee-deep in planning. Treading water in unfamiliar waters. And that . . . I don't know. That you could use some stress relief."

"That's thoughtful of you."

He holds a brown paper bag up by its handles. "I brought you flowers."

"Flowers?" I stare at him like he's crazy as he sets the bag on my desk in front of me with a big *thunk*.

"Flowers," he reiterates.

My tongue feels thick in my mouth as I struggle with what to say. It won't go over well if Rossi happens to walk in here and see flowers from another man—his teammate no less.

And at the same time . . .

"Go on," he encourages.

I rise from my seat and peer into the bag prepared to see daisies or roses or something with petals. Something that I'll have to thank him for but acknowledge that I can't accept—not just because of Rossi's reaction but because of the warring emotions accepting them would make me feel.

Emotions that already seem to be warring even without flowers.

It's been crickets. Or almost crickets seeing as how I've barely heard a word from Rossi. Not much more than a "working hard with the team" during his time at Sterling. Yeah. That working hard, according to various pictures on my socials, included a few clubs and several bars.

He had all the time in the world to do that, but not a single minute to call his girlfriend or return a text with anything more than a one-word response.

His silence spoke volumes.

Clearly, he wasn't too upset over not getting to spend the week together because he never once mentioned it.

I fought the urge to pry more—to insert myself—into what he was doing, but I refrained. Rather, I threw myself into my work. Into the gala. But even with being busy with that, I've dipped between anger and sadness at his silence. At feeling like I've been pushed aside.

And yet this man in front of me is showing me that he's thought about me.

"Oh." The lone syllable escapes my lips when I see the stack of books and the few scattered peppermints within the bag. There's no way he just did that. "You brought me flowers," I murmur, now understanding what he meant, before looking back up at him with eyes wide with surprise.

"I did." He nods, a proud expression on his face. "And I was promised they were loaded with lots of good betrayal and attraction to sink your teeth into and to help you relax."

He bought me flowers.

"Lachlan." I look at the bag full of books and then back up to him.

He holds his hands up in front of him. "It's no big deal, really. I was on a rare outing, exploring the city while at Sterling, and I came across this cool bookstore. I thought of you, of our conversation from a few weeks ago, and wondered if you needed 'flowers' for when you have some downtime. Or perhaps to force you to pause and relax. It wasn't anything."

But it's everything. Doesn't he see that?

This is the sort of thing Skylar would do because she knows me so well. And yet, this man, my newest friend, seems to get me too.

Not to mention, he's Lachlan Evans. He just can't walk in anywhere. He gets noticed. His actions are reported on. He . . . he made an effort for me. *He listened to me.*

"I don't know what to say." Does my voice sound as overwhelmed to him as it does to me?

"You don't have to say anything." His smile is shy. "I promise it's nothing more than what I said. It's just books."

"You mean *flowers*."

He chuckles. "Right. Flowers." He rocks on his heels, awkwardness settling in all of a sudden. "Well then . . . I hope you enjoy at least one of them."

"I'm sure I will." I pull one out and run my hand over its spine.

"I have to get back. It was my first free moment and I've been lugging these around, so I wanted to get them to you before I creased the cover or bent a corner or whatever it is that ruins a book." He shrugs. "My mum is a stickler about those things."

"I love her already." I laugh. And why do I find the way he says *mum* so damn adorable?

His cheeks flush as he adjusts his hat on his head. "Okay then. I'll see you around."

"Lach?"

"Yeah?"

"Thank you. Truly. That's the nicest thing someone has done for me in a long time."

He simply nods and walks away. I listen to his footsteps as they fade down the hallway. I hear him say hello to a few people.

And then I'm left in the silence of my office with a bag full of books and head full of thoughts.

I sort through the titles again, my head shaking and the smile on my lips soft. Wanting to remember this moment, much like a cork or a bottle cap, I snap a quick picture of them.

The picture is interrupted when my phone rings. If a smile wasn't already plastered on my face, it would be now.

"Skylar!" I answer the phone, everything I'm feeling more than evident in my tone. *Does she know how much I've missed her?*

"Wow. Someone is clearly in a great mood." She laughs.

"I am. I just got the best bouquet of flowers ever."

"Flowers?" She snorts. "But you don't even like flowers."

"I like this kind," I say, so lost in looking at the books, I don't realize what I just said. Skylar knows me well to catch the flub.

"And who gave you these flowers?"

"A friend."

"A friend?" she asks. "So *not* the man who's supposed to be giving them to you, then."

I open my mouth to make an excuse for Rossi but then stop myself. If anyone knows the truth about me and Rossi, it's Skylar. She's often challenged me whenever I've stood up for or made excuses for Rossi, and as I've watched her and her husband more closely as of late, I'm beginning to understand why. So, honesty it is.

"Correct," I say.

"And would this friend happen to be a man or a woman?"

"This friend . . . it's a long story, but the flowers weren't flowers. They were books. I—"

"Okay. This is making more sense. I can see why you liked the 'flowers.'" She pauses. "Explain why you're hesitating to be honest here. Why won't you tell me who gave them to you?"

"Sky." I sigh her name out.

"Nope. No, *Sky. No excuses.* Whoever bought you these flowers—er books—has clearly made you happy." She clears her throat. "Sounds like something your mom or one of your crazy siblings would send you." She's not wrong. "Which you totally deserve by the way. So this person is a good one to have in your corner from my perspective."

"Thank you. It's been a while since someone has made me feel like this— happy, appreciated, I don't know—and I hadn't realized I was missing it, if that makes sense."

"It makes total sense. Rossi hasn't cared for you *well* for a while now. And it's worried me." Interesting Sky has noticed that, and yet, it's only recently hit my radar. I nod, not that she can see.

"It just came out of the blue, you know?"

"Yeah, I hear you. Definitely not something Rossi would do. *Selflessness* isn't in his wheelhouse." I chuckle and for once I don't feel the need to defend him. "Look, you deserve to feel everything your flowers made you feel. We both know that. It sounds like you need to make some choices here. Perhaps look at your relationship with Rossi with a different perspective." *A different perspective.* Interesting that Skylar mentions that term after Lachlan did a few weeks ago.

"I know," I say softly as I run my fingers over the jackets of the hardbacks.

"Good. I'm glad. Sometimes doing what's best for you is the most courageous thing you can do in life. It's not easy. You often have to go through some pain to get to the other side. But it is well worth it. I promise."

"Just like you did," I say softly.

"Just like I did," she repeats. "And send me a picture of your flowers. I want to see them!"

We talk for a bit more, and when we hang up, I read over the synopsis on each book while Skylar's words linger in my mind.

When was the last time someone who wasn't part of my family did something thoughtful like that for me? A care package from my mom is one thing, but this was an intentional gift.

One he put time and effort into.

One that says he was thinking about me.

Because that's what friends *do. Right?*

Chapter Nine

Lachlan

"**P**USH. PUSH. PUSH." HENRY'S VOICE COMES THROUGH MY EARPIECE as I let up coming into the chicane.

"Understood." The car vibrates around me, and the signature whine of its motor fills my ears. "The split?" I ask, referring to my time to this point on the track versus the current pole sitter.

"Point zero three."

"Ten-four," I say and readjust my grip on the wheel as I come into the straight. And prepare to fly.

The world outside of my cockpit becomes one big blur. Green from the grass. Yellow from the walls on one side of me. Red from the walls as I enter the last straight. And a blend of colors as I push through the grandstands' straight, entering my second qualifying lap.

"Great first lap. Point zero four behind the leader."

"Got it."

"Time to fly, Lach," Henry says.

"Currently flying," I say, but the grin on my face has nothing to do with what Henry says and everything to do with the damn woman I can't get out of my head.

The one I need to.

The one whose dream it was to fly.

Blair Carmichael.

"Point zero three," Henry says at my first split, shocking my thoughts back to where they need to be.

To this.

To the track.

To my own damn dream.

To putting the next puzzle piece in place that will let me win a world championship one day.

I hold my own on the lap. Trying to trim the line of the track where I can. Pushing the car as hard as I can when possible.

"Great job. That's a P4," Henry says when I cross the start/finish line.

I'll be in the second row for tomorrow's race.

That's the best place on the starting grid that I've had in the last five races. I pump my fist knowing it's a solid day for the car and my team. The time and adjustments we made at Sterling were worth it.

And when I cut the engine and climb out of the car, the expressions on my crew's face say they feel the same.

"Damn good driving out there," Henry says as he helps me out of the car and clasps my hand.

"It's a start," I say, set my helmet down, and look to my crew around me. "Great work, everyone. You kicked arse for me, and I appreciate it. The car felt great. Ran great. I'll try and build more on it tomorrow during the race."

Fingers crossed my position stays where it is. There are only two cars left to finish qualifying today, but I'm sitting pretty solid so I'm not worried.

I chat a bit more with my race engineer and a few of the mechanics, but even with all the distractions, I know he's here. I don't have to look over my shoulder to know my dad is standing on the periphery, taking it all in, not interfering, but a significant presence in the garage, nonetheless.

Just like he always has been.

And I'm not wrong. He's on the fringe of the garage, just outside of the chaos. Close enough so I know but far enough away so he doesn't interfere.

"Dad," I say and move toward him. Our hug is quick—just like it always is.

"You put in a good showing out there. A great starting position. I'm proud of you."

"Thanks." I run a hand through my hair and sigh. "It's been a struggle but with the extra time we've been putting in, I think we might have ironed things out and be on the right track."

"That's what Gio thinks," my dad says, referring to the owner of Apex Racing, Gio Dumount.

"You talked?" I ask looking around, surprised he was here considering he wasn't planned to be.

"We did."

"About?"

He shrugs. "His plan for the team. If and where he sees you fitting in with it."

"Chandler's handling it," I say of my agent and what feels like the endless negotiations for a ride next year.

"I'm well aware. It doesn't hurt for me to ask too."

I nod. "Gio knows other teams are interested."

And they are but not in the way I want them to be. Isn't that what is compounding all this stress?

"He mentioned that. Do you think that's the best course of action if this is where you want to stay?" He meets my eyes. "You do want to stay here, don't you?"

"Everywhere else that would be a step up already has their drivers locked up for next season. That leaves me . . . fuck if I know where that leaves me."

"Gravitas would be an equal move. They've insinuated that they would welcome a driver shake-up. Sure, they'd have to buy out Schilling's contract—"

"They'd never do that."

"They're looking for new life. Navarro is locked in. Schilling has been underperforming. And frankly, their cars are outperforming yours right now."

"New life? C'mon." I wave a hand at him.

"Schilling was told he needs to start performing or is out."

"Like you know." I make the statement but know deep down he's right. Everyone talks to my father, Erik Evans. He's the nice dad with the endless praise and kind smile. Secrets just spill out around him.

"I do." He nods. "His father was distraught over it. Needed an ear. I lent him one earlier in the paddock."

This changes things.

"Gravitas talked to Chandler, but we thought they were just blowing smoke," I say. "Just feeling drivers out for future contract options."

"Apparently not." He glances over his shoulder and then back to me. "I know you want to stay here, but don't discount Gravitas. They have a good team, have a good engine . . . and sometimes change is a good thing."

I run a hand through my hair and sigh as I wait for crew members to walk past so that our conversation stays private.

Teams have shown interest, but ones that are farther down the Constructors' standings. They've discussed decent contract terms, but they'd be a step down from where I've worked fucking hard to be.

But until now, I thought Gravitas talk was just that—*talk*. And now . . . now I need to wrap my head around the idea that they might be in play.

Just when I thought rosters were locked up for the next year, this comes about.

A stark reminder that every contract has an option that can be bought out. One that could upend the fragile balance of the driver world I walk in.

"There's a reason we chose Chandler as your agent," my dad says. "He's dogged and always has something up his sleeve."

"True."

"And you've been in this world long enough. When someone wants you, they want you. It's on you to perform even when the car doesn't. That increases your worth."

"I'm well aware. Believe me, I'm well aware."

My contract *is* ending at season's end.

I need to make something out of nothing.

And, it's Rossi I'm competing with for the lone seat at Apex and now apparently the seat at Gravitas.

There is also an incredible crop of rookie drivers waiting in the wings to push us out and make our seats their own.

Pressure.

It's fucking everywhere. All the time. Every minute of every day. While I wouldn't have it any other way, at times it wears on you.

But my dad is the only person who I'll let see that exhaustion.

"I told Gio the season's about to turn around and that he'll wish he grabbed you before someone else does."

My dad lifts his hand and waves to somebody. I follow his gaze, thinking it's Gio and in no way do I want to seem like I ignore the man who pulls the purse strings here at Apex.

But while my search ends up empty for him, my eyes stutter over the sight of someone else.

Over to Blair in pit row. Her boss—Paolo, I think it is—is at her side. They're walking, both have sunglasses on, and both with intense expressions as if they're discussing something of utmost importance.

Jesus. The woman takes my breath away. She's in a pair of white pants and a red T-shirt. Nothing fancy. Nothing sexy. And yet every part of me is aware of her and wants. Desires.

"And dare I ask who that is?" my dad asks, his question seeping into my thoughts. But I can sense the moment he realizes who she is and why I'm looking.

His body tenses.

His exhale is audible.

The man knows me better than anybody else.

"Lachlan." His voice is a warning I don't want to hear or heed.

"That's Paolo," I try to cover as I tear my eyes from Blair. "He asked if I'd participate in a few more of the outreach programs. Just a cameo here and there but you know, to help reach disadvantaged youth."

"Good to hear it. It's always good to remember where you came from."

"Yep."

We talk a bit more. About the car's potential. About the team's time at Sterling. About my mum and a crazy case she's in the middle of as a criminal defense lawyer. About how I'm doing—something he always asks as if I'm still a teenager.

But it's comforting and normal for a big weekend where we as a team and I personally need to perform.

"Dinner?" he asks.

"Sure. Something low-key. I need to keep my focus."

He flashes a proud grin. "Of course. I'll text you later."

"Sounds good." I turn to go back to my team and my duties.

"Hey, Lach?" he says, pulling me back toward him.

"Yep?"

"You couldn't fool me way back when. You still can't fool me now. Pick any woman but her. You're trying to win a seat. The last thing you need to be known for is disrupting a team over a woman. You have a teammate you need to keep happy. You have a reputation to uphold. Nice try, though."

"Nice try?"

"It was creative." He smirks but gives an admonishing shake of his head.

"I look forward to seeing you participate in those outreach programs though. Charity always looks good and makes you feel good."

Fuck.

He shoves his hands in his pockets and strolls away with me looking after him and shaking my head.

I just lied to my dad to hide my desire over a woman I can't have.

What is wrong with me? When have I ever let a woman threaten all that I've worked for?

And yet here I am, skimming the crowd like a teenager waiting for a glimpse of her.

Wondering why I always have to be the good guy. The one who takes the high road. The one concerned about everyone else instead of taking care of my own needs and wants and desires.

Team.

Teammate.

Crew.

What the fuck, mate?

What the actual fuck.

You want a seat with Apex.

That must be your one and only focus.

Not delivering "flowers" to a woman who can never be yours.

Even if her smile of thanks made my fucking year.

Chapter Ten

Blair

I'M IN A STATE OF SHOCK.

I shot for the moon, expecting to land on the stars and instead . . . landed on the actual freaking moon. There was no way that the biggest pop star on the planet, Tori Michelle, would say yes to performing at our masquerade ball. Not a chance in hell.

But I asked anyway.

I wrapped my request in commentary about how she'll be in town the same weekend, how it's a charity benefitting various charities she's been affiliated with in the past, and how it's an event surrounding one of the most popular sports on earth. I packaged it all up, sent the request to her management company, and then laughed at how ridiculous it all sounded.

But holy shit.

She. Said. Yes.

And now? Now I just want to celebrate a hard day's work even if that means snuggling up to Rossi and watching mindless television.

There are muffled voices behind his door when I knock. The television sound lowers. The door opens.

"Hey." Rossi's eyebrows furrow as I look beyond him and see a couple of people—women and men—on the couch behind him.

And it's not like this isn't normal. This is his home for a week while he's at a race and so people being in and out of his suite is common. The difference is usually when he sees me, he pulls me into him, hugs me, and then kicks them all out.

He chooses me.

"Hi. I missed you. I thought maybe we could hang for a bit." I step into him and he takes a step back.

Whoa. What the hell?

"I'm kind of busy."

I take a closer look at the people on the couch. They're crew members he hangs with on occasion. They're FIA staff members. All of whom appear to just be having a drink, relaxing.

"Can I come in?" *Why do I have to ask?*

He glances over his shoulder and then back to me. "Nah. Not right now. Like I said, I'm busy."

"Rossi."

"What?"

"We hardly talked when you were gone last week at Sterling. You've been busy all week with your team. I had a really great day and I wanted to share it with you. Celebrate with you." I shrug almost as if that should be enough of an explanation for him to agree.

But he doesn't. He just stands there with that impassive look on his face. "Of course. Your job. Your success. You. You. You."

"Yes. Me. For once. God forbid."

"Then go celebrate."

I stare at him, blinking, with my lips lax and my brain unable to process that he really just said that. "I wanted to celebrate with you." My voice is barely a whisper as the writing on the wall becomes bold and flashes in neon yellow.

"Yeah, well, I said I was busy, and I meant it. We can do something next week. Call Trina and have her put it on my calendar," he says.

"Trina?" I laugh his personal assistant's name out like he's joking but his expression says he isn't.

"Yes. Trina. She knows my schedule."

"Since when do you need to pencil me in, Oliver?" I ask, arms crossing over my chest as if that's going to protect me from the hurt already burning in its center.

I stare at the man in front of me. For so many years, I've counted him as one of my closest friends. *Now . . . he feels like a stranger.* But over the past two months or so, he's definitely pushed me away. Canceled last minute—*if he made plans with me at all.*

And when was the last time we had sex?

He's disregarded me as if I mean nothing to him.

And asking me to book time with him via Trina? *What the actual fuck?* Does he not consider that I've seen the pictures from the media or from bystanders on the socials where he's been at clubs with women on his arms? Or the ones of him out partying, mouthing off to anyone who will listen, and reveling in the attention of his adoring public?

We have lines we've said we'd never cross. Ones I've never thought he had. Ones I thought he respected me enough and that he never would.

But now? Now I'm not quite sure about anything.

Clearly, I've been looking at this relationship through rose-colored glasses. *Yes, Skylar. You were right about that one.*

We barely see each other despite seeing each other. Has he just assumed we're in one of those off-again times we've been through in the past? But even so, in the past we'd address it. We'd agree to it.

This . . . this time just feels different. Like it's so much more than a "break."

I grew up in a home of chaos. One full of love, but also one where I craved to feel significant. Seen. To be the center of someone's world.

Rossi was the person who made me feel that way. Like I mattered. But . . . if I'm honest with myself, not for some time.

Isn't that what hurts the most?

Death by a thousand cuts.

Is that what this is?

Fuck.

"Since you seem to think you're bigger than you really are." He offers a strained smile. "I'll see you when I see you."

"No, you won't."

He stops the door in mid-swing as he goes to shut it. "You always come back like a dog to its master."

What the fuck?

"Not this time."

His chuckle is condescending and yet somehow indifferent. "Yeah. You'll come back. You'll never really leave me."

Those words. It's like I hear everything they say and maybe he has been saying for the first time. *You'll be here regardless of what I do or how I treat you.*

I glance over his shoulder again, not wanting to have this conversation with an audience but not exactly given any other choice. "No. I won't." I shift on my feet willing the words to come. Willing me to say the words to the person who has been as constant to me as breathing for the past ten years. "This just isn't working anymore. I deserve better than this."

"And you're saying you can find better than me?" he asks incredulously.

"Maybe not." I shrug, the numbness settling in much easier than I expected it to. "But we're over."

He scoffs, shakes his head, and says one word—"Perfect"—before shutting the door to leave me standing there staring at it.

Long enough to hear his laugh through the door. To hear him seemingly unaffected, whether it's because he thinks I'm joking or because he really doesn't give a fuck. Both are equally disheartening.

Walk away, Blair.

One foot in front of the other.

Oddly enough, I listen to myself. I take a few steps back with my eyes glued to the door like he's going to open it back up and tell me he's sorry.

But that never happens.

It's only once I step outside the hotel lobby that I feel like I can breathe. I gulp in huge breaths of air, one after another, as if I've been suffocated.

I'm naïve to think this hasn't been coming. That we're not in different places, different spaces, and that a break was coming.

But damn it stings.

He cast me aside without a second thought.

I'm worth more than that.

I lift my hand to hail a taxi and draw in my first steady breath as the car pulls away from the curb.

I just booked Tori Michelle—a huge feat in and of itself—that will speak volumes professionally.

And I just left Oliver Rossi.

The funny thing is, there's definite sadness with it. A sense that I failed at something when I know better than to take the blame for something we're both responsible for.

And yet . . . that sense of failure, that weight of sadness, doesn't come with the soul-crushing despair I'd expect it to have.

Right now, as I watch the city lights flash by outside my window, I almost feel . . . lighter.

Relieved.

It's just the newness of it all, Blair.

At least that's what I tell myself as I get ready for bed. As I check my phone numerous times to see if Rossi's texted to talk, apologize, fight . . . whatever.

But there's nothing.

Nothing but me crawling into my bed, snuggling under a comforter that's mine for the week, and waiting for misery to hit.

Because isn't this when it normally does? When it's the middle of the night and the only person who'd pick up if you call is your best friend?

Guess I'm screwed since Skylar is on the opposite side of the world in a different time zone and my next closest friend is Rossi.

But the night wears on.

My mind runs.

My emotions swell.

The anguish never hits, but the need to connect with someone does.

And when I roll over and grab my cell, I call the only person I can think of. The only person I want to call.

"Blair?" his sleep-drugged voice says. "Are you okay?" This time more alert.

Shame washes over me in a way I can't explain.

"I'm sorry." My voice breaks as tears well in my eyes. I clear my throat. "I dialed the wrong number."

"Hey. You sure?"

The kindness in his voice undoes me and I swallow back the sob that threatens. "Yes. I'm sure. I just dialed wrong. Good night."

I end the call and then clasp a hand over my mouth to stop the sob.

Why does this hurt so much?

"You always come back like a dog to its master."

Hurt? Nah. I'm wrong.

This is anger.

At Rossi's words. At his nonchalance. At him casting me aside like I've never meant anything to him.

And what does that say about me?

That when I needed someone, *I called Lachlan?*

But why did I lie to him and tell him my call was an accident?

And why do I want to call him again?

Chapter Eleven

Lachlan

"WELL, PULLING YOUR HEAD OUT OF YOUR ARSE AND NOT BLAMING everybody else would be a good start," I mutter. The mic of my headset is angled up and away from my mouth but the words are out there nonetheless.

The sudden quiet in the debriefing room means everyone heard it.

And everyone is waiting for the fallout.

"You got something to say, Evans?" Rossi barks from across the room.

I meet his eyes. I see the fire in them. The rage. *What the fuck is his problem?* "I think I already said it. You can take it how you want to. We had a solid team effort today. The cars were stronger. We placed better. So what the fuck is your problem?" I ask.

He glares at me. The muscle in his jaw pulsing and his hands fisted.

You want to come at me, fucker? Come at me. I'm not scared of you.

"Nothing." He pushes away from the desk, readjusts his headset, and looks at the monitor in front of him that holds all the telemetry data from the race. "Let's get this over with. I've got shit to do."

"Charming," I mutter as I sit back in my chair and lower my mic as Johann continues on with the rundown from the race.

Not a stellar performance for the Apex team of old, but a respectable one for the cars we have this year.

So Rossi's little tantrum is bullshit on all kinds of levels . . . and Johann asking me to stay behind once the meeting is over says as much.

"That was good stuff today," Johann says when the room clears.

I nod. "Not good enough."

"You're going to battle with what you have. That's all we can ask of you."

"It's not enough, Johann. You know it. I know it. The public doesn't fucking know it though." My sigh is one of exasperated exhaustion.

"It's being noticed by who needs to notice it."

Our eyes meet. "If it's being noticed then why isn't there an offer yet?"

Johann clears his throat, my misdirected question clearly leaving him uneasy. Gio's the only one who can answer that question. "Keep doing what you're doing. That's all you can do."

His non-answer, answer rubs me the wrong way.

"Right. Great." I sigh and run a hand through my hair in frustration. "Time to go meet the media." My lack of enthusiasm is apparent. I adjust my Apex baseball cap and start to walk away.

"Lach? You know what his deal is?" he asks with a lift of his chin in the direction where Rossi stalked out.

"Not a fucking clue." *See that, Johann? I'm the team player, not Rossi. Tell Gio that I'm the most deserving of the contract.*

"Well, I need you guys in sync. Can you figure it out so you can be again?"

"I can't control his fucking attitude now, can I?" I snap and then wince. *Shit, now I'm sounding like fucking Rossi.*

"I thought our time at Sterling did wonders for the two of you. Last thing I need is that shit falling back apart on us. There are a lot of decisions to be made soon and . . ."

"Yep. Got it," I say. Where in my contract does it say I need to be Rossi's therapist and babysitter? Like . . . what the fuck?

Because that's what he's asking for.

Be the team player, Evans. He'll remember that over being the hothead. I hope.

Fuck.

⌒

I wait for her. I have the brim of my hat pulled down low over my brow and have absolutely no Team Apex apparel on to try and avoid recognition.

Sure, this is the hotel that F1 employees stay at, but fans aren't exactly hanging out here to stalk them like they do at the drivers' hotels. Like they currently are at my hotel.

But here I sit, waiting for a woman so I can ask her what the fuck is wrong with her boyfriend ... even though *I* want so much more from her.

I didn't call her back.

When she called the other night, I didn't call her back.

I wanted to.

I started to several times.

Because that break in her voice? It nearly killed me.

What was wrong, Blair?

Isn't that the question I've asked myself over and over? It's not like I could ask her. I've been busy doing my job, keeping focused, and have purposely made an effort *not* to go and look for her.

And maybe that's for the best.

The last thing I need is to get between her and Rossi.

Fuck. That's it, isn't it?

Rossi thrashing around. Being an arsehole. Blair calling me at midnight. Then being nowhere in the garage when she usually sneaks in for the pre-race shit. Why didn't I think of that sooner?

They're fighting.

Yep. I don't want any part of this. I rise from my seat, thoroughly pissed that I wasted all this time waiting for her to come back from the track so I could figure out how to approach Rossi.

Now I know and want no part of it.

I don't even take two steps to leave before I come face-to-face with her.

"You're here," she says, surprise startling her eyes open wider.

"I am." I don't trust myself to speak for some reason.

"Not on the jet back home?"

"We're flying out tomorrow," I explain like she doesn't already know Rossi's schedule.

"Oh. Right."

I resist the urge to reach out and wipe away the bruises beneath her eyes from lack of sleep.

She looks like hell.

I mean ... she's beautiful. Nothing could ever change that. Her auburn hair is swept up and her outfit showcases her full curves, but if you look closely enough, you can see the stress there. The sadness. The exhaustion.

She averts her eyes from my scrutiny.

"Hey." I dip my head down so that I'm eye level with her and wait for those lashes to flutter up and meet mine. "You okay?"

"Of course. I'm fine." Her smile pulls tight at the corners of her mouth as she clearly tries to fake the cheer she's infused in her voice.

I study her, my fingers going to her chin so she can't look away. "You're lying to me."

She forces a swallow, takes a step back, and lifts her chin, giving me a glimpse of her usual composure. "It's been a rough couple of days."

I nod and lower my voice. "Want to talk about it?" The question is as automatic as my next breath, and it's the last thing I want to ask.

Because I think I know the answer.

And because the answer opens a doorway I think way too much about walking through . . . but know I can't.

She clears her throat. "I broke up with Rossi."

She broke up with Rossi. Not *Rossi broke up with* her.

That shouldn't change things in my mind, *but it does.*

And that "doorway" just opened a bit wider.

Fuck me.

"Blair." It's all I can say as I struggle with how to comfort her. My instinct is to pull her into me and wrap my arms around her. It might help her but fuck if it won't hurt me. The heat of her body against mine? Her face against my chest and her hair tickling my neck? "I'm sorry. I don't know what to say."

"There's nothing to say. Just because it was a long time coming—something I can see now—doesn't make it any easier."

"I can understand that." I say the words but don't really know seeing as I've never allowed myself to seriously date anyone. The job comes first. My success comes first. And then once my time in Formula 1 runs out, then will come time for me. Then will come time I can share with someone else.

Isn't that what's been drilled into my head my whole life?

So why, standing here, looking at a woman who makes me feel things I don't normally feel, do I feel like I've been missing out? *I've never felt that way before.*

"For the record, I won the award for best listener in primary school, so . . ." I hold my hands out and get the smile I was working for from her.

"In primary school?"

"Yes. That's kind of like your elementary school, I believe." I shrug and cross my arms over my chest. "You're welcome to experience the marvels of an award-winning listener. I mean, I don't offer these services to just anyone."

Her smile widens and her head angles to the side, her vulnerability like a badge on her sleeve. "I became a fixture in his life. One that sat pretty on a shelf but that he no longer saw or thought needed attention." She purses her lips. "It sounds stupid but that's the best way I can describe it. I became an old memento . . . a toy Rossi wanted to hold on to because it made him feel good but one that he didn't think was important enough to bring out to play with anymore."

Jesus. I blow out an exaggerated exhale. "That's brutal."

"That's the truth." She glances over her shoulder for a beat and blinks away tears. "But it's for the best. I can move on. He can move on. And . . . you know." The break in her voice this time is ten times worse than over the phone because I can see her expression when she does it.

"Is there anything I can do for you?"

"No." Her smile is quick and melancholy. "Letting me say it out loud is more than enough. It's . . . never mind."

"No. Tell me." I tap my ears and smile. "Do I need to show you the award to prove it?"

"It's the stupid things I worry about."

"Meaning?"

"I have other friends, and my family, don't get me wrong, but Oliver has been my go-to person of sorts. He understands this world that we exist in, and few people do. He's who I'd call at two in the morning when I have a bad dream. With our travel and the constantly changing time zones, it's not always easy to call my best friend or parents with the time difference. Who am I going to go and do stupid things with that make me laugh so hard I can't breathe? Who is going to laugh at my lame jokes and understand my penchant for reality television?"

Me.

And I think what she's not saying is even more telling than what she is. *Not.* Who am I going to go to when I need a big hug or to be comforted?

Me.

"All very valid points. Ones I'd probably worry about too. Especially someone finding out about the reality TV bit."

"You like trashy reality television?"

"Carmichael, I live it every day out there on the track. Dodging drivers who are in bad moods. Avoiding crew members who are having a spat with another one. Checking over my shoulder for rival teams trying to take me down."

"It's a life of danger."

"So very dangerous," I say. She grants me a genuine smile for the first time since she walked in here.

"Thank you." She reaches out and squeezes my hand. We both stare at our joined fingers as if that simple touch would ever be enough.

You're such a dick for even thinking that. The woman just broke up with her boyfriend of how many years and all you can think about is how much you wish she were yours like a damn fucking sap.

Screw your wants, Lach. Hers are what matter right now.

This season. The contract. Next year's ride. Those should be your focus.

Before I can process it, Blair steps into me and wraps her arms around my waist. I stand, frozen in that middle space between knowing what I should do and what I want to do.

What I should do is pat her gently on the shoulder and not touch her any farther.

What I want to do is wrap my arms around her and notice how perfectly she fits here. The way her head rests under the line of my neck. The soft curves of her body against the hard planes of mine.

"I needed this," she says softly, almost as if it's hard for her to admit.

I swallow forcibly and decide on a middle ground. I give her the quickest hug known to man—one that doesn't memorize the feel of her but sure as fuck hopes I get to. "Glad I could be of service."

It's when I step back—create the distance I so desperately need—that I catch the tears pooling in her eyes. That I can sense the brave face she's putting on instead of letting the quiver of her chin win out.

"I should go pack," she says.

"You should." Distance will do me a world of good right now.

But neither of us move. Much like we did in the lounge a few weeks ago after staying up all night, it's as though we find comfort in simply being with each other. *Does she not want to leave me as much as I don't want to leave her?*

I clench my jaw, shove my hands in my pockets, and force myself to take a step back. "Have a safe flight." The words are strained.

"You too."

Chapter Twelve

Lachlan

"LACHLAN? IS THAT YOU REALLY CALLING ME?" ZOLA CHAMALET asks and then laughs.

Heiress, sometimes acquaintance, and maybe a woman I went on a date with.

"I am. Hi, Zola. How are you doing?"

"I'm doing good." I can all but hear her trying to figure out why I'm calling her. "Tough race, huh?"

"It seems like they all are this season." I glance up to the hotel in front of me like I have been for the past few hours and wonder which room's light is Blair's.

"Hmm." It's the only sound she makes before she falls silent. Her throaty laugh fills the phone. "And?"

"And I was wondering if I could ask a favor of you."

"Of course you are." I can hear the humor laced with curiosity in her voice. She's about as down-to-earth as she can be but at the same time thinks the world revolves around her. It's a weird dichotomy that she wears well. "What do you need, Lachlan?" she asks in a singsong voice.

"I need access to Golfpark Plateau tonight."

She barks out a laugh. "Tonight." I can hear her snap her fingers. "Do you think I'm a genie? I don't have a lamp."

"No, but you have friends in high places."

"Lachlan," she groans but I know she loves the attention. The sense of feeling important. She's told me as much in the past.

"Call in a favor for me. Throw your name around and get your ex to give me access. Tonight. Privacy. You know the drill." And she knows what I'm talking about. Her ex-boyfriend's father is part owner of the conglomerate that owns the club. God knows how I remember that, but I do.

"Ooohhh," she says as if it all clicks. "Lachlan Evans has a date tonight and he doesn't want the media to know."

Something like that but the devil's in the details and Zola is more of a big-picture girl.

"Pretty please," I say as a response.

She huffs. "Well, Lachlan Evans . . . I guess. And only because you're asking me nicely."

I fist-pump the air. I've been out here wracking my brain over what I could do to help Blair. To give her a reprieve from . . . everything. "You're the best. Awesome. You'll call right now?"

"Everything has its price, Lach."

Of course it does. "Like what?"

"Be my date. My mother is throwing a party on the yacht."

"Zola . . . we tried this, remember?" I laugh. While the woman is drop-dead gorgeous and knows how to live life, she's simply not my type. And if she were, the distraction and everything her last name would bring wouldn't exactly help my focus.

Says the man who's trying to commandeer a golf course for another woman.

"Look. I need your help. She's determined to set me up with the Count von something or other, and you need to save me from his sweaty palms and horrible personality. She loves you. She'd buy the notion that we're seeing each other again. I wouldn't ask if I weren't desperate."

"Yes, you would."

"You're right. I would." She laughs. "Please. Just go with me. Help me. *Save me.*"

My grin widens. "Leave it to you to add the dramatics."

"Always. Besides, cozying up to me can only help you. You know my mother has no problem wielding her influence where it needs to be wielded."

Ah, yes. The carrot has been dangled.

The one I was waiting for her to drop.

The same damn carrot I would've ignored a few weeks ago, but now am so very conscious of.

"Make the call, Zola."

"Be my date, Lachlan."

Chapter Thirteen

Blair

THERE'S NO WAY THAT'S ALL GOING TO FIT IN THERE.

I stare at my two open suitcases on my bed and debate how I'm going to shove the remainder of my belongings into either of them.

How do I have the same amount of stuff that I came here with but now it doesn't all fit?

"Well, shit," I mutter as I put my hands on my hips like that's going to help me figure out my quandary.

I startle at the knock on my hotel door.

My heart leaps in my throat.

Rossi.

Then dread sinks into the pit of my stomach. I don't want to talk to him. I don't want to fix this. It's broken and as much as I love Rossi . . . these past few days have proven to me that I don't think I have been in love with him for a while.

I should feel like I've lost the love of my life. *But I don't.* We've been so disconnected—are so disconnected—that whatever was holding us together has simply disintegrated. *And I'm okay.*

Those are the same three words I typed to Skylar over and over earlier.

She thought maybe I was bolstering so she wouldn't be worried about me.

But I wasn't. I truly am . . . okay.

I may be the old toy on the shelf he didn't want to take out and play for a while, but haven't I treated him the same way?

It's run its course.

That is my mantra for the day. Was before I saw Lachlan down in the lobby. Still has been after.

"Who is it?" I ask before I step up toward the peephole.

"Lach," he says at the same time I see him in the distorted view finder.

I open the door without thinking, surprise leading the way. "What are you doing here?" I ask flummoxed. "How did you know my room number? How did—"

"I have my ways." He winks and then holds out his hand much like Rossi did weeks ago at the track. His words are eerily similar. "Come with me."

The difference is my urge to say yes is almost automatic.

My smile is shy. "I'd love to but I can't. I have to leave for my flight soon."

"Screw the flight. I'll get you another one."

"Lachlan."

"You need the night off." His grin is as tempting as his words.

"Where do you want to go?"

A roguish twinkle lights up his eyes. "Do you trust me?"

The answer shouldn't be so easy, but it's there as sure as the books he got me—which are packed in my carry-on. "Yes."

"Good. Grab a jacket. Let's go."

Despite knowing the city well, I have no idea where he's taking me. We drive in silence, him hunching down behind the wheel to see street signs and follow directions it seems he knows.

Missing a flight to go on a mystery adventure? *Who am I right now?* I don't really know and to be honest, I don't really care. All I'm thinking about is how welcome the warm, summer night air feels as it whips through my hair on what feels like an old country road, and how the man beside me brings a sense of calm to me like I've never felt before.

I'm pulled from my thoughts when Lachlan turns into a deserted parking lot. There's a row of trees in front of us and a light in the far-off distance.

"C'mon," he says enthusiastically as he exits the car, opens my door for me, and holds his hand out again.

"Where are we?"

"You'll see in a minute."

I narrow my eyes at him but climb out, curious and excited.

It doesn't take long for me to realize we're on a golf course. A very closed, very empty one at that.

"Lach," I whisper. "We can't. We're going to get in trouble."

His laugh is loud and boisterous and so very opposite of my whisper that says I'm afraid we're going to be caught. He turns to me and grins. "You said you wanted to be taken out to play. We're here to play."

"What? How? I don't even know how to play golf."

"But that's the beauty in it," he says and holds his hands up while taking a slow spin to make a show. "No one is here to tell us how to play. I called in a few favors to the owner. He's given us free rein here. We can play or not play or simply do whatever the hell we want."

I bark out a laugh. *We're here to play.* Leave it to Lachlan to take my words and bring them to life for me in some misconstrued way.

"I don't . . . I'm a woman rarely at a loss for words but you seem to continually make that happen."

"That's a good thing." He steps toward me, his usually stoic expression animated and his eyes wild with mischief. He reaches out and taps me on the shoulder. "Tag. You're it." And then he sprints down the pathway and onto the green.

"Lachlan." I laugh his name out but give chase like a teenager.

We run down a fairway and onto a green. Our hands flailing and laughter floating in the summer night air.

The man is good at bantering, at being serious, but playful is not something I pegged him for and God, how glad I was wrong about that. He shrieks and hollers and does funny pirouettes down the fairway. Anything to make me laugh.

Everything to show me he cares.

I follow suit, my goofiness coming through as I do cartwheel after cartwheel, laughing so hard at my horrific form.

But he stands and claps, shouting out ratings for each one before taking off again with me in hot pursuit.

We run till he collapses and then proceeds to roll over and over down an incline like a little kid. Without thinking, I drop and follow, only stopping when my body ends up bumping against his.

I can barely breathe through the laughter and the exertion, but I can't remember the last time I felt this alive.

It sounds so silly but it rings so true.

"Oh my God," I say as I roll onto my back to mirror his position beside me.

"I'm out of shape," he jokes.

"Hardly," I snort, knowing how much physical conditioning that each driver puts in to be able to withstand the g-force the car and track exert onto their bodies. He is most definitely not out of shape . . . but I appreciate the comment so my lack of conditioning doesn't feel so obvious. "My heart is racing."

"Mine too. Feel." He reaches out and grabs my hand, placing it onto his chest. His heart beats an insane staccato. One that reverberates against my hand and jolts shock waves down to my own heart.

One that has picked up its own pace . . . but I have a feeling it's not because of our sprint.

It's because of my hand on him. His hand on mine. And everything else that's so unique about this moment he's fabricated for me.

"Lachlan," I whisper.

"Look!" He points to the dark sky above. "A shooting star."

I yelp and lift my hand off his chest to point out in reaction at the streak of silver across the sky. "Wow."

"Make a wish," he says.

"A wish?"

"Yep." We fall silent for a beat as I try and think of one.

To remember this feeling forever.

That's it, isn't it? This feeling. The laughter. The ease in my chest and the carefree feeling riding through me. All are things I haven't felt in forever. All things that Lachlan elicited when he took me out *to play.*

He shifts beside me and props his head on his hand. I can feel the weight of his stare on me, know he's looking, but that doesn't make my grin go away. It doesn't make me self-conscious. It makes me feel seen. Regarded. Noticed.

"Your smile says it's a good wish," he murmurs.

"Hmm." I turn my head to meet his eyes. "What was yours?"

"Can't tell or it won't come true," he says.

"Uh-huh." I snort but look back up at the sky in case another happens to fall from it. "I've never seen one before."

"Never?" he asks incredulously.

"Never. I guess I never took the time to stop and look for one."

"You can't look for one, Blair. They just happen. Kind of like the most important things in life do."

Turning slightly, I study him in the dark. The lines of his face. The wave to his hair. The strong line of his jaw. The intensity in his eyes.

I resist the urge to reach out and touch him. It owns my thoughts in ways it shouldn't. In ways I want it to.

"You have grass . . ." He reaches out and uses the pad of his thumb to wipe grass off my cheek. His hand lingers.

My breath stutters in my chest and every part of me is keenly aware of him.

"Blair." He says my name like an oath. Like a promise. Like it's written in the sand and waiting for the water to wash it away. "I . . ."

"I know," I whisper. But even I don't know what I mean by that.

I know because I'm attracted to you too.

I know that if you kissed me right now the world might feel right for the first time in a long time.

I know that us even thinking this is wrong despite feeling so damn right.

"You bring something out in me that I like," he states.

"I think that's one of the best compliments anyone has ever given me," I say softly.

Our gazes hold across the darkness as the air between us charges. And I want it to charge. To ignite. To explode into a wildfire.

I've been sitting here for weeks telling myself what a great guy Lachlan is. What a great friend he's becoming. How the way I search for him in the paddock even if it's just to lay eyes on him is because I'm lonely.

But I've been lying to myself.

I've been walking that fine line of want for some time now, so why am I still trying to walk it? I'm no longer with Rossi. I don't have any ties to hold me back. I haven't betrayed anyone unless we're talking about myself.

It's okay to want this. To want him.

Jesus, that feels good to think. To acknowledge. To say even if just in my head.

Lachlan has put more effort into me in the past few weeks than Rossi has in months.

I am okay.

And it is okay to want this.

I reach out to touch him. My fingertips grazing over his arm.

"This isn't a good . . ." Lachlan shoves up to a seated position so that I'm forced to look at his muscled back. The confusion woven in his voice echoes in my ears.

I should feel rejection, but I don't. He wouldn't be here if he didn't want something more. It's just the uncertain territory we'd be treading into that makes this more than complicated.

"What do you mean that this isn't—"

"Are you hungry?" he asks and then springs up without warning and runs across another green toward what looks like a clubhouse.

"What?" I laugh out as I jog after him, still trying to process the headiness of the moment we just shared and his obvious need to put distance between us.

And when I catch up to him, he's at a vending machine pushing all kinds of buttons until that telltale thunk of food falling to the bottom of the machine can be heard.

"Here we are," he says and holds out a handful of treats. Cookies and candy and chips. "Snacks of champions. Can't say I don't know how to take a woman out for an expensive meal." He laughs and then lifts his eyebrows. "Which ones are you going to pick, Carmichael?"

"Um . . . I'm good." My stomach growls. "The last thing I need are snacks."

"Nope. Not going to hear it," he says, his grin infectious. "You need to eat to keep your energy up."

"In case you haven't noticed, I seem to eat plenty."

"And thank God for that." He looks me up and down more in appreciation than predatory and damn if that single look doesn't make me feel like a million dollars. "I'd be hard-pressed to find another woman who can fill out a pair of jeans like you do."

"Whatever." I roll my eyes.

He takes my hand with his free one and holds my arm out as he takes me in before murmuring, "Damn, girl. Just damn."

"Lach." His praise is unexpected and overwhelming. I blush and struggle with what to say.

"Own it. I won't accept you doing anything other than that."

"Now you're just being ridiculous."

"No. Now I'm telling you what you deserve to hear. You're stunning. Truly." Our eyes meet and as much as I'm uncomfortable with the attention, his does things to my insides that should be illegal. "Now, pick a snack, Tink, or else I'm going to be offended that you think I'm a cheap date, which will prompt me to buy every single snack inside that damn machine."

This time when he holds them up, I don't hesitate going for the cookies. They're not ice cream but they are most definitely a good substitute.

"Good choice." He nods resolutely. "Definitely a good choice and worth missing a flight for." He looks around us. "Now let's talk options for how exactly we're going to *play* next."

Chapter Fourteen

Blair

"**Y**OU ARE NOT BEATING ME THIS TIME," LACHLAN YELLS AS HIS GOLF cart inches in front of mine.

"Watch me!" I shout over to him as we race against each other down a fairway.

The golf carts aren't exactly fast. The governors on their throttles have obviously been adjusted so assholes like Lachlan and me can't race over the golf course.

But we're doing so, nonetheless. Doing so and laughing so hard that my sides hurt and my cheeks are sore.

I push the cart's limits until the whole thing shimmies and shakes as we bounce down the uneven grass. I'm gaining on his slight advantage with every foot we go.

"Eat my dust, Evans," I yell over to him as I pull in front and then throw my hands in the air and shout out in victory when I win. "Woohoo!!!"

"Two out of three," he says as he pulls up beside me.

"Two out of three?" I shriek and jump out of the golf cart to go to his. "That was more like eight out of ten." I huff on my knuckles and shine them on my shirt. "I'm beginning to think I'm in the wrong line of work."

Lachlan leans back, his arm slung across the back of the golf cart's seat, his smile smug but contrite.

Jesus. He's never looked more handsome.

"I'm beginning to think you are too." He shrugs and lifts his other hand from where his wrist rests on the steering wheel. "Or you could assume I let you win so you'd feel good about yourself."

His words stop me in my tracks as I stare at him. "You wouldn't dare." I tug on his arm and force him out of the golf cart to stand in front of me. I jab a finger in his chest. "I know you, Lachlan Evans, and you are too damn competitive to let me win for the sake of winning. One race maybe, but not eight. So don't you dare say that."

"Yes, ma'am," he says and laughs. "But do you really know me?"

We study each other through the night as I struggle with that question even though I feel like I know the answer. "You like animals and wanted to help them, which says a lot about you. You are a sleeping giant in the garage. Quiet and inquisitive but a looming presence whenever you step foot into it," I say. He quirks an eyebrow up in response. "You have a good sense of right and wrong and always opt for the least amount of drama. You are close with your family—choosing to go to dinner with your dad instead of out to a club or an event. And you . . . you . . ."

"Am struggling with stepping back right now"—he answers for me and locks his hand around the wrist of my hand currently on his chest—"instead of doing what I really want to do."

"And what is it that you want to do?" The words are breathless.

"This." He reaches out with both hands to frame the sides of my face seconds before his lips meet mine.

There is no hesitation in his kiss. No caution. He's all in from the minute our lips touch and the urgency of his tongue seeking access to mine.

I should be staggered.

I shouldn't want it. *Want him.*

But God, does it feel good. Everything about him and this night he's created just for me. The softness of his lips. The taste of peppermint on his tongue. The coarseness of his stubble. The sound of desire that reverberates deep in his throat. The masterful skill with which he leads us.

He's in complete control, complete possession of me, and I've never wanted to be swallowed whole more in my life.

My body buzzes with adrenaline and aches with a desire that slowly burns its way through me. It's an intoxicating, all-consuming feeling.

And when the kiss ends, when a soft protest falls from my lips as he steps back and simply stares at me, all I want is for him to do it again.

Lachlan clears his throat and retreats yet another step. "I should get you back." I can see the disengagement and that confuses me even more than his kiss just did. "Your flight is in three hours."

"My flight?" Reality struggles to break its way through this alternate universe I want to remain in where golf courses are playgrounds and the man in front of me is mine.

A ghost of a smile crawls over his lips. "Did you think I was going to make you miss your flight and not book you a new one?"

"But . . . how?"

"I have my ways." He winks and lifts his chin to the golf carts. "Race you back?"

And without waiting for a response, he climbs in his golf cart and handily beats me back to the deserted clubhouse.

He moves with a purpose putting everything back where it was, almost as if his actions will prevent us from discussing what just happened.

The kiss I can't forget and the one it seems he doesn't want to address.

We don't talk about anything with significance on the way back to my hotel. In fact with each passing second, I can sense Lachlan withdrawing even more. There's a pensive silence in the car that suffocates me and slowly strangles away all the joy and happiness we just shared over the past few hours.

I steal glances his way. Trying to figure out his sudden silence. Trying to comprehend the fact that he's like a drug that I'm beginning to crave.

Does he regret kissing me? Is that what's going on? He gave in to the moment and now regrets it?

Or is he thinking about how he wants to do it again?

I'd love to ask the question, but we arrive at my hotel before I get the courage to.

We walk in silence to my door with an awkwardness to us when no part of tonight has been awkward at all.

"Well, here you are," he murmurs quietly, conscious of the fact it's now three in the morning.

"Here I am," I say playing with my key card in my hand. When I finally have the courage to meet his eyes, the worry fades away. It's just him and his kind eyes and warm smile looking back at me. "Thank you, Lachlan. Tonight was . . . it was what I needed. To not think. To just laugh. To . . . just be."

"Good. Then the objective was achieved."

Lachlan shifts on his feet, looks down for a beat, and clears his throat before looking up to meet my gaze with a clarity that is almost unnerving. "I meant to do that, Blair. To kiss you. I don't want you to think otherwise. None of this, *it was a mistake, it was just the moment,* bullshit. I hands down meant to do that and goddamn it"—he laces his fingers at the back of his neck and pulls as he chuckles—"I'd do it again if given the chance."

I struggle to swallow over the lump of emotions lodged in my throat.

"But I can't. It's not right. You told me I was a man with a good sense of right and wrong and what I did back there wasn't right."

Can this man be any more perfect?

"That's for me to decide," I say.

He nods as he purses his lips briefly. "Yeah, but . . . there's too much riding on this goddamn season, and I'm not the type of man who takes another's woman. Between the shitstorm us being together would cause and . . . that's not who I am."

"I'm not anyone's—"

"But you were. For a long time." He takes another step back as if the physical distance will help him believe the emotional distance he's attempting to create. "I make no qualms about wanting you, but I refuse to take advantage of you and your vulnerability right now."

"You weren't taking advantage of me. I wanted the kiss too," I whisper.

"That makes two of us." His flicker of a smile makes my stomach flip. "But I'm not about to fuck up my team when everything I want is just within reach. I've worked so goddamn hard for this—for my career—and while I think you're damn fucking worth it, I can't risk the fallout."

"I wouldn't want you to. You don't think there'd be fallout for me too? A race chaser hopping from one driver to the next? I mean . . ."

"Exactly. We both have a lot on the line and that's something we need to consider if we choose to pursue this."

"If we choose to?"

He nods, that muscle pulsing in his jaw like this whole situation is tormenting him. "I'm not a rebound, Blair."

"Lachlan. That's not—"

"I know that's what you think right now, but you need time to sort your feelings out. To know for sure what you might want. I'm not a half-arsed kind of guy. That might be what you're used to, but that's not me. That's not how I operate." He glances down to my lips and then back up to my eyes. "It takes twenty-one days to make or break a habit. To know what you want or don't want."

I chuckle. "What are you saying?"

"I think . . ." He swears under his breath almost as if he can't believe he's saying this, and the simple act alone makes him even sexier. The torment his next words hold are everything. "Twenty-one days. You need to take them, take time for yourself, before jumping into something with me."

"You think twenty-one days is all it takes to fall in or out of love?"

"No. I don't know shit. But I know how I am, Blair. I know I'm all or nothing. And you need to know who you are and what you want. I know what I want."

"What do you want?" I'm afraid to ask because I might not like the answer.

"I want to stay with Apex, but I've been warned not to make waves. That all eyes are on me and Rossi and neither of us can make a mistake. And honestly, I never believed I'd want to juggle a relationship and this crazy life of mine. Too many distractions. Not enough time. Too much outside noise. But even in this brief time we've gotten to know each other, you make me think I could. That I want to. And as you could see tonight, it's fucking with my head."

"I understand," I say softly.

"No, I don't think you do." He smiles incredulously. "I adore everything about you, Blair. The things I've learned. The things I know I'm going to learn. You make me feel things I'm not used to, and it's only been a few weeks. *That's not normal*. It's you who makes me want to take the risk and try to do this. But it's also you who needs to be damn sure you want this too . . . that's why we need the twenty-one days to break . . . whatever it is we need to break."

His words are like a balm to my soul that has been craving intention and conviction and . . . everything he represents. Is it way too intense?

Yes. But isn't that Lachlan Evans? Intensity and passion rolled into one? Isn't that the man I've learned to like and want to spend more time with? Isn't that the person I'm desperate to get to know better?

And where he's intense, I'm the polar opposite. I need levity to balance me out. To let him know I heard him but that I get a say in how this goes too. That I matter.

"And what if I want you to be my habit?" I tease.

His grin is lightning fast. So is his step back as his entire posture eases and he holds his hands out to his sides. "Then, baby, here I am . . . but only after twenty-one days. That's the rules and I don't ever break my own rules. Team. Teammate. Crew."

"Rules were meant to be broken."

"Not in my world they weren't."

I bark out an exasperated laugh. "You know this is ridiculous, don't you?"

"We'll suffer if this is really what we want, but you'll thank me for it later."

"I can thank you for it right now." I take a step toward him, but his hands stop mine from touching him.

"You are . . . incredible." He whispers the last word and chills chase over my skin because of the complete reverence with which he says it. "Twenty-one days, Tink. I need you to be sure."

"I am sure."

His chuckle is pained at best as his eyes wander up and down the length of my body. "Now you're just being mean and trying to tempt me."

"Can you blame me?"

He groans. "It's best if I go. The longer I stand here, the harder it's getting to determine what's right and wrong."

His honesty is so . . . refreshing. Unnerving. Real.

"You are . . . incredible."

The irony is that Lachlan Evans is standing in front of me talking about being together, having a relationship, and every part of me would tell anyone else they're crazy. That I just broke up with someone and so I need time and space and whatever it is most people need to figure themselves out.

And yet, I'm not saying any of those things.

Instead, I want to argue against every single logical thing he's saying because when I'm with him I feel more real, more whole than I have felt in years.

And it's not just because it's attention when I haven't been paid much of it. It's his attention. The way he listens. The way he hears me and tries to give me what I need. The way he makes an effort. The way he wants to be with me, wants to make me feel good, and has a way of reminding me how fucking good it feels to laugh again.

So is this insanity in all forms that it's been days since I broke up with Rossi and I want Lachlan? Hell yes, it is.

And maybe that's why I stop myself. Maybe that's why I listen to him. Maybe that's why I'm willing to go along with his stupid twenty-one days.

To prove his theory wrong.

And to prove my instinct right.

Love at first sight is bullshit. Instalove is even more so . . . but hell if Lachlan Evans doesn't make me feel in spades—good, bad, incredible, alive.

It doesn't make me weak to want that. It makes me more real than I think I've ever felt before. And if I'm honest with myself, it feels like my life is moving forward, like this is a grown-up relationship. And I can now see that it's been in limbo—with Rossi—for quite a few years.

"Twenty-one days? That's a lllloooonnnggg time to want something, Lachlan."

"Mm-hmm. It is. But the reward will be damn worth it."

"It will be. I know it."

"Me too."

I nod with so much to say but not enough words to express them with, so I say what I can. "Thank you for taking me out to play."

"It was the best night out I've had in a long time," he says, holding out a peppermint to me. But he doesn't say the words this time. *To remember me by.* He knows there's no way I could forget him, forget tonight. "Fly safe, Tink. See you soon."

I take the peppermint. "See you soon."

Chapter Fifteen

Lachlan

A GOOD SENSE OF RIGHT AND WRONG.

Guess I just proved that fucking theory wrong.

I kissed her.

I fucking kissed her and would kill to do it again.

Her taste is seared in my goddamn brain.

Her laugh is echoing in my ears.

Her smile has stained my every thought.

I want her and I can't have her unless I risk every goddamn thing I've ever worked for.

You don't fuck with your teammates.

Your team comes first.

But when I look out the window of the jet to the city beyond as we cruise higher and higher, I want her with every bone in my body.

Twenty-one days. Where the fuck did that come from, huh? You actually think that ridiculous bullshit is going to work? That it's going to make you want her less? Want to fuck up your carefully balanced world less?

News flash, fucker. Absence makes all things grow stronger. Or harder in my cock's case.

Twenty-one fucking days of torture when you know what the outcome is already going to be on your end.

"Hey."

I glance over to where Rossi is holding a bottle of scotch out to me. Just like he always does on the jet ride back to Monaco.

But unlike my usual response—*no thanks*—this time, I fucking take it.

"Ohhh, a rough day?" he asks from behind a pair of dark sunglasses.

"Something like that." I pour myself a glass and pass it back without looking his way.

I can't. Guilt is a mean, nasty bitch.

I've never particularly liked Rossi. We're two completely different men, which is what made our pairing such a good gamble for Apex. But now we're competing against each other. And not just in a race car.

That's a fucked-up thought.

I lift the tumbler to my lips. I savor the sweet oak-y taste of the alcohol on my tongue, but nothing erases the taste of her kiss.

Fucking nothing.

I pushed it to the final damn minute—me kissing her—until I couldn't hold out anymore. Missing my flight wasn't an option. It was my last tether to my control. Anything more than a kiss would result in me getting lost in her like I've thought about more times than I can fucking count.

And then I would've missed this flight.

I swallow the mouthful.

I invite the burn.

I welcome the purgatory of sitting next to my teammate. Of sitting with a man who has no clue I've spent the night with Blair.

I should feel bad for him. For his complete lack of awareness when it comes to Blair. But I don't. He's the one who's in the wrong. I don't pretend to know the entire truth behind the two of them—clearly it takes two to be in a relationship—but I know the man showed such little regard for her, that she broke up with him.

Does he still think she'll come back to him? Does he even care if she does? I'm thinking no to both questions, but then again, I have some serious skin in the game.

Or I will.

After twenty-one days.

It's then I'll know what Blair decides. It's then, hopefully, I'll have a contract signed and not have to worry about any blowback when it comes to my career.

Do I talk to Johann about it? Give him a heads-up?

Do I ask my father for advice on this?

No.

This is about me. My personal life. I'm allowed to live it as I want. And fuck does that feel weird—and gratifying—to think.

The thoughts will keep coming over the next three weeks. I know they will. More doubt. More questions. More fucking everything. But they don't matter.

None of them do.

She does.

Stepping into her fire is a foregone conclusion. All I can hope is that the world doesn't burn down around me when I do.

Chapter Sixteen

Blair

"**B**EE! HOW'S MY GIRL?"

I close my eyes and sink into the sound of my father's voice and the comfort of a nickname he's called me forever. "Dad. Hi. It's so good to hear your voice."

"Everything okay?" Concern floods his tone and has me slouching on my stool. Why did I think he wouldn't notice when he's the most astute person I know?

"Of course it is," I lie. "Why wouldn't it be?"

"Because you haven't called me like you usually do to regale me with all the funny stories from behind the scenes."

"I've been busy."

"With the masquerade ball? Or with . . . other things?"

"All of the above."

"Want to talk about it?" he asks, treading lightly.

Yes. No. I don't know.

"The ball is a shitshow. The previous planner had good intentions but wasn't great at follow-through. So there are a lot of ideas but just no implementation."

"But Mom says you got that girl with two first names to perform for free. That's good, right?"

"Tori Michelle?" I laugh. Leave it to my dad to try and stay hip on popular culture but not completely make the connection. "Yes. We signed the contract for her appearance yesterday."

"I mean, that's huge. Or at least the girls say so," he says of the pop-loving twins. "You know me."

"I know. If it isn't classic rock, it doesn't matter."

"Exactly." He laughs. "What'd you do? Flash that pretty smile her way?"

"I think I had some outside help. Hell, I'm still busy trying to figure out why someone as famous as her would agree to perform for us for free."

"I'm sure it's a write-off," he says.

"You say that about everything."

"Well . . ." We both laugh. "So what else is going on? You're swamped with work, rushing to get things done that already should be done. And Rossi? Things are good with him?"

"He's . . ." I hesitate.

"He's Rossi, huh?" He falls quiet as I try to process my ever-changing emotions.

"Pretty much." If two words summed up the past few weeks, those would be them.

"You know we love him, but we love you more. You're ours. He's just lucky enough to get us by association."

He can't see my smile, but it's there. "I know."

"I know you know, but it's worth repeating in case you doubted it. A man does not and should never define you, Bee. You are incredible in every aspect and any man would be lucky to have you as their partner. Your worth is more important than any man's ego."

"I broke up with him."

He blows out an audible exhale. A sound I can't quite read as he's always been fond of Oliver. I mean . . . he is basically part of our family. "Probably for good reason, right? For reasons that matter to you. It's hard to step away from someone who has been your shadow for so long. You okay?"

Guilt from a kiss I can't stop thinking about hits hard.

Just like it has all damn week long.

But it hasn't made me want it to happen again any less.

"Yeah. I'm okay. I think . . . I think who we were as fifteen-year-old kids isn't who we are now. We've adjusted and readjusted to try and make it work, but I just think we're in different places. I get he is who he is—and I wouldn't want him to be anyone else—but I am who I am, and that doesn't mean I have to take a back seat because of it."

"There's my girl," he says proudly and digs a little deeper into my guilt. "That's a hard thing to recognize. I'm proud of you for being able to. I'm sure whatever is meant to be will be. Either Oliver will get his shit together and you'll take him back—if that's what you want—or you'll find another person who appreciates you that much more and you'll go from there."

"True."

"You've got a great head on your shoulders, so I know you'll do what's best for you. And if you need a break from the chaos of it all, we have chaos here at home that will welcome you with open arms."

"I know." And this is why my family is so important to me. Is why my dad is so easy to talk to. Both my parents have hearts of gold and always let me know that I can come home to them if I need or want to.

They have my back, support my decisions, and have always encouraged me to chase my dreams, especially regarding my career.

I'm the luckiest girl in the world and don't ever take their love and support for granted.

We chat for a bit more about the team he started coaching, about his big plans for my mom's birthday, and about work. All things that help me to feel like I belong. It sounds odd, but it feels so very needed.

Especially in the state of unrest my life seems to be in.

When I end the call, I close my eyes and draw in a deep breath.

What is it that I want? And why does it feel like if I even knew, it wouldn't matter anyway?

And in those two thoughts I'm proving Lachlan Evans and his ridiculous twenty-one day theory right.

Confusion hits the minute I touched down and came home to a flat that was littered with little pieces of a life with Rossi. A life I loved living but that clearly isn't me anymore.

Sure I've felt sadness but not because I wanted to get back with Rossi. It was more because I was trying to find who I was in the mess of the items I was gradually putting into a box and moving to the back of the closet. I was trying to figure out when she faded away and this new me stepped into her shoes.

Soon after the confusion came the guilt. The shame. The desire for more kisses eclipsed the guilt, though. Do you know how ridiculous it is to feel guilty that you don't feel more guilt?

Like . . . *what the fuck.*

But a few days and a few bottles of wine later and my resolve didn't change. I still knew what I wanted.

And I wanted Lachlan.

So I'll play his game. I'll prove to him that I know what I want. That I, too, understand the calculated risk we share in being together, and why we have to be cautious.

And then I'll reap the damn rewards because if the way he kisses is any indication of how he does other things, then . . . *damn.* Just damn.

But it's more than the physical. So much more. I had the physical with Rossi. It's the talking. Feeling heard. Feeling understood.

There are risks though. Risks that feel like a splash of cold water every time I think about them. The ones that so clearly conflict Lachlan too.

And while I hate that he even has to think about it, I also love that he has. It says huge things about his character and the man he was raised to be.

But in wanting him, I could risk all he's worked for. All I've worked for. How fucking unfair is that? And would it be worth it?

My job.

His relationship with Rossi. I can just imagine how Rossi would react if he found out his teammate started dating me.

His contract? Would that affect a team and how they perceive him? Someone willing to screw over a teammate for sex?

Those are the real questions.

Then again, why does it have to be anyone's business? And why doesn't it make me want him any less?

Seventeen days left.

I open my eyes and am met with the scene on the canvas in front of me. The green of a golf course, the dark night sky, and a shooting star streaking across it.

What did you wish for, Lachlan?

And why do I feel selfish wishing it were about me?

"You need help," I mutter to myself as I grab my paintbrushes and head to the sink to clean them. I get lost in the mundane task of cleaning them as my thoughts drift.

Rossi hasn't called at all. First and foremost, I think that's more telling than anything. It means my decision was the right one. It means he doesn't think I'm worth fighting for . . . or that his effort is better aimed elsewhere.

Have I gone to pick up the phone to text him about something random that happened? Of course I have. Old habits die hard.

But I've also picked up the phone to call Lachlan more than my need to text Rossi.

Does he have the same urge? To text? To call? To hear my voice? Is he reliving the moments we've shared over and over in his head much like I am?

My dad's words come back to me.

"Either Oliver will get his shit together and you'll take him back—if that's what you want—or you'll find another person who appreciates you that much more and you'll go from there."

So far it looks like it's the latter.

Who knows? Maybe I've already found that person. Even if it's just for the time being. No one said this is forever. Maybe he's just a new habit. Then again, maybe he's something more.

All that matters is that he makes me feel good about myself. That he makes me feel important and beautiful and heard. That I smile when I think about him.

The same things Skylar swears Russ makes her feel.

Lachlan Evans isn't the reason I broke up with Oliver Rossi.

That's for damn sure.

But he's not a bad distraction either if I'm going by my train of thought.

I'm not a rebound, Blair.

Those words have been on repeat in my head about as often as the memory of his kiss has replayed.

And now my dad's have been added.

If that's what you want.

Funny enough, what I want hasn't wavered. Not once. I'm just hoping Lachlan Evans is willing to bend the rules he's lived his entire life by to allow me to have it.

And if he's struggling with that, then I just might need to remind him why he should.

Chapter Seventeen

Lachlan

Fourteen days.

IT'S ALL BLAIR'S TEXT SAYS AND FUCK IF THOSE THREE SYLLABLES DON'T make me fucking hard as a rock. What I should be doing is what I came to my private driver's suite for—to clear my head.

And now both heads are at attention with no fucking relief in sight.

But I said twenty-one days and I meant it.

Had to.

Because she needs to be sure. I need to face my own fucking failure in going against everything I've ever been told.

And that's just fucked up in so many ways.

So I'm holding out. It's killing me but I'm a man of my word, and I need to at least hold on to that.

"Every fucking race."

I glance over to Rossi. The King of Muttering in what seems to be his pre-race default as of late.

Doesn't he know I need to focus as much as it seems he needs to mutter? The last thing I want to do is engage with him right now. He's been a bear during the last month, and it seems like in almost every interaction we've had, he's gunning for an argument.

That's the last thing we need right now. An argument. A verbal sparring match. Whatever you want to call it. My damn contract is no closer to being offered and so I need to keep my nose clean and take the high road.

I get up to close my door. "Good luck today, mate. We've got weather on our side, that's for sure. Gonna close this for a bit and—"

"She's been at every fucking race of my career. Every goddamn time like clockwork. She shows up and gives me a good luck kiss. Leaves before anyone sees her." He throws his hands up so they slap against his legs like a toddler does. "And this time . . ."

Fuck. I cannot have this conversation right now.

"I mean, I'd give you a good luck kiss if you'd like but I doubt you'll enjoy it," I say with a cheeky smile.

Do I want to tell him to shut the fuck up? Do I want to tell him he's acting like an entitled arsehole? Yep and yep. But it's race day—the best day of the week—and the last fucking thing we need is for me to create more stress.

"Right. You want to kiss my ass as well as Johann's, do you?"

For fuck's sake. Did the man put the A in antagonism because that's all he seems to want to do?

"No, mate. Just trying to get in the right headspace before we perform our death-defying job and all that."

"Jesus. Take a load off, will you? It wouldn't hurt you to let loose and get off every once in a while. All work and no play makes Lachlan Evans a dull boy," he teases.

What the fuck? What does that have to do with any part of this conversation? I'm trying to be nice. He's still trying to be an arsehole.

I cross my arms over my chest and glare at him.

What's the most un-fucking-believable thing about this conversation? It's that he still thinks she's coming. That even though they're broken up, he expects her to be here, to be bowing at his feet and piling adoration on him when he couldn't even give her the fucking time of day.

But I keep my face impassive, unable to show that I know about their breakup. The only thing I can do is entertain whatever tangent Rossi is taking me on now.

And apparently, it's how he thinks I have a stick permanently shoved up my arse.

If he only knew . . .

"Is that so?" That's safe enough to say.

"It is. I mean we have the job every person would kill to have. Use it to your advantage. Have a woman. Have some women. I mean, isn't it time you actually got serious about something?"

Ditto, Rossi.

But I bite my tongue. *Hard.* Johann asked me to keep the peace in his garage and fuck if I'll fail at that.

Besides, Rossi's little tizzy has nothing to do with racing and everything to do with Blair not being here for him.

Has he called her? Texted her to ask for a second chance? Apologized to her? By the way he's acting, I highly doubt it. So, I shrug.

"My time will come, mate."

He narrows his eyes at me, very possibly pissed off that I'm not engaging like he wants.

"I was going to marry her someday."

I stop my door mid-swing. *Fucking hell.* That's the last damn thing I expected him to say.

Really? *Marriage?* I've been around the two of them—at a distance, but around them—for the better part of three years while on this team and not once did I ever think, *now that's a couple who'll get married someday.*

The man barely looks interested when she's in the room. He baits her. He ignores her. And I'm not talking about at the track where they have to maintain their professionalism, but rather at private Team Apex events.

Marriage? Is he delusional?

Fourteen days.

It's been a torturous week since I last talked to her. I've spent way too much time thinking about her, wanting to be with her, hoping she's ridding Rossi from her system. And as seems to be par for the fucking course, now I'm stuck hearing him bitch and moan about missing her.

The guilt I'm suddenly feeling? Yeah, it's eating at me in ways I've never experienced before.

"What was that?" I ask.

"That was the plan. Eventually. To marry her."

Think you forgot a very important part here. The Blair wanting to part.

"Wow. Okay. That's surprising to hear."

"What the fuck does that mean?"

"You don't exactly act like marriage is on your radar."

"Like you'd fucking know."

"You're right. I wouldn't." I lift my hands up in surrender. "Look, Rossi. We have a race to prepare for. Can we go back to that for now? I'm sorry you and Blair are going through whatever it is you're going through, but we need to table it until after the checkered flag. You good with that?"

See, Johann? I'm putting my teammate first. Putting the team first.

"Whatever, Evans." The muscle tics in his jaw and the tendons in his neck go taut. "Blair and I have an understanding and lines we don't cross. There's history there you know nothing about."

No doubt he can see the skepticism in my expression. My poker face can't mask this one. *I don't want to know about your history, mate. I give zero fucks.*

"Blair . . . she's different. She's okay with all this. With me being me."

I snort and think of Blair's analogy about being a toy on the shelf. I recall the hurt in her eyes, and it infuriates me. "Or maybe she wasn't?"

"What the fuck? You're supposed to be on my side. Teammates and all that."

Do not engage. Step the fuck back. Nothing you say is going to change his delusions of grandeur.

The team.

The race.

Deep breath and plaster on a smile.

"Okay, *teammate*," I say, forcing as much false cheer into my voice and expression as I can. "Time to focus. Get our prep in. Get shit done."

"Yeah. Whatever," he grumbles and then turns, slamming his door.

I roll my eyes. *Such a prick.*

But shutting the door doesn't shut him out like I'd hoped it would. He's already in my head. His words. His arrogance. His fucking entitled arse.

I slip my headphones on and take a seat to chill out, but I'm restless. Antsy. Needing to move but wanting to avoid the crowds amassing everywhere outside.

And now I feel trapped.

She's texted me. A daily countdown.

And rather than pick up and invite the chaos I created, I punished myself for it. I hiked the hills above Monaco. I did a century on my road bike. I beat the shit out of myself in the gym.

Then I forced myself into the simulator for hours upon hours until my eyes hurt and my tailbone ached.

Anything and everything to drill into my head what's important. The work. The team. The championship I crave.

And yet when I close my eyes and lean my head back, it's her I fucking see.

It's her I still fucking want.

It's Blair—the only distraction I've ever allowed in my career. Fuck if I have a clue what to do about it. My new damn habit.

I gave us twenty-one days to cool things off. To make sure we understand the consequences and the possible fallout.

And it just doesn't seem to fucking matter in my head.

If I give in to what I want—her—my disloyalty to my teammate ruins my team.

If I hold out then my distraction over Blair does.

It's a no-fucking-win situation I'm rather sick of being honorable about.

There's a knock on the door.

"It's time already?" I ask reluctantly.

"It is," Lana, my PR minder, says.

I grumble but change my shirt and make my way out to the garages. To where the media, dignitaries, and garage pass holders mill about, shooting the shit, and trying to feel important in a world where only the drivers and the cars they drive are.

We're required to be here. To be present. These are our garages. Our team. And our presence is noted and documented.

"Grin and bear it," Lana says under her breath as we're spotted for the first time by the crowd.

I plaster on the smile I don't feel and greet those who come over to me. Normally I don't mind this scheduled socializing and playing the game. But today, not so much.

I've got too much on my mind.

"Lachlan. Good to see you."

I look over to see Hannah Brown from Motorsports Today. "Hi, Hannah. How are you doing?"

"Good. Glad to be back."

"He's two months now?" I ask of her newborn son, and her face lights up immediately at the mention of him.

"Yes." Her grin radiates. "He's growing so fast it's crazy."

"I can't imagine." I glance around the garage out of habit, well aware that her cameraman has his camera trained on us. "What can I do for you?"

"Answer a few questions?" she asks sheepishly.

"Of course."

"So coming off the small improvements from the Austrian Grand Prix, how is the mood and optimism in Team Apex right now?"

"I think we're always optimistic. Every race is an opportunity to prove ourselves and our competitiveness. Sure, we've had a few bumps in the road this year adapting to the changes implemented at the beginning of the season, but everyone has had to adjust, not just us."

"True, but Apex has struggled."

My smile is quick and reticent. "It would be stupid for me to deny that considering everyone can hear our race communications and see the results every Sunday afternoon, but at the same time, I believe in our engineers and mechanics and know that they are doing their diligence to turn this around."

"Is that what you worked on at Sterling Ridge?"

"What happens at Sterling Ridge, stays at Sterling Ridge," I tease and get the laugh from her I was working for.

"So it's top secret, huh?"

"Working on how to better communicate is never a negative."

"Very true. One more question, if you will?" she asks. "There are a lot of contract rumors buzzing around."

"Is that a question or a statement?" We both laugh, and I continue. "Contract rumors are always buzzing, even when everyone is signed and has a home. But sure, yeah, there's a buzz in the background."

"So there's no truth to the fact that there is in-fighting between you and Oliver Rossi?"

I glance over to where Rossi is talking on camera in the front of his garage, much like I am. He's looking up at the viewing area that sits directly above the bay. There's a strange expression on his face. One that's fleeting at best, but I catch it.

And I follow his gaze right to where Blair is standing at the railing, hands braced, and looking down below.

Right at me.

Our eyes lock. I'm fucking sucker punched.

Blair.

Our look is brief but it's enough to tell me that the want between us didn't dampen. Not in the fucking least.

I tear my eyes away, knowing Rossi's watching, and I'm on camera. I swallow forcibly as I wrack my brain for what question Hannah asked.

I struggle to find words.

"All I can say is that my focus is one hundred percent on Team Apex and making sure we get the most out of this current season. What happens after that? I'll leave it up to the agents and lawyers."

"Fair enough," she says. "Thank you for your time. Good luck in the race."

"Thank you."

And when I look back up, Blair is gone.

But it's Rossi's stare I can still feel.

Chapter Eighteen

Blair

THE WATER LAPS AT THE HULL OF THE BOAT.

It's a subtle sound but one that has the stress slowly draining from my body.

The soft growl of a motor is the other constant as water taxis bring people toward the extravagant superyachts in the Monaco harbor.

I look over to Monica Chamalet as she sits down with a glass of champagne across from me and curls her legs up beneath her. The diamonds on her fingers and ears glisten in the sunlight and seem so very commonplace while sitting on this massive boat. In her mid-sixties, she is flawless in every way possible—from her style to her manners to her aging. The inherited owner of one of the largest luxury watch companies in the world, Monica is the definition of affluence, success, and always a force to be reckoned with.

And, strangely, she's taken a liking to me during our numerous exchanges with the community outreach program.

Her involvement with Formula 1 has been accompanied with numerous scandalous rumors. Ones that center around the notion that upon her husband's death, when she found out about the many—and I mean *many*—lovers he'd taken during their marriage, she repaid the favor by spending ridiculous amounts of money on the sport he, for some reason, abhorred.

Her involvement has been more hands-off with a large focus on the charitable aspect, but behind the scenes there are murmurs she's looking to make a large investment in buying a portion, if not an entire team.

She's a good person to know—professionally and personally—because doors open automatically for her by simply being associated with her.

Consequently, I never decline an invite when it's extended.

"Darling, I'm so glad you could join us today," she says in that rich, velvety voice of hers.

A soiree on a superyacht in the Mediterranean? Who in their right mind would say no to that?

"The sun. The sea. Champagne. Good company. It's what the doctor ordered," I say and lift my own glass of champagne to my lips. I glance around at her other guests. A few I know, a few I know of, and others I've never met but feel like I have since they frequent movie screens. "And I have to thank you. Tori Michelle's agent said you put in a good word for me and tipped the scales to agree to perform at the gala."

Her smile is sly. "It was mentioned in passing and I thought I could help. I knew I was overstepping, might have even added in some heavy guilt about the charities the gala benefits and how her donated performance would be wonderful publicity for her." She rolls her eyes and flutters her fingers. "And I'm so very glad I did. She can afford it."

No one ever complains when Monica oversteps. I sure as hell won't either since it's usually a good thing.

"Well, I appreciate it. Truly."

"Anytime, darling." She perks up a little brighter in her seat and lifts her glass in a mock toast to someone across the deck. "And you're well? Over the whole Rossi thing or maybe with a few more glasses of this liquid gold and a hot romp with one of these gorgeous men here, you will be?" she asks.

The woman knows everything about everyone and somehow knew about my split with Rossi when she called me. In fact, I believe that was the basis for her call and invitation and why she informed me she wouldn't accept no for an answer.

"I am. I'm good. I think the breakup was a long time coming. I'm in a good place. I really am."

"That's wonderful. And it's perfect that you're here today to watch my magical matchmaking skills in action." She wiggles her fingers, prisms moving everywhere from the sun reflecting off her diamonds. "And once you see them, then maybe you'll let me use them on you."

I cough out a laugh as my mind goes to the only person I can see being matched with.

Seven days.

"Your magical matchmaking skills?"

"Mm-hmm. I need to do something to entertain my time."

"I don't know if I should be scared or amused," I tease. "Dare I ask who you're trying to play matchmaker to?"

She purses her lips and nods as she looks around at her guests. "I've had a man in mind for quite some time."

"For you?" I cough the word out.

"No. God, no." She huffs impatiently because I'm not following her. "For Zola," she says referring to her late twentysomething daughter. "I had my sights set on another—Baron von Steubing—to be exact." As if that name means something to me but no doubt the man has more money than he can spend in a lifetime if Monica is *picking* him for her daughter. "His mother and I have been busy plotting their nuptials. Lake Como. Four grandchildren. Family vacations in the Seychelles."

"Oh. Wow." Sounds . . . horrific.

"In fact, I invited him here today to try and work my magic between him and Zola, but then she showed up with a date. And . . . as disappointed as I am that Baron is going to have his feelings hurt, I will not be deterred from getting them together."

Poor Zola.

"Who knows, maybe she'll talk to Baron today, things will click, and plans will fall into place," I offer politely.

"Perhaps," she murmurs. "But truth be told, as much as she must at least test the waters with Baron for my sake, she seems quite smitten with her date. And if I'm honest with myself"—she leans in and covers her mouth so only I can see it when she whispers—"so am I."

"Wow. That's high praise," I say, more to be polite than anything, but with a huge dose of curiosity.

"It's Lachlan Evans. I'm sure you know him from the circuit. The real question is, *do you like him?*"

Her words are like cold water being thrown on me. I snap my head up and, luckily, she's looking the other way. *If only she knew how much I liked him.*

I open my mouth. Close it. Open it again. "Yes. Of course. He's—"

"Simply charming. Witty. Intelligent. Has that adorable Australian accent. And my oh my, is he handsome," she says dreamily. *I thought she was a fan of Baron von Whats-his-name? Can she go back to adoring him and leaving Lachlan out of her master matchmaking plans?*

I follow her stare and as if on cue, Zola steps out of the sliding glass door in a bikini that highlights every sculpted inch—no doubt from her hard work in the gym and the pristine skill of a plastic surgeon—of her incredible body.

Well, *fuck*.

I glance down at my own body—one I'm not ashamed of by any means—but one that sure as hell doesn't look like hers and . . . sigh.

A billionaire heiress who looks like she belongs on the cover of *Vogue* versus a working-class, plus-size army brat.

Like that would be a hard decision to make.

But before I can fall down that rabbit hole of insecurity, Lachlan strolls out right behind her.

In an equally devastating piece of swimwear. His shorts are a bright blue and then there are what feels like mile after mile of his own bronzed skin, stretched taut over corded muscle. There's a tattoo that snakes up the side of his torso that I can't exactly decipher but that my fingers itch to touch.

Who am I kidding? They itch to touch every damn inch of him.

Jealousy streaks through me. It's red hot and tinged in green.

I've waited fourteen fucking days. Fourteen days of silence. Of long looks across the paddock. Of wondering if he's going to let his principles override whatever it is between us.

And this is how I get my answer? Seeing him on a yacht catering to Zola the beauty queen? The same Zola who Monica plans on setting up with him?

I grit my teeth.

For a woman who didn't give a fuck if women hit on Rossi, I sure as hell do when it comes to Lachlan.

But why?

"He's even got you staring," Monica teases as we both study him unabashedly.

But while she's mentally cheering the small touch of Lach's hand to Zola's back as he hands her a glass of champagne, my entire body is tensing from it.

He's a gentleman. I know that firsthand. And so he's simply doing gentlemanly things.

But that doesn't make watching the two of them together any easier for me.

"They make a beautiful couple, don't they?" Monica asks as we both study them from behind our sunglasses.

"They do." The words feel like poison on my tongue.

"Lachlan," Monica calls out. His smile is automatic but his body freezes when he sees me sitting there with her. And then a slow, catlike smile crawls over his lips.

Jesus. My insides twist in the most deliciously jealous way.

Lach excuses himself from Zola and the circle of people around them and moves toward us. His eyes hold mine before moving back to Monica's . . . and that glance alone has me sitting taller.

"Ladies." He kisses Monica on both cheeks before doing the same to me.

I'm hit with the sandalwood scent of his cologne. With the feel of his hand against my lower back. With the slightest exhale to know my nearness affects him just as much as his does mine.

"You two are acquainted, yes?" Monica asks Lachlan as she looks back and forth between us.

"It's been a while since I've seen you, Blair," Lachlan says.

"It has. Like, what? *Fourteen days?*" I ask.

Lachlan's eyes widen and nostrils flare ever so slightly as a smile ghosts his lips. "Something like that. Good to know you were counting."

"Always." I lift my flute of champagne and turn back toward Monica to explain. "We shared a golf cart ride."

"We did," Lach adds.

"And now you're here with Zola. She said your dinner date was incredible last night."

He smiles and nods without responding.

"So does that mean I'll be seeing more of you around here?" Monica asks.

"Lachlan?" Zola asks from her place across the deck, her eyes darting from her mother to Lachlan and then back. "Come. I want to introduce you to somebody."

Lachlan nods and stands. "I'll catch up with you ladies more in a while."

"No need, darling," Monica says. "Please enjoy your time."

A fleeting glance is all I get from Lachlan as he walks away. *Why do I hate that so much?*

Because I already care about him. That's the truth of it.

My head hurts. Too many glasses of champagne on a stomach that can't tolerate food right now. Because all I've done is watch. Let's be real here, *and pine.*

It's not his fault she wants him. I understand that because I do too.

But that doesn't make me seeing the two of them together any easier.

And they are just that—*together.* All afternoon long. Chatting with other guests. Eating food. Riding jet skis. Spending time together.

What do I get? The woman who has been waiting fourteen days to break a bad habit?

Nothing. Not a glimpse. Not a second glance. Not a fucking nothing. Is this Rossi 2.0? How many years did I sit back and watch Rossi flirt with other women? Doing so while I was in the same damn room? Acting as though I truly never really *had* him?

But that feeling I had when Rossi would flirt? It's ten times worse watching Lachlan do it and that tells me something very significant.

This is crazy. I've only really been interested in him a month or so, but damn if my heart doesn't already know what it wants. Him.

So why is he here with her? Why do I feel like I don't exist?

"You sure you can't stay for dinner?" Monica asks.

If I have to listen to Zola giggle like an air-headed ditz, and watch her put her hand on Lachlan one more time, I might tear my eyes out.

"I can't. I'm sorry. I already made other plans."

"That's your first mistake," she says and winks. "When I throw a party, you never make plans for afterwards because we always like to see where the night takes us."

"Noted for next time."

"I'll have the captain call for the water taxi for you then."

"Thank you. I appreciate it. I'm going to head toward the restroom before it arrives."

"Perfect."

I set my empty champagne flute on the tray of a passing server and head down the maze of hallways toward the restroom.

I'm halfway to it when I'm pushed in a stateroom. I bite back my yelp as Lachlan puts his hand over my mouth to quiet me. But the minute he shuts the door at his back, I jerk my head back and forth to rid his hand.

"Don't touch me," I grit out.

His flash of a grin does nothing to abate my festering anger. "Now that, I can't do."

His lips find mine. It's a kiss full of need and greed and fucking hunger and peppermint. One I want to fall so deep into I can't see my way out. One I've craved and relived over the past fourteen days but fuck if my fury doesn't override my desire.

I tear my mouth from his—my body hating me, my mind needing to.

"A dinner date? Zola? I can't even get a fucking response from a text to you and you're out schmoozing with her?"

"You're jealous." His smirk infuriates me.

"You're damn right I am." I push against his chest but there's no give. The space is small and he is strong. "She's a fucking goddess."

"Blair." He laughs my name out like I'm being a ridiculous child and it only infuriates me more.

"You say you're different, but you're proving to be just like Rossi." My rebuke is sharp and fueled out of the jealousy and desire clouding every facet of my being.

"You don't mean that." He dips his head to meet my eyes.

"I do," I lie.

"Fine." He lifts his eyebrows. "Then I have my answer."

And just like that he drops his hands from me and reaches for the door to walk out. I yank him back toward me so our bodies land squarely against one another's. The feel of him. Jesus. It's heaven and hell and every slice of debauchery in between.

I kiss him. It's hard and reeking of desperation. God it feels good to finally take what I want without repercussions. Without thinking.

Don't end.

Don't fucking end.

But he frames my face with his hands—something about the action makes me feel wanted and desired—and leans back to look at me. His labored breathing feathers over my lips as my heart all but beats out of my chest.

"Zola helped get us on the golf course that night. I'm returning the favor. Her mom is the queen of trying to set her up. I'm saving her from some old guy by pretending to be her date."

I tsk in response at his far-fetched bullshit. "You sure as shit are playing the part well, now, aren't you?"

His grin widens. "I like this side of you." *I don't.* He bends his knees so that he's the only thing in my line of vision. "Look at me. Monica Chamalet is the private advisor to Gravitas Racing. Yes, I'm helping Zola out here, but

I'm also well aware of the game I'm playing. The one I need to play to guarantee I'm on the grid next year. Nothing less. Nothing more. What I want—you—hasn't fucking changed one goddamn bit."

I open my mouth and then close it. The conviction in his voice is as much of a turn-on as his hands on my cheeks.

The rumors must be true. If Monica's advising now, I can see why people are saying she might take a step toward ownership.

I had no clue she was that involved. Or that he knew Zola well enough for her to ask for his help in fending off her mother's matchmaking.

"So there's nothing there? Between you two?"

"I only have eyes for one woman," he says resolutely.

"And everything else is you just playing the game?" I whisper.

"It is. And obviously it's rather convincing." His smile lights up his eyes.

But watching him play the game is like having acid drip . . . it burns every time it hits but it doesn't kill you outright.

"You think I don't want you, Blair? That I've changed my mind?" He runs a thumb over my bottom lip, and I lean in to the touch. "You're out of your goddamn mind. I've tried convincing myself of every damn reason why we shouldn't. Why I can't risk it. And all I keep coming back to is how I don't have a fucking choice because I'm going mad without you."

His lips slant over mine once more. He takes them like a man starving for air and I'm his only source of oxygen. There's a potency to it I've never experienced before. I've been ruined by it because it's all I'll ever want going forward.

"Seven days," he murmurs against my lips.

"What?" I all but shriek as he covers my mouth once again to keep me quiet.

"I told you, I don't break my rules for anyone."

"Lach?" Zola's voice floats down the hallway. "The help said you were down here."

His wince says it all. *He's playing a game.*

"Hey, Tink?" He pulls me firmly against his body so that I can feel every deliciously hard inch of him. "These?" He runs his hands up and down the length of my bathing suit-clad hips. The heat of his touch against my bare skin is the sweetest seduction known to man.

The darkening of his eyes says he feels the same way.

"This is what I get off to. This body. These curves. This mind. You. Not hers. Believe me . . . it's you."

And just like that, the fury is gone, and the goddamn inferno of desire returns as he slides out the door of the stateroom, leaving me a puddle of want. Well . . . that just happened.

"This is what I get off to. This body. These curves. This mind. You. Not hers. Believe me . . . it's you."

And I can't wait until it happens again.

Chapter Nineteen

Lachlan

Knock. Knock.

Christ. I hang my head and roll my shoulders.

The doorman didn't say anyone was coming up so that only leaves one person—my elderly neighbor who's prone to asking for chores to be done at odd times at night.

I scrub a towel through my freshly showered hair, and then head to the door to see what she needs help with this time. I'm not exactly in the best mood to deal with her right now, but I can never say no to her.

But when I swing the door open, I'm met with the best fucking surprise.

"Blair."

"If you're going to pretend in public that you're with her, then you're going to prove to me in private that you're with me," she says with a defiance that has my jaw dropping and libido fucking sparking.

And if her confidence didn't make me hard instantly when she strutted past me, her presence in my place in heels and a yellow sundress with tiny buttons on its front sure as fuck does.

"Well, hello to you too," I murmur.

"We have unfinished business," she states as I fight the urge to haul her against me and take until I can't take any more.

But I'll play the game.

"I thought we had seven days. I thought there were rules." I grin as the ache in my lower belly spreads and my balls tighten.

"You can break your rules for me. *For this.*" She starts to undo the tiny buttons on the top of her dress. I can't look away.

I groan and drag a hand through my hair. *She's not playing fair.* "How do you know where I live?"

"I have my ways," she says coyly, repeating my line back to me from when I knew what hotel room she was in. When I force my eyes off her dexterous fingers and the scrap of white lace that's becoming apparent beneath the dress, I meet her eyes again. My swallow is forced. My chest constricts. She angles her head to the side and smirks. "What? Are you going to say no to me, Lachlan?"

"You're making it really fucking hard to."

"*Good.*" Her eyes glance down to where my cock is begging to be free of my sweats. "Hard is just how I like it."

My laugh is strained and desperate. So is my need to touch her again. My hands on her hips earlier were the biggest cocktease ever . . . and now she's here. Within reach. Looking like that. Like a 1950s pinup girl full of curves and sass and exuding sex appeal that could wake a man from the dead.

"Blair." Her name is a groan as her dress falls open.

White lace. A ton of cleavage. The hint of a garter belt. And an expanse of tanned skin just beneath.

Christ almighty.

"You think I don't want you, Lachlan Evans? You think that twenty-one days is going to stop me from wanting that? You're all I think about. What you taste like. What you feel like. What you'd feel like inside me. How fucking good we'd be together." She hums. "I've played along with your self-imposed time frame. Your twenty-one days to form a habit. I call bullshit because all it took me was thirty minutes."

"Thirty minutes?" I ask, finding it difficult to focus on her words when her body is right there.

"Thirty minutes outside of a sponsorship party for me to want to know you more."

"That's not enough," I taunt and take a step closer as she slides the dress off her shoulders so it falls to the floor and pools at her feet.

She's breathtaking.

Simply fucking breathtaking.

All I can think about is mapping every line and dent and curve of her body with my hands. With my mouth. With my tongue.

"All it took was one night in a bar, to know there was something there between us. Something indescribable. Something I've never felt before."

I slide my hand beneath my waistband and wrap my hand around my cock. The sight of her like this is fucking unbearable. I've jacked off with less of a vision of her—now this one? I'm ruined for life.

My groan is guttural as I slide my hand back and forth over my hardened shaft.

"One night? That's it?" The strain in my voice is audible. "How do you know that when you've only ever been with Rossi?"

She runs her hands over her breasts. I can see the dusty rose of her nipples through the lace. I can see them pucker. Can smell her fucking arousal from here.

"I want to watch," she says and looks down to my pants.

Like I need to be any harder but those words . . . those words fucking do it. With my free hand, I slide my sweats down over my fisted cock and my hips and step out of them.

The entire time I'm watching her. The shudder of her shoulders when she sees me. The gasp of breath when I groan. The chills that chase over her skin. Her eyes finding mine again.

I quirk an eyebrow. *There you go, Blair. What are you going to do about it?*

"Three hours." She takes a step toward me. "Three hours playing on a golf course." And another step as I tighten my fist. "But it was really only one minute."

My breath hitches when she reaches out and runs a hand down my chest. Her fingernails scrape softly over my skin.

"One fucking minute," she murmurs as she steps into me so that we're a feather width apart. So that her exhale is my next inhale. So that I can feel her body desperate for mine. She wraps her hand over mine and helps me stroke this one time. "One. Fucking. Minute. When your lips touched mine that I knew I had to have you."

Her voice never wavers. It never even hesitates. It's as sure and steady as her confidence walking in here.

"That's a bold statement," I breathe out.

"You might think I've only ever been with Rossi, but my heart stopped beating for him a long time ago. Not just weeks ago. We *are* history, Evans. I'm only looking at the future now. I'm only looking at you."

She grabs hold of my cock and slides down, rubbing her hand over the top and then back to its base.

It's fucking heaven.

Our eyes hold. I fist my hand in her hair and hold her head back so she's forced to look at me. So she won't be distracted. So she'll hear me loud and fucking clear.

"Well, I'm going to need a hell of a lot more time than one minute tonight to fuck the desperation out of me that I've felt since that first night."

She lifts to her tiptoes so that our lips whisper over each other's when she speaks. "I'm willing to take that punishment," she says, her hardened nipples brushing against my bare chest. "To risk that reward." She licks her tongue over the seam of my lips. "And, Lachlan, it's going to take a lot longer than a minute." This time she licks a line up the side of my throat and tugs on my ear.

My growl fills the room. From one beat to the next I have my hands threaded through her hair and my lips on hers. I don't ask. I simply take. Her taste. Her tongue. Her moans. Her kiss.

It's all I can think about. All I want to think about. I savor it. Savor her.

Make it last. Make it fucking last, Lach, but that might be impossible with her body in my hands.

"Lach," she moans out when my hand cups her breast, my thumb and forefinger rolling over the tightly puckered bud. "I want you." Her hand slides between her thighs, digs into her wetness, and then slides it over my cock.

It's the sexiest thing I've ever seen, ever felt. The proof of what I do to her. The knowledge that she wants to give that to me.

I grab her wrist and take her fingers to my lips and suck on two of them. The sweet taste of her consumes me. Fuels me. Ruins me and my patience.

From one beat to the next, my lips are back on hers, and the two of us are stumbling down the hall toward my bedroom. It's like those damn fourteen days have been torture and we can't bear to part.

"On the bed," I tell her and watch as she bends over slowly and crawls on all fours up the mattress. The white lace splits over her arse and pussy and gives me the most glorious view as she makes a show of it.

Then she turns over and spreads her legs to give me an even better look as I roll a condom on my cock.

"Good God, woman," I mutter as I fill the space between her thighs and take in the glistening pink and the unmistakable scent of her desire. I use my hands to spread her thighs even wider as I dip my head down and run my tongue from clit to slit.

My feral growl owns the fucking room. I've never tasted anything better—never been harder—in my whole goddamn life.

My eyes are locked on hers from above her mound as I swirl my tongue over her clit, again and again, before tucking two fingers into her and making sure she's ready for me. She grips my fingers with her muscles as her thighs tense on my shoulders.

Her hips buck beneath my touch as I work her into a frenzy, but no matter how intense her sensations become, she keeps her eyes on mine and her hands gripping the sheets at her sides.

She's a sight to fucking behold. I dip my tongue inside her just as she moans. *My girl likes that.* Her body shudders—once. Twice. Three times. And before I can wipe my chin off or process what's next, she's pulling me up and guiding me into her.

"I need you. In me. Now," she pants between breaths. Then the last one is capped with one long, guttural groan from both of us as I push slowly into her.

Fuck.

Just . . . fuck.

My head rolls back on my shoulders and my eyes fall closed as her sweet pussy grips every hard inch of me. It's the best kind of torment. The kind I want to withdraw so I can feel all these sensations again when I push back in but also, never want to leave.

"Blair. Jesus, woman."

Her chuckle is a low rumble as she lifts her hips and milks my cock with her muscles.

"Please," she whispers.

And she doesn't have to ask twice. I grip her hips, my fingers digging into the flesh, before pulling out and driving into her again.

The way she stretches around me.

The glisten of her fucking arousal.

The way her tits jolt with each push in.

The way she fucking feels.

I think in sensations. Her taste's still on my tongue. Her wet heat's wrapped around me. Her begging mewls soft but demanding. The scent of us together.

The pressure builds. Brick by goddamn brick with each drive in, each grind against her clit, and every fucking slide back out.

It's addictive. Everything about the moment and looking down at her as she gets pulled under the tsunami of pleasure, as she comes again, is the sexiest fucking sight I've ever seen.

Her teeth in her bottom lip. Her breasts heavy and nipples hard. Her eyes glazed but on mine. Her hair fanned out over the pillow. And her pussy absolutely drenching me as she pulses around me.

I can't look away.

I don't want to.

And then my own orgasm hits. It's a sucker punch of pleasure that robs me of all thought. That heightens every sensation. That I know will own me for fucking ever.

Blair Carmichael is it.

Looking down at her as I come harder than I've ever come before in my life, I know it.

I broke my rules for her.

And I don't break them for anybody.

Chapter Twenty

Blair

"**B**LAIR."

If satisfaction and exhaustion could be woven into a sound, it would be Lachlan's deep voice.

"Hmm?" My eyes are closed and my body's still vibrating from him, from the mind-blowing sex . . . from everything that has to do with him.

The man knows how to take care of a woman. With his words. With his actions. With his clear attention to detail.

His ability to make me feel cherished and like an object of desire simultaneously is something any woman can appreciate.

"You're too far away," he says and slides a hand around my stomach and pulls me against him so that my back is to his front.

His cock is nestled between my ass cheeks and his hands never stop touching me. A lazy slide up and down the swell of my hip. His fingers trailing back and forth over my abdomen. His chin and the soft scrape of his stubble against the curve of my neck. The heat of his body behind me.

"Mmm." It's all I can muster.

"What does that mean?"

I shrug but open my eyes and take in his bedroom around me. It's sparsely furnished but clearly lived in. It's whites and creams with a touch of browns on rustic wood furniture. It's the polar opposite of Rossi's place full of sleek wood and modern black.

Just like the two men are polar opposites.

But there's no comparison between them for me beyond that. That's the funny thing. I don't see Lach and think Rossi would do it this way or that way. It just seems like when I'm with Lachlan, there never was a Rossi except to set a bar that my next boyfriend needs to be above.

"You're not talking."

"I'm looking at all your stuff."

"Snoop away. I have nothing to hide," he murmurs into the crown of my head.

"You have pictures of your family."

"Is that a bad thing?" he asks.

"No. It's very good. It means you like them."

"Why wouldn't I like them?" He chuckles.

I shrug again. But the fact that there are pictures in his room of his family says they're not for show. It means he truly loves them and that makes me smile.

"You're quiet again."

"I'm just thinking."

"About?" he asks.

"It's just . . ."

"Talk to me, Tink."

The nickname makes me smile and the safe space he's created around me makes me comfortable enough to utter my next words. "This has never happened to me before."

"The sex?" He snorts. "If you tell me you're a virgin, Blair, I'm not exactly buying it."

"No. Not that." I roll my eyes and offer a smile he can't see while pulling his hand still on my stomach up to my lips. I kiss his fingers, and the fact that they smell like me is oddly satisfying.

"Then what?"

I sigh as I struggle with the words. "I know we just had sex and it was amplified by the waiting and the wanting and all, but—"

"Please tell me you're not playing this down because I don't mean to brag, but that was fucking incredible. *You* are fucking incredible."

He kisses his way down my shoulder as his fingers slide between my thighs. My body sinks into him as he draws lazy lines up and back over my already hypersensitized skin. It's the slightest caress but it ignites the still-smoldering ache.

"Lach." Breathless, I moan his name out, and I can feel his lips spread into a smile on my bare shoulder.

"Touching you is my new favorite thing." And just as I spread my thighs wider to give him unfettered access, he says, "And I'll continue right after you finish what it is you were going to say." His fingers stop, just atop of my clit. It's enough pressure to know he's there and to remind me how much I want his touch. "So? I know we just had sex, plan to have more sex—*I'm adding that last part for myself*—and it's amplified because of the wanting and the waiting part but . . ."

I open my mouth and then close it, feeling ridiculous that I opened this door. How can I verbalize my thoughts to him when my logic says it's absolutely ridiculous to feel this strongly for someone in this short amount of time?

"Blair?" He rubs his finger in a subtle circle to remind me of my choice—be honest and be rewarded or keep to myself and miss out.

"I'm not a firm believer in insta-anything."

"Insta-anything?"

My cheeks heat in embarrassment. I'm just glad he can't see them. "Mm-hmm."

"As in lust? Chemistry? Belonging? Love? What?"

"All of the above."

"And let me guess, you're busy trying to tell yourself none of those things are possible while I'm here about to tell you it is. There's a reason I said twenty-one days. I don't believe in that shit either, baby, but *all of the above* is exactly what we are, and I'm fucking fine with that when in a million years I'd never think I would be."

"Lachlan." It's just his name but it represents the dozen questions I have running through my head.

How can you say that?

How can either of us think this and not be absolutely batshit crazy?

How is this even possible?

"You think this is easy for me? All I've ever done my whole life is race. I've stayed between those lines and looked straight ahead, only focusing on the podium. I've been with women, sure, but nothing has ever distracted me from racing. Not like this."

"Now you're telling me you're the virgin," I tease.

He chuckles and it rumbles through my back. "Now, did what just happen between us feel like what a virgin would do?"

"Um. No." That little pop of his hips that hits all the right places? Most definitely not.

"Why do you think I said twenty-one days?" He presses a kiss to my shoulder.

"Because you're a masochist."

"Perhaps." Another rub of his stubble over my shoulder. "Or perhaps it was because if I'm going to break all my rules, I need to make sure. But . . . *fuck, Blair,* the thought of you only grew stronger. More pervasive."

"Great, so now I'll be the one to blame for a bad season," I joke.

"Uh-uh." He tugs on my hip so I roll over and come face-to-face with him. I reach up and run a hand over his cheek, my fingers touching lightly over his lips. "You are just the distraction I need. The person who might help me put things into perspective. You're *all of the above.*"

It should unnerve me. Those words. The conviction with which he says them . . . but they don't. He doesn't. And simply because I feel it too.

Because I know it too.

I tip my chin up and brush my lips over his as his hand slides down to cup my ass, the tips of his fingers so very close to where I want their touch.

"How do we do this though?" I murmur against his skin.

"How? Well, it starts with me touching right here." A gasp falls from my mouth as his fingertip finds purchase and pushes its way into me, moving leisurely.

"Not that." The words are a moan that coincides with my fingers tightening on his chest. "That's not what—"

"Then this?" He palms my breast so my nipple is at a perfect angle for his lips to close around it. The warm, wet heat of his tongue is like a mainline to my core. His cock thickening against my thigh enhances the sweet ache singing through my body.

"I'm not going to complain about that," I murmur as he brings his lips back up to mine so that our tongues dance against one another's for a slow, sensual kiss. "I mean this. Us. The outside world."

He rests his forehead to mine, a sigh on his lips that's so contradictory to the sensations I'm feeling with his fingers slowly pleasuring me.

"There are a lot of consequences to us being together," he says.

"I know."

"But more than anything is how you'd be perceived. Because of our positions, because of my job, the public's perception . . . you would be perceived negatively. The track bunny. Society is so fucked up the way women get blamed."

I want to tell him that I don't care if I'm to be blamed. I want to express my disregard for outside opinions . . . but I've worked so hard to get where I am, and I'd genuinely hate for all that to be negated because I'm with him.

"We're in very sensitive times in our careers," I say.

"My contract renewal. My teammate. Your reputation. Your career. Your want to keep Rossi as a friend. My—"

"Zola," I say cattily, earning a chuckle and the added pressure of his palm to my clit.

"I assure you, I'm not thinking about Zola right now." He adds a second finger to the mix that has my back arching. "Or ever."

"Good to know," I pant out. But rest assured I'll bring her up again if this is what my punishment is.

"You've worked hard to make a name for yourself as a dedicated, honest, woman—*God*, you're soaking me," he groans, and I slide my thumb over the crest of his cock. He shifts his hips away. "No. You first. You second. Maybe even a third or fourth had. *Always.* Then me. Then I get mine. I can wait."

Can he get any more incredible?

Death by orgasm. Not a bad way to go.

He laces open-mouthed kisses up the underside of my neck. Too many sensations. Too much stimulation. Not enough him. For some reason, I doubt there ever will be if this is how he makes me feel.

"So we . . ." It's getting hard to concentrate.

"We stay discreet. For now."

"A part of me likes that. The part that says I get to keep you all to myself."

"Yeah well, I'm struggling with this. The last place you need to be is hidden on a shelf. Hmm," he murmurs sexily as I buck my hips into his hand. "I told you once if you were mine, I'd show you off. This is preventing that, so I'm not exactly thrilled."

"In time."

"In time." He nips my shoulder and increases his tempo. "So long as I get all of the above."

"You're making it hard to concentrate on talking. On thinking. On—"

"Good." He tucks a third finger inside and fills me, my body burning with need. "Come for me, Tink. Drench me. Scream for me. And then we'll do it all over again but with my cock next time."

Chapter Twenty-One

Blair

It's a beautiful morning. The sun is out and the sea is sparkling in the harbor beyond. And last night was . . . too spectacular to even put adjectives to.

But as I stand in the boulangerie, looking at the glass case of baked goods in front of me and a clerk standing there waiting and staring at me expectantly, I realize how unrealistic my optimism is that this will work out.

I know what Rossi's order would be right now. What he takes in his coffee. And the fact that he even eats breakfast.

But I have no damn clue about any of those when it comes to Lachlan. Not his habits. Not his dislikes. Not his routine.

And as I stand here dreamily thinking of the warm bed I left not long ago to take a work call and then come grab us breakfast, the realness of this hits me.

Hard.

The clerk lifts her eyebrows and stares at me as confusion owns me. "Um, two coffees please. And . . . a mixed assortment of these," I say pointing to various bakery items. All of which look good. None of which I know if Lachlan likes or even eats.

"Of course. One moment."

"Thank you," I say and walk to the end of the case to inspect some of the other items on the menu. I've passed this shop dozens of times but have never had the need to stop in here. Rossi's place was always professionally stocked, and I knew where everything was. At Lachlan's, I felt like I'd be snooping if I were to open cupboards and look for something to make.

"Blair?"

I freeze at the voice behind me. Oh. Shit.

I turn to face Rossi. It's the first time we've been alone together since we broke up weeks ago. And it feels familiar and strange at the same time.

"Hi." Oh shit. *My order.* Two coffees. A dozen pastries. This early on a Sunday morning. "How are you?" I ask with both caution and concern.

"Good. Been better." He scrubs a hand through his hair and I can see it now. The exhaustion. The confusion. The unshaven scruff. The things that only someone who's known him the better part of a decade might be able to see. "You?"

I shrink hoping he doesn't see the exact opposite in me. The happiness. The relief. The . . . everything that Lachlan has made me feel. "I'm okay. Just busy. Just focusing on my work."

"Yeah. Right. The masquerade ball." He lifts his eyebrows up and shifts on his feet.

"Right." I try to keep the bitterness from my tone, but it's there, front and center. "Things turning around with the cars?" I ask like I don't know. Like we're strangers.

And the awkwardness kills me while the guilt comes in waves.

"Ma'am? Your order. Two coffees and—"

"Yes. Great. Thank you." I stare at the box of baked goods and the two coffees when clearly, it's just me standing here. "It's for—they're for—a meeting. For the gala."

"On a Sunday?"

"Yes. The countdown is on, and I still have so much to do," I ramble.

"Here? In Monaco? Why not in Nice by your flat?"

I blink blankly at him and lie. "It's a neutral spot."

He just nods slowly, his eyes holding mine and distrust firing in them. "Got it."

"When do you leave for Hungary?" I ask, changing the subject as subtly as I can.

I'm sure he notices.

"Monday. Just like every other race I've gone to over the past how many years?"

I glance down to my twisting fingers and then back up to him. "This shouldn't be this hard," I whisper softly.

He nods. "Yeah well . . . you got what you wanted, right?"

I suck in a breath, the sting real. My nod is contrite. "There's no right way to answer that, Oliver. No one wanted this. No one wanted either of us to be hurt. No one wanted—"

"You're hurting?" His eyes narrow as he stares at me.

"Change is hard. We grew into different people."

"No shit. You changed and—"

"*We* changed," I correct but I have a feeling he's not going to hear me. He never did. "And you're proving my point."

"Got it. Great. Enjoy your coffees and your"—he glances over his shoulder as if he's expecting to see whoever the second coffee belongs to—"*meeting.*"

"I will." I gather my items off the display case, a little sad that this conversation couldn't have gone better. When I go to move past him, there's an unsettled feeling in the pit of my stomach.

He blows out a breath. "*Blair.*"

I turn to look at him over my shoulder and for the first time in a long time, I see the teenage boy I met at the track all those years ago. The one with the crooked glasses and hair in need of a haircut. The one who used that space and this sport to erase the chaos from his home.

My chest constricts and that grief I've been waiting for finally hits me. But it's not grief over us not being together. It's grief because I miss my friend.

"I . . ."

"I know." I smile softly at him. "*I know.* You're still one of my best friends, Oliver. I hope we can be that again to each other one day."

He drops his head for a beat, his eyes on the ground before he meets my eyes. There's honesty in them. Gone is the bad boy persona of Rossi, the reckless driver. Instead, it's Oliver Rossi from Vicenza who just might actually miss me.

He nods his head subtly with a melancholic smile on his lips.

But he doesn't say a word. Rather he just watches me walk out the door, and I swear I can feel his eyes on me way past turning the next corner.

I keep glancing over my shoulder the entire way back to Lachlan's place. Rossi lives the opposite way and yet . . . this town is too small, with too many

F1 drivers and people I know. How did I think I could stalk into Lach's apartment and not be seen? That I could keep this under wraps and remain discreet?

Talk about going from the highest of highs to the lowest of lows.

Change is hard. Didn't I just say that to Rossi? Then why am I struggling with it? Why am I wanting to rush back to Lachlan while my heart is hurting for the man I just walked away from?

Fuck.

I'm lost in these thoughts and my naivete over how this would go with Rossi and exhaustion over a very active night is showing as I quietly push open the door to Lachlan's place.

I'm met with a very stoic Lachlan when I enter. He's sitting in an armchair in nothing but the sweats he had on last night. He has one ankle resting on the other knee, his elbow bent and finger on his lip, and he's staring at me with an undecipherable expression.

"Hi," I say as I shut the door behind me. "Everything okay?"

"I thought you left."

"Left?" I ask as I hold up the coffee and pastries in my hand.

"Yeah, as in you woke up, thought we made a mistake, and ghosted me." I'm stopped in my tracks by his intensity.

But I know how I am, Blair. I know I'm an all or nothing.

His words come back to me.

I set everything down and move toward him. Toward the bronzed skin taut over corded muscle. Toward the unshaven jaw and the confused eyes. I straddle him, digging my knees into either side of his hips and frame his face.

"I didn't ghost you. I woke up and wanted to do something nice but in doing that, I realized I don't know anything important about you."

"You know the most important things," he says, leaning his cheek into one of my hands.

"No. I don't. I know how you make me feel, but I don't know how you take your coffee. What you eat for breakfast. Do you shower at night or the mornings? Are you an over the sheets or under type of guy?"

He chuckles. "That was what you were thinking when you were looking at my naked body in a nice warm bed?" He quirks a brow. "Clearly, I didn't do my job good enough last night."

I lean forward and press a kiss to his lips. The simple action erasing that mini-panic attack I had. "I kind of freaked out. I didn't want to open your cupboards to find coffee. I didn't want you to think I was snooping. I didn't want to . . . I don't know what your boundaries are and, when the barista asked me for your coffee order, I didn't know it."

He grabs my hands, pressing a kiss into my palms. "This is a side I haven't seen from you yet. Relax, Tink. I'm an open fucking book to you. I have nothing to hide. No skeletons in the closet that might jump out. No ghosts who'll jump out of my cupboards when you open them." He links his fingers with mine and sets them in our lap. "I take my coffee with milk. Any kind, I'm not picky. Sometimes I eat breakfast. Sometimes I don't. It depends when my workout is, and so if it's early, I drink a protein shake. They're in that fridge over there." He lifts his chin to show me. "But something else is bugging you. Regrets, then?"

"No. God, no. I'm here, aren't I?" I try to joke.

"*Something* else is bugging you."

"I saw Rossi at the bakery."

"And?" he prompts cautiously.

"It was hard. I played it off why I was in town, but . . . it was hard."

"I'm secure enough in who I am and whatever this is between us for you to say you miss him."

My smile stutters. "I do . . . but for silly things. For nostalgic things. Not for the relationship part."

"Okay. I can understand that."

"It was just . . . a lot. Heavy."

"Sounds like it."

"And it also made me realize that if we plan on being discreet, that I can't come here. This town's too small. Too many people see things. Gossip. Especially with you being you. So that might pose a problem."

"Then we go to your place," he says matter of fact.

I chuckle disbelievingly. "My place is nowhere as nice as this."

"Do you think I give a shit? So long as you're there, that's all that matters."

"Rossi hated going there."

"Well, Rossi is a pompous prick who forgot what mattered most."

"Perhaps."

"Lucky for me then," he says as his hands find their way to my hips and his fingers dig in as I also feel his cock pulse against my core. "Hey, Blair?"

"Hmm?"

"Open the cupboards." He brushes his lips against mine. "Search my closets." Another. "Grill my housekeeper when you meet her." Our tongues touch this time and all I want is more. "*I don't fucking care.*"

"You don't have to say that—"

"And the shower part?" He meets my eyes as he shifts beneath me, showing me just how quickly he's become hard. "Morning. And night. And I think right now is a perfect time to give you a personal tour of it."

"A tour?"

"There's a seat in there."

"For shaving legs?" I ask as we stand and he takes my hand in his.

"No. For riding me."

Chapter Twenty-Two

Blair

MY TO-DO LIST IS A MILLION MILES LONG AND THE DAYS ARE counting down to the gala. A classic case of too much to do and not enough time to do it in.

And a major case of the best weekend ever that I can't stop reliving in my head over and over.

Skylar's high-pitched squeal is still ringing in my ears from our conversation earlier. From her excitement over me and Lachlan and what she called was me being unmistakably smitten.

I stare out the window, a soft smile ghosting my lips and so many memories dancing around in my head.

There's no way this is real. Can't be. And yet Lachlan's texts keep coming at random times throughout the past few days to make me realize it is real. A glance at my screen proves it.

> Lachlan: Lach Ness. That's what my mates called me at school when they wanted to make fun of me.
>
> Lachlan: I prefer pesto over a red sauce any day.
>
> Lachlan: Not one for sparkling water. The bubbles make it taste funny.
>
> Lachlan: Bucket list destination is Iceland. But I don't understand why it's called Iceland when it's the green one and Greenland is called that when it has the ice. Shouldn't it be switched?
>
> Lachlan: Shh. Don't tell anyone but I loathe Vegemite.

Lachlan: One leg out of the covers at all times. That's how I like to sleep.

Lachlan: Not a fan of spiders or snakes. Not exactly easy phobias when you grow up in Australia.

I told him I didn't know him—his ins and outs, his preferences, his everything—and now he's set out to show me via random texts throughout the day.

It feels silly and juvenile, but it makes me smile every time my phone alerts a text and I look down and see his name.

And it means he cares that I was concerned over it.

"Good news or bad news first?" I look up to where Paolo is standing in the doorway of my office. The far-off sound of engines revving in a garage somewhere peppers the air.

"Good news. Always good. I don't want my mood ruined," I say.

He nods and takes a step into my office. "Are you sitting down?" he asks and then laughs because I clearly am. "You know you seriously upped our fucking game, don't you?"

"Okay." I draw the word out, assuming he's speaking of the whole Tori Michelle thing but figuring I'll wait to see where he goes with this to be sure.

"You're going to have the world watching, Carmichael, so please don't fuck this up."

"Paolo. No pressure or anything."

He looks at me and his smile looks disbelieving. "I'm being serious. You'll have the world watching. We just signed a contract to broadcast the gala and her performance."

"What?" I bark out as his grin grows and his eyebrows shoot up.

"Exactly what I said. We just signed a contract for it with Worldcom Media. It'll be the first time that something other than the actual race is broadcast simultaneously around the world."

"You're serious."

"I am." He leans back and folds his arms over his chest like a proud papa. "Everything Tori Michelle touches right now turns to gold like she's fucking Midas. Worldcom thinks that between the draw the drivers have and her in general, people will tune in like gangbusters. And tuning in means advertising dollars and advertising dollars mean money and money makes everyone happy."

"Any of that money going to the charity?" I ask.

"Yes. Built into the media contract."

"Good." I nod but try to wrap my head around it.

"I'm serious when I say that whoever helped or intervened or talked Tori Michelle into agreeing to perform? You need to do some serious kissing of his or her ass because they just made you a huge name." He stares at me. "Are you going to say something?"

"That's supposed to be the good news?" I croak out.

"Well, yeah," he states like I'm an idiot.

"Because to me that feels like the bad news," I joke as the pressure tightens around me like a vise.

"Carmichael," he warns.

"Okay, if that's the good news, then what's the bad news?" I ask.

"If something goes wrong, we're seriously fucked," he deadpans. "Your job. My job. Fucking toast." He chuckles, and I'm not sure if he's joking or being serious. I think maybe a little of both.

"Jesus, Paolo."

"What? I'm not one to sugarcoat things. We have a lot riding on this and now the global spotlight included. I put my ass on the line suggesting you to be the part and so . . . you need to be that part."

"Just pile the pressure on. Please."

Monica Chamalet. She's how this happened. Clearly, I owe her a lot more than a thank-you over a glass of champagne.

"Opportunities don't come without consequences," he says.

"I know but we're talking—"

"You knew you were being thrown into the fire. This is just proof of it."

"Lovely." Sarcasm drips from the two syllables.

"So here's the deal. I need your focus here. At work. On the gala. I'm going to have you skip attending the next few races until it's over with. I—"

"That's the best part," I protest because it is. The adrenaline. The high of a race day. The anticipation of it all. The buzz that you can all but feel in the paddock.

And that also means not being at the track during a race. There's nothing more nerve-wracking than watching a race from home, knowing if there's an accident you feel like you're a million miles away and helpless.

Truth be told you're also helpless standing on the premises during a race, but at least you feel like you could do something if needed.

"I know it is. And I know how much you love that aspect, but I need you focused on details and deadlines. On last-minute problems and flawless execution. We have to get this right."

"I know. I understand." And I do.

"Great." He rises to his feet. "This is going to be huge for us, Blair. A game changer. If it goes well, we'll look like trendsetting heroes. The bar to set every other event against. If it goes bad though . . . Christ. Don't let it go bad."

On that more than ominous note, he leaves my office with me staring after him.

Holy. Shit.

When life decides to let you have new chances . . . it definitely ups its game, doesn't it?

Global television.

"Jesus," I murmur as I pull my hair up into a messy bun and try to grasp the magnitude of it.

Chapter Twenty-Three

Blair

"IS NOW A BAD TIME TO TALK?" MY MOM ASKS.

"No. I have time before they start their engines. Then I won't be able to hear shit." I look up at the monitor in the hospitality tent where I'm standing and watch the broadcast. There's a poetry to the synchronized chaos of the garages. To the dozens of people milling about who all have their set places and know when and where to be. To the drivers who have their headphones on and their focus being tuned to the challenging race ahead of them.

"Good. I'll be quick. I got your text and wanted to call and tell you how very proud we are of you. To sign that big star and to have the event be televised is such a big deal. You should be so very proud of yourself."

"I am. And scared. And nervous." I chuckle.

"You've come a long way, kiddo. Who knew volunteering at races would lead to this job that you love?"

"I know. Crazy, isn't it?" I think back to those days where I used to dream of getting to work for the owning entity of the sport let alone segue it into my dream job.

"It is. But please make sure to take care of you. I know you thrive on the stress, but you also forget to stop and take a breath. And on the knees of the breakup . . . I don't know. I just worry about you."

I mouth the last five words of her comment and smile. *Like clockwork.* She's said the same or something similar the numerous times we've talked since the breakup. She's held back many of her opinions on the matter and simply cared about me and how I'm doing. She's let me talk. She's let me vent. She's even stayed on the line when I've fallen silent as I processed everything.

And her quiet understanding and support has given me more confidence than she'll ever know. In myself. And in knowing that what I'm doing with Lachlan is the right thing.

"I love you, Mom. And I'm fine. I promise. I'm . . . more than good," I say cryptically about the same time they pan over the Apex garage.

"You sure?"

"I'm sure."

"Well, it wouldn't hurt for you to escape for a few days to come home and reset. I know you're super busy with the event and the planning, but we miss you and would love to help you have a few days to yourself before the massive stress of the event. You even said your boss suggested you take a few days off before the gala to center yourself. If you don't listen to me, then maybe you'll at least listen to him." The dog barks in the background. "I can make you your favorite meals and we can . . . just hang out."

Why does the offer—one that always stands—cause emotion to lodge in my throat?

"Thank you. I'll keep that in mind."

"Please do." She sniffles and my heart squeezes in my chest over how much I miss her sometimes. "I know you're busy so I'll let you go. Just know we're here for you. Always. We love you. Always. Okay?"

"I know. I love you too." I pause. "Thanks, Mom."

"No need to thank me. Bye, Bee."

I end the call and smile. Her calls make me happy. And today's in particular has distracted me from how lost I feel right now.

I'm used to having a purpose at races. A crew of families to see to. An agenda to take care of. A quick sneak into the Apex paddock to wish Rossi good luck.

But I don't have any of that to do today.

And the last place I need to be seen is in the Apex garage but it's killing me to not be able to see Lachlan before he gets in the car.

The past week has been chaotic with eyes on us the whole time. Rossi's suite was situated next to Lachlan's at the Apex team hotel and my room just happened to be next to Paolo's boss—my boss's boss.

So sneaking out hasn't been an option for either of us.

Maybe tonight. Maybe with the race over, we'll get a chance to see each other before I head back home.

That helplessness has me wandering through the paddock from suite to suite, needing the mental break from my job, but also needing somewhere to channel my energy.

But I also know I'll get the best view from my office in the paddock. From the ten screens we have up in the command center that monitor every aspect of the race and not just what the national broadcast will show.

And to be honest, you see so much more on the monitors than you can at any seat on the track.

So I head back to our command center of sorts, where I've been able to watch every race since the start of my tenure here.

"Are you watching in here?" Fanny asks as I walk past her.

"Yep. Just like always."

"You want to go over RSVP numbers while we watch?" she asks.

"Sure. Yeah. Let me stop by my office and grab my laptop."

"See you in there."

I head to my office, to grab my things so I can settle in for the race with Fanny and the rest of us, and when I enter my doorway, my feet falter.

On top of my closed laptop, on my desk, is a single peppermint candy.

He was here.

He came to see me almost in a reverse *wish him luck* scenario.

And he left something to *remember him by*.

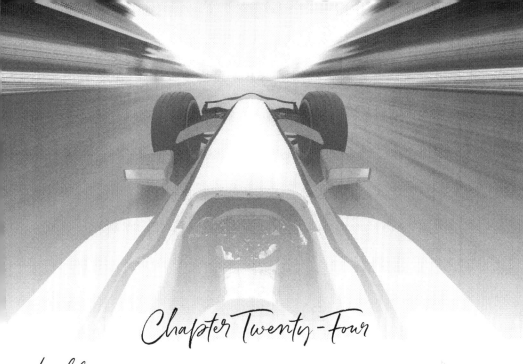

Chapter Twenty-Four

Lachlan

NAVARRO IS WITHIN MY SIGHTS.

That damn orange car. The one I've been chasing all fucking race. I push the button and engage the DRS.

C'mon, baby. C'mon.

There is a surge of power as I pull up and begin to pass him on the right. I'm half a car length into him when . . . nothing.

The engine has no oomph. No real power to overtake.

He surges forward as I slip back behind him and into his slipstream.

"*Fuck!*" I shout to no one in particular.

Classic fucking par for the season.

This goddamn car is a piece of shit. All goddamn year. It's making me a tenth-place driver when I'm a top-fucking-four.

Come. The. Fuck. On.

I need this overtake. Especially against Gravitas. Against Schilling. For so many more reasons than just this goddamn race.

"Henry," I grit out into the radio. It's all I need to say for him to know how frustrated I am.

"I know. Next straight we go again."

"Ten-four."

But it doesn't feel like ten-four. It feels like a million kilometers away and I've only traveled five of them.

"Rossi's behind you."

"Okay?" As in okay, are you telling me I need to give way to him? Or as in okay, he'll block for you?

Because each one has a different set of consequences and a different dynamic that states exactly where we both stand with this team.

"Johann will make the call," he says.

Great. A fucking wait and see. Just what I fucking want.

Out of your head, Lach. Focus. Fucking focus.

I take each curve, shaving the distance as thin as possible. I practically kiss the wall. I ride the white line. I cut across the switchback with the closest of margins. Anything to get me fucking closer to Navarro. Anything to get me farther from Rossi.

"You're within point oh five," Henry says in my ear. "DRS in three. Two. One."

I engage the DRS system. "C'mon, baby," I murmur, knowing damn well that if I have DRS on Navarro, then Rossi could easily have DRS on me.

And that's an interesting scenario for Apex in general.

"Push. Push," Henry encourages as I increase my speed and gain on Navarro's orange car. My vision's so focused on him. On gaining this spot to put us on the podium for the first time in for-fucking-ever.

Smack.

The car hits me out of nowhere.

The jolt as he clips my back tire.

"*Fuck.*"

A flash of blue in my periphery.

The noticeable whip of my neck as the car spins with an ungodly amount of force.

The vibration and roughness as I hit the gravel.

The *oomph* that comes out of my mouth as I hit the water barricade on its far side.

Then nothing.

The eerie ringing of silence as everything settles around me. And then as my body becomes wracked with adrenaline and begins to shake.

"Lachlan?" Henry's voice breaks through the quiet.

"I'm fine," I grit out as anger overtakes me.

"Good. Good to hear."

"What happened?" I ask and the flash of blue comes back to me.

"Safety crews are there to help," he says.

I'm out of the car before they get to me, setting my steering wheel on the top of the car, but it's Rossi's car in pieces on the opposite side of the track that has my anger firing to epic proportions.

I jog my way back to the garage.

Back to a space where there are no cameras—*and I can process what the fuck just happened.*

My own teammate just hit me?

Fucking took me out?

"What the fuck, man?" I throw my helmet down and come at Rossi.

He looks over at me as he removes each earbud and shrugs. "It's racing."

"It's racing?" I growl. "Both of our cars in the goddamn gravel? *Nah.* That's called carelessness. It's called lack of skill. It's called—"

"Relax. No one got hurt," he says and turns his back on me as our crew pushes people out of our area and shuts the doors.

Fury fires.

My fists clench.

My body tenses.

"And no one fucking placed either. The whole fucking point of this exercise, isn't it?"

He shrugs. "Shit happens."

"Shit happens?" I shout, my hands clenching into fists to hold me back from throwing one. "Are you the one footing the bill for all the money Apex just lost? Are you the one who has to explain to the sponsors why we can't get their goddamn name on a podium? Are you the one who is going to explain to everyone that I'm a good fucking driver whose own teammate just took him out?"

There's a clatter as he sets his helmet down on the table. His chuckle grates over my skin like sandpaper. "Ah, always about the contract with you, isn't it?" He looks my way and angles his head to the side as he studies me. "Pity. Have you not signed with anyone yet?" He lifts his eyebrows as his question eats holes into me and causes doubt to fester.

Has he signed on?

Who signed him?

Am I going to be hung out to dry?

My head spins with the unanswered questions he's thrown out there as a fuck you. The mind games have begun.

"Check the fucking replay for your answers," he says and then struts out of the room and slams the door behind him.

I wait a beat and follow him to the Apex control room. My team already has the replay cued up for me, knowing I need to see what happened.

And when they push play, I see the incident in slow motion. Me chasing Navarro. Rossi chasing me. McElroy on Rossi.

"Ah," I say as McElroy touches tires with Rossi causing my teammate to careen out of control and hit my back tire as he flew through the air. "Christ."

"Pretty much," Henry says as he meets my eyes. "A shit day all around."

Fuck me.

Now I need to go eat crow. Need to apologize to Rossi for accusing him. *Fucking hell.*

I was so bloody close. I take deep breaths to calm down my racing heart. *So. Close.*

"It's racing."

Yeah, as much as it pains me, I need to go apologize to Rossi.

But first I need to speak to my agent.

Because I need to know if Rossi was taunting me . . . *because he already has a contract.*

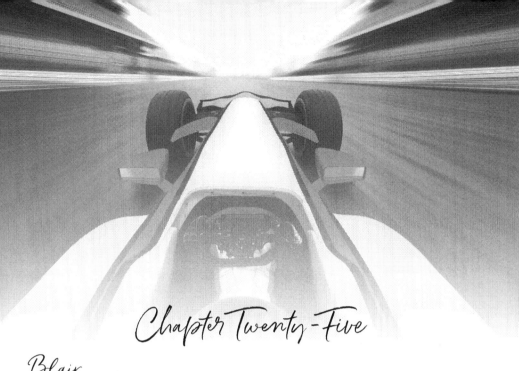

Chapter Twenty-Five

Blair

"L ach?" I look back and forth outside my front door to see if anyone saw him before yanking him into my place.

"Is that a good *Lach* or a bad *Lach* or somewhere in between on the scale of happy to see me?" he asks.

"Good." I press my lips to his and take the kiss I've been holding on to since I left Hungary without getting to say goodbye. "Definitely a good *Lach*," I moan as his hands run over me until they rest on my ass, pulling me against him.

I've missed him. Plain and simple. We were at the same place all weekend but couldn't exactly act like this.

And now that I can, I feel the ball knotted in my chest unravel.

"Now that's a hello if I've ever had one," he murmurs against my lips.

"It's been . . . days."

"It feels like forever." He chuckles and then presses a kiss to my forehead and wraps his arms around me.

"I know." I press my head to his chest and just hold tight, listening to the steady beat of his heart. "That scared me," I whisper.

The crash has replayed in my head over and over. It's replayed from a place of me knowing that everyone was all right, but that doesn't erase the downright terror that owned me for those few fleeting seconds.

He presses a kiss to the crown of my head. "I know, but I'm okay. I'm fine. You can see and feel that for yourself." He runs his hands up and down my back to reinforce his words. "I'm sorry I scared you."

"Don't be." My voice is muffled against his chest. "It's just never easy. The helplessness. The waiting. The not knowing."

He puts a finger under my chin and lifts it so I'm forced to look in his eyes. "I'm here. I'm okay."

"I know." I lean up on my tiptoes and brush my lips over his, reveling in the reassurance of the action. "What are you doing here? Didn't you—"

"Just land? Yes. Yes, I did. And my first order of business was to see you." Another brush of his lips.

"Lucky me."

"Nah, pretty sure I'm the lucky one," he says.

I brush his hair off his forehead. "You're really okay? That was a rough one."

"I'm a little sore." He chuckles and cups the back of my neck. "But I wanted to see you and . . . I don't know, just do nothing with you."

"Do nothing?" I ask as my hands find the back of his neck and start rubbing. It has to be sore from the way he hit the gravel. I swear my heart leapt into my throat.

I yelped out loud as the crash unfolded. I couldn't help it. I'm just lucky that both Lachlan and Rossi were involved so that my gasp could be mistaken for my ex-boyfriend and not solely for Lach, which would make people look a little closer at me.

"That feels good," he murmurs as his eyes close and his forehead dips to land on my shoulder.

"Is this where you're sore?" I ask.

"Mmm," he says.

"Let's get you settled. Get your shirt off, get you relaxed, and I can give you a proper rubdown."

"You're heaven-sent. But . . . the porch." He points to where I just shut the door.

"What?" I ask as I open the door to find bags of takeout food.

"Dinner. I didn't know what you like so I . . ."

"Picked up everything you could find?" Oh my God, there are bags upon bags of food.

"Exactly." He angles his head to the side, looking so much like a sleepy little boy I want to fold into my arms and not let go of. "You're right. The not knowing part is daunting."

"You're doing a good job of informing me about you with your texts."

"You like them?" he asks as he hauls some of the bags to my kitchen table. Soon my place smells like a food court in a shopping mall with so many different types of food.

"I do. They are very helpful." Mexican. American. Chinese. Italian. French. He literally picked up one of everything.

"Then I think you should start doing some to me too. Help a guy out so he knows whether to get pad thai or enchiladas."

"Neither," I say and step forward to kiss him again. "I'm boring. I like it simple."

"Noted." He nods. "But I'll be expecting texts now."

"Fine. I will text but you can ask me too. Over dinner."

"Dinner can wait."

I lean back and meet his gaze. He lifts his eyebrows as his eyes darken. My insides twist in anticipation. "It can?"

Thank God.

"Mm-hmm." He grabs his shirt at the nape of his neck and pulls it off on the first try. I'm met with an expanse of deliciously tanned skin that calls for me to reach out and touch it.

"How could I forget? You needed a rubdown."

"I do."

I reach out and run my hands down his chest and love watching his abs constrict from my touch alone.

"Where does it hurt?" I ask coyly. "Here?" I point to his lips.

"A little."

"Here?" I skim my fingernails over the back of his neck and watch chills chase over his skin.

"Mm-hmm."

Then I trail my fingers down his shoulders and then down the mainline of his chest to his waistband. "Anything in need down here?" I ask, my eyes looking up at him.

"Mm-hmm." His eyes hold mine as my fingers dance over his cock pressing against his pants. "It might be in need of a rubdown."

"A rubdown?"

"Mm. Yes. A two-handed one."

He groans as I drop to my knees in front of him. "Maybe if I kiss it, it'll make it feel all better." I pull his waistband down so that his cock springs free as he pushes his pants down to his ankles. I push him back so he sits and admire his cock. It's thick and heavy and rests against his lower abdomen.

Jesus. The sight of it alone has my body aching and my desire simmering. I hold his eyes as I lean forward and use the tip of my tongue to circle around its crest. I dip it into the slit and welcome the salty taste of him.

Then I tease him. With my lips around the tip, I take him just deep enough to clear his crest before pulling back off him.

His thighs tense. He shifts his hips up in a silent plea.

It's a heady feeling.

"You're teasing me, Tink."

"No, I'm just making sure I take care of every inch. I wouldn't want any part of you to be neglected now, would I?"

"God, no. We wouldn't want that."

I close my lips around him again as my fingers grab his balls and he emits the most guttural growl I've ever heard. It's so fucking sexy. His head rolls back and his eyes close.

"Lach?"

"Hmm?"

"Eyes on me."

And when those heavy-lidded eyes of his meet mine, I take as many glorious inches as I can all the way to the back of my throat.

His hands fist in my hair immediately as a *fuck* falls from his lips. And I keep him there for as long as I can until I can't any longer. And when that happens, I hollow my cheeks out on the way back out.

"Jesus, baby, that feels so fucking good."

His praise is music to my ears. It's now that I go to work. With my lips and my two hands in a synchronized series of actions. A twist of my hand at the base of his shaft while my lips suck at his tip. Over and over. Then a deep swallow of his cock to start a new rhythm.

His taste owns me. His groans even more so.

And when he comes, when the warm spurt of come hits the back of my throat and his hands tighten in my hair, my own body aches with want for him.

"Blair. Now. Come here," he demands and hauls me up to straddle him. His lips find mine. He doesn't say a word about his taste being on my lips because he's too damn consumed with the moment, with the desire coursing through him, and with me.

All he wants is to be closer. To feel me. To need me. It's in his touch. In the hurried movements. In the repetition of my name as he holds my head still and kisses me breathless.

He's hard again. I don't know how. I don't question it because he's moving my pajama shorts to the side and urging my hips to sink down on him until I'm so full I can't lower any more.

Jesus. Christ.

This man. He feels . . . incredible. He makes me feel incredible.

He grabs the globes of my ass and with his lips still fused to mine, urges me to move up and down.

To ride him.

To see how much more of him I can take with each and every rise and fall onto him.

It's bliss. The slide of his cock over every sensitized nerve inside as I move on him.

It's urgency. His fingers digging into my flesh, urging me to move faster, harder, to take him deeper.

It's everything I didn't know I needed and everything I'll forever miss if I lose him. I grind over him as his tongue licks against mine.

It's Lachlan.

Just Lachlan.

Chapter Twenty-Six

Lachlan

THE EARLY MORNING SUN STREAMS THROUGH HER WINDOW AND lights up her room. It's a mishmash of the person I'm beginning to know. Sophisticated in the sleek power suits hanging in her open closet, but then there's a stuffed unicorn taking up residence in the far chair across the room.

She too has pictures of her family in here but from what I saw last night, the only constant in them besides her are her mum and dad. Everyone else changes.

She has jewelry strewn across her dresser and just like she said, a hurricane vase is filled with corks and bottle caps. *Are there any corks in there from our time together yet?* Her hamper is overflowing and her bag from the last race is unpacked and tucked in the corner.

And then there's a canvas propped against the dresser that catches my eye.

At first, I think it's a painting she's bought until I look closer.

It's one of hers. It has to be because it's our night at the golf course. The shooting star. The crooked tree we almost hit. The golf cart in the foreground with snack wrappers on the ground near its tires.

I'm not sure why seeing it is so satisfying to me, but it is. She paints things that make her feel good.

Isn't that what she said?

My smile remains as I turn my head on my pillow and study her.

The bedhead with strands falling across her face. The lightest row of freckles across the bridge of her nose. The tan lines on her shoulder from her bathing suit. Those lips parted and full.

Jesus.

At the mere sight of her, every part of me wants, and I don't know what to do or how to process it.

Yes, infatuation is a real thing. It's something I've had with other women before. Hasn't everyone? But it's different when it comes to Blair. It's like I wake up wanting to talk to her and go to bed needing to hold her.

And it just feels . . . right. There's no other way to describe it other than *right*.

A phone rings on her nightstand. It startles us both but it's Blair who jolts out of bed, eyes wide and lips startled into a big O.

"Oh my God. *Work*," she says as she scrubs a hand over her face, clears her throat, and picks up the phone on the fourth ring.

"Paolo. Of course I didn't forget. I was running behind on another call." She rises from the bed and searches for something—anything. I hand her my T-shirt from the floor beside me.

"Thank you," she mouths as she puts her boss on speaker and pulls my shirt over her head.

Good. God.

My shirt stretches across her tits. Across the hardened peaks of her nipples pressing through the white cotton. All I can think about is dipping my head forward and taking a taste of them, but she's already flustered from waking up late.

My needs can wait.

Hers come first. Always.

She's flustered. I can see it on her face, in the way she keeps blinking. I find small satisfaction in knowing the sex was so good that she slept like a baby. The other part of me feels bad that we didn't think to set an alarm.

But lucky for me that gives me one hell of a view this morning.

And I enjoy every minute of the next fifteen minutes as I watch her multi-task. She paces, moving out of the bedroom at times, and then seconds later I hear her fingers clicking on the keys of her laptop. She moves back into the bedroom where she peeks out the window at the sunshine outside.

Her feet don't stop as she runs a meeting in my T-shirt with the bottom of her arse hanging out.

She is in her own world and it's so damn sexy listening to her answer questions off the top of her head and spout figures from memory that there is no way I'd be able to remember.

It's like every single thing about her becomes more attractive the more I'm with her—her body, her mind, her personality, her emotions.

"Sounds like a plan," she says and then groans as she drops the phone on the bed and her arse beside it. She covers her eyes with her hands and scrunches her nose.

I take her in. All of her. It's like I can't look away and frankly, why the hell would I?

The silence stretches until she lowers one hand and peers at me with curious eyes. "Why are you staring at me?" she asks.

"Because you're beautiful."

"Wrong answer," she teases and adjusts herself on the bed so that her head can rest on my shoulder. "Try again."

"Because you're good at this," I murmur and press a kiss to the crown of her head.

"What? The sex part or the work part?"

The being mine part.

I open my mouth and then close it. *Down, boy.* Words like that just might scare her away.

"How about all parts? The sex? No complaints there. The work? Paolo better have no complaints there considering he's not letting you come to my races anymore. You in my T-shirt? You can have every single one I own if this is the visual I get when you wear them. The art?" She stiffens. "Impressive."

"You weren't supposed to see that," she says and chuckles. "When I was on the phone, I was casually trying to figure out how to turn it over without you noticing . . . but clearly it would have been noticed."

"It would have. I did notice and I love it." I twirl a lock of her hair. Touching her is my new habit. "Maybe in time you'll let me see some of your others on purpose."

"Maybe."

We fall silent. The only sound in the room is our breathing and the slightest rasp from my finger trailing up and down the length of her spine.

"I really should get up and work." She sighs heavily. "I have so many calls to make and things to button up. My computer is calling me from the other room."

"Okay." *Please don't.*

"Paolo is expecting updated spreadsheets on budget numbers and . . . just so much to do."

"I'm sure there is." I press a kiss to the crown of her head and just breathe her in. "And I'm sure you'll kick arse at every single aspect of it."

"Mmm."

"Mmm? That's all I get?" I chuckle.

"I'd much rather do this with you. I like this," she murmurs against my chest.

"What part of this?" Because let's face it, there are a lot of great parts to all this.

"The doing nothing together part."

"Me too, Tink. Me too. But . . ." I shift so that she's forced to look up at me. "I refuse to be a distraction in your world. I mean . . . I love being one, but not like this. How about we get up, I make you breakfast—"

"You cook?"

"We won't go that far, but I can scramble some mean eggs." She smiles and just the sight has my balls drawing tight and the knowledge that we need to get up or there's going to be a whole lot more than doing nothing happening in a few seconds.

"Really?"

"Really. So you work. I'll feed you. I'll make some calls." Because contract talks are in full swing. "And then . . . then we can meet right back here for some more doing nothing when you're done."

"Promise?"

"Promise."

Chapter Twenty-Seven

Lachlan

THE HILLS ABOVE MONACO ARE A BRUTAL FUCKING HIKE. STEEP AND slippery and never-ending.

But they afford the best views of the harbor beyond. The turquoise water. The various yachts milling around the harbor. The king's palace.

And more than that, the arduous hike not only gives you peace of mind and perspective, but it also gives you time to think.

Too bad mobile service still works.

"Dad. Hi. What's up?"

"Hi."

"I just got to Tête de Chien," I say in labored pants as I put my hand on my hip and just stand still for a beat to catch my breath.

"Good to see you're putting in the work on your off days."

"I always put in the work. What is that supposed to mean?"

"Nothing. It wasn't a dig," he backpedals.

"Uh-huh."

"So what's going on? Still the same?"

"I met with the owners of Moretti and then of Gravitas," I say, only because no one else is around.

The meetings were held in uber private locations with switched cars and fake names. Anything and everything to avoid the press and their speculation.

I'm actually surprised there haven't been any leaks already, but secrecy was tight for this reason. Chandler and his team know what they're doing.

"So Rossi hasn't signed with anyone yet, right?" he asks, knowing how confused I was by Rossi's comment after the last race.

"Do you think anyone's actually talking? Nope. Everyone's playing the field. Maybe he has. Maybe he hasn't. But all the players I'm interested in are talking, and that's what I need to focus on. If they weren't talking, then I'd know. I'm sure he's doing the same." And trying to fuck with my head while he's at it.

"What is Apex saying?"

"The same shit they're all saying."

"You need a good race under your belt? That they need to see more of the season?"

"Pretty much, as frustrating as that is."

"What's your dream scenario, mate?" he asks when he already knows. But he also knows me well enough to know that talking about it helps me clear my head.

"A multi-year contract. I don't want any of this let's just finish out the year and we'll do a one-year contract extension bullshit."

"That's daunting."

"It is. I want a home where I don't have to be worrying about this shit next year. There's enough pressure as it is to perform. Knowing each race hinges on if I have a ride or not the next year makes it even tougher."

"Lach, every race matters whether it's a multi- or a single-year contract. You know as well as I do that you can have a contract one minute and be out of a seat the next. Look at McElroy a few years back. His team bought out the remainder of his contract and he was out a ride for a year. And off the grid is never a good place to be."

I scrub a hand over my face and sigh. "Don't I fucking know it."

"So who's offering a multi-year contract?"

"No one is offering anything yet. That's the problem. Until words become actions written on a goddamn paper I can sign, I'm in the fucking bubble."

"Just like Rossi."

"I think?" I push out a laugh. "I mean, all the players are still talking to me so that means he's full of shit and hasn't signed anywhere."

"So that means it's yours for the taking."

"It means I need to have a good fucking finish is what it means."

"True. What does your gut say?"

"Moretti won't offer. They're talking but they have Riggs and just signed Bustos for two years. No way they're going to renege on the Bustos contract and, let's face it, Riggs is marrying a Moretti so he's not going anywhere."

"And Gravitas?"

"There's interest there." A lot actually and unexpectedly.

"And you've been spending time with Zola Chamalet. That doesn't hurt."

Great. If he knows, then everyone knows. "That's a whole other situation we're not getting into."

"*Situation?*"

"Don't believe everything you read, Dad."

"That's why I'm coming straight to the source and the source isn't exactly answering me." He makes a noncommittal sound. "I'd say dating a gorgeous woman who has connections in the right places isn't exactly a hardship."

"It's strictly platonic."

He snorts in response. "Sure it is."

"I'm being straight with you. I was helping her out from her mum by running interference and she's helping me out."

"I'm hoping by helping you out you mean by having her mum put in a good word for you with Gravitas. Monica holds a lot of pull."

"I'm well aware." I stretch my quad and look at the trail back down the hill. "Stay out of my love life, Dad."

"Love life? I wasn't aware you had one."

Shit. Didn't mean to say that.

"My dating life. My love life. My sex life. Do you need a diagram?"

"Relax." He chuckles. "Now is not the time for a distraction. That's all I'm saying. This might be the contract that sets you up for the rest of your career. You've had good ones so far, but Lach, I have a feeling everything is going to fall into place more than it already has."

In my *actual* love life, yes.

Everything else though?

Shit. Everything else feels like how I did when I hit the wall the other week.

Confusing.

Unknown.

A clusterfuck.

Chapter Twenty-Eight

Blair

"So I'm thinking a nice dinner. Caviar. Cristal. Maybe a top pastry chef flown in. A few drivers attending will be an added bonus—"

"A few drivers?" I ask Monica Chamalet. That's an out-of-the-blue request. Not only is she asking that I have a Michelin-starred chef fly in to cook dinner for Tori Michelle, but now that I throw in a few drivers as well.

Jesus.

"Yes. A few. Ten maybe. I mean that would be a requirement of course."

That's half the fucking grid. I put my face in my hand and scrunch my nose. This phone call is not going how I'd planned. When I sent her flowers as a thank-you for the help, the last thing I expected was her calling to thank me . . . and put in a formal request for billionaire-like things for Tori. Yes, I'm more than grateful for her performing at the gala and was planning my own thank-you, meager as it may be compared to these requests, but still . . .

Now to try and head this off at the pass—without offending her.

"Monica . . . I appreciate all your suggestions. They are quite . . ." *Ridiculous.* "Fabulous. I'll gladly present them to my bosses and see what they say. Because we are a charity, we're on a budget—"

"But sometimes the more you spend, the more you'll take in."

Says a woman who eats caviar like it's ramen.

"Agreed." *Have patience, Blair.* "Time is winding closer . . . and while we clearly want Tori to know how appreciative we are, and you for encouraging her to donate and perform for the gala, there's only so much we can do in such a short amount of time."

Her laugh is deep and rich and reverberates through the phone line. The sound of a helicopter—at least I think that's what it is—whop whops in the background. "Money can buy anything, Blair. *Even time.* And admittedly, when you're my age and have what I have, you can make ridiculous requests and expect people to fulfill them. Right or wrong, it's how the world works."

I lift my eyebrows and just shake my head. Clearly spoken by someone who has way too much money to comprehend boundaries and who uses it every chance they get.

"Like I said, I'll do my best but can't make any guarantees."

She sighs in resignation. "I'm sorry. I know I'm being my pushy, old self. I just want this night to be perfect. This gala is going to be everything."

"That's the hope," I murmur, looking over my shoulder to where Lachlan just came into my apartment. He has a baseball cap down low over his forehead, a hoodie with the hood over the hat, sunglasses on, and is carrying a bag with him.

Every time I see him like this—trying to remain unrecognizable as he walks the streets of Nice and sneaks into my flat—I laugh. And I feel honored that he's going through all this trouble to see me, in my shitty little place, when he is *him* and has this grandiose place with a view of the Mediterranean.

God, is it good to see him.

"Between you, me, and the fence post, Blair," Monica says like she's about to tell me a national secret—but her giddy little laugh tells me I might not like what she's about to say—"I think this might be the coming out party for Lachlan and Zola as a couple."

I choke on my breath. "Why would you say that? I thought you were set on Baron von Whats-his-name?"

She makes a noncommittal sound. "I am. Believe me I am. The power and influence our two families would have if they combined is ridiculously alluring, but every time I mention getting them together, Zola's off with Lachlan. I mean, they're becoming quite the adoring couple."

"How wonderful." I choke over the words.

"Wonderful, perhaps. But they're keeping it all so secret. She said they're just in the beginning stages of whatever this is and wants to keep it private. I can respect that but, darling, do you have any idea how torn I am? Between wanting to show them off when Zola doesn't want me to say a word yet and keeping my promise to Greta von Steubing about our children matching up? It's simply dreadful."

"I can't imagine," I say as Lachlan angles his head to the side and studies me. He's curious who I'm speaking with.

"You can't. It's excruciating. I must try harder to get them together." She pauses and I can *feel* her thoughts across the connection. "I'll make a renewed effort, I think. One last time to get Zola to try and see Baron through different eyes, but . . ."

"But what?"

"I do have a soft spot for Lachlan." Her voice softens. "Handsome. Talented. Charming. An athlete. And Zola really is smitten with him, it seems. It's a pity I didn't think to match them sooner so I could take all the credit."

No.

No. No. No.

Let's not venture there.

"Maybe a surprise dinner date for the two of them?" I suggest and then correct myself. "I mean Baron and Zola. Not Lachlan. Something quiet, so they could get to know each other."

His head perks up. That got his attention. Lachlan narrows his eyebrows at me and then I can see the recognition dawning on his face over who I'm speaking with.

"A great idea, yes. I just . . . maybe Lachlan is the one for her. Hmm. It seems all roads lead back to Formula 1 for me, doesn't it?"

I have no idea what she's talking about so I just make a noncommittal sound. I find any words are hard considering there's a lump of acid lodged in my throat.

"Maybe I can convince Zola to make the gala the debut for her and Lachlan. Then everyone would know I was the one behind them meeting and"—she squeals as if she just figured something out—"that could be absolutely perfect."

"Um . . . okay." I refrain from sighing heavily. What the hell am I supposed to say? I glance over to Lachlan as he pulls a ridiculously expensive bottle of wine out of the bag beside a baguette and some cheese.

"What if I pulled on some of my strings and got him over to Gravitas?

Then he'll be part of my racing family, part of my real family—my husband would loathe it. *It's perfect.* Can't you picture what gorgeous grandbabies they'll give me? I simply can't wait. I mean, I couldn't tie it up any prettier in a bow if I wanted to."

I'll get him to Gravitas.

Grandbabies.

Jesus.

She's delusional. She went from Baron to Lachlan to now it's a revenge thing against her late husband.

"I think the more you interfere, the more Zola will push the other way. Maybe you just let whatever's going on run its course. I know I'd be livid if my mom tried to meddle in my relationships." I pause, hoping I didn't just offend her. "Besides, Lachlan has a reputation for preferring singleness. From what I've heard, he's one hundred percent focused on his career and winning a championship."

The topic of this conversation laces his fingers behind his neck and leans against the back of the couch, curious eyes and an amused smile directed my way.

"Perhaps," she muses. "Only time will tell. And no doubt that time will include pressure from Baron's mother."

"Everything will work out as it's meant to be in the end," I say. "And in the meantime, I'll see what I can do on this Tori Michelle request you've had."

"Sure. Yes." By the tone of her voice, she's clearly distracted now. "I knew you would. Cheers, darling. Off to Ibiza now."

Monica ends the call and I look over to Lachlan.

"What?" he asks with a cheeky smile.

"I'm mad at you."

"What did I do?" He chuckles. "Were three orgasms last time not enough and you want to go for an even five this time?"

"Five is not even."

"But it made you smile," he says as he moves toward me, his eyes questioning as he tries to figure out what's wrong.

"How many times have you 'hung out' with Zola?"

"Twice. Why?"

"Twice?"

"Yes. You've known each time. The yacht and then we met up for coffee. Well technically three times because there was the dinner date before the yacht party, but that's semantics. Oh, and she told me there might possibly be one more time. Some dinner event coming up. I don't know. We both have to go so we figured since clammy-hands Baron will be there, that maybe I could go with her and save her from that and her mother's pushiness."

I feel for Zola. I truly do. But . . .

"Well, for the record, it looks like you two have sold it so well, Monica is believing it."

"Don't be ridiculous." How can his smile be so disarming? He really has no idea how good-looking he is. "Their family's ties to the von Steubings have Baron and Zola's wedding planned. Has been for some time."

"Ugh," I say as he puts his arms around my waist and pulls me into him. I feel an automatic security in this. In him. And I let him comfort me in a way I've never let anyone else. It's like with each passing day, the time we've spent together should be catching up with the strength of our feelings, and yet there's nothing stopping this freight train of emotions I feel for this man. "She is planning, Lachlan, and her planning isn't always a good thing."

"How about she plans me up a contract with Gravitas so I can stop stressing about it?" he jokes into the crown of my head.

"Oh, she said something along those lines too. She's giving away her daughter with a contract, apparently," I say sarcastically.

"No, more like a contract with her daughter thrown in," he says, but I'm beginning to think it's not so much of a joke. "But hell, I'll take her help any way I can get right now." And I know he's joking, but a small part of me knows he means it. I've watched him go through the gamut of emotions over the past few weeks. Excitement to despair to frustration have been a constant as he takes calls from his agent and is rushed off to secret meetings here and there.

"I feel bad for Zola." I look up at him, and he brushes my hair off my forehead.

"I do too. Why do you think I'm helping her? She's a great person. Always been a good friend to me." He shrugs. "And she'll probably end up with Boring Baron, but she wants more time to live her life first."

How depressing.

"Then I guess I'll let her keep borrowing you in public so long as I get to keep you in private."

"Lucky for you because the private part is so much better." He runs a thumb over my lower lip before he leans in and brushes a kiss to it. "Six is a good even number, don't you think?" He flashes a grin.

"Stop trying to distract me with multiple orgasms talk."

"But it's so much more fun than talking about Monica and Zola and expectations I can't control."

"And yet they're still there."

"And so is the chance this association might help me get a deal with Gravitas, according to what you're saying. Is it a cheap shot letting Monica think Zola and I are together? I don't know. Everyone is playing the game and if I don't, then I'm out. What matters most is that Zola knows the truth and that she gets what she needs out of this."

And there he goes trying to be the hero and save the day for another woman.

"Why do you have to make so much sense?" I roll my eyes.

"Because it's how I keep you mine. Sense, great wine." He lifts his chin toward the food and bottle of wine on the table. "Incredible sex and multiple orgasms."

"I'm not complaining about any of the above."

He brushes his lips against mine. The kiss lingers and chills chase over my skin. "Come with me to Belgium, Tink."

"You're forgetting I was told not to."

"Fuck Paolo," he murmurs against my ear. "He said you weren't allowed to be at the track." He leans back and looks at me. "Go to the race with me. Work from the hotel. A different hotel away from the teams. We can work during the day, and I can steal my nights away with you. Out of the public eye. We can . . . just do nothing together."

"Just like you said to me, I don't want to be a distraction for you."

"You're not." He cups my face with his hands. "You're what centers me."

Chapter Twenty-Nine

Blair

THE PRIVATE RENTAL IS JUST ON THE OUTSKIRTS OF THE BUSINESS district. Sounds from the city float up to its open windows where I sit with my laptop open and a list of last-minute . . . *everything*, in front of me.

"Thank you for the update," Paolo says. The irony is I can hear the whine of the engines in the background from his place at the track and I itch to be there.

And it's only miles away.

"Not a problem. I'm feeling confident that everything is in place as much as it can be for a month or so out."

"And I'm hearing the same from your team. I don't know how you've done it," Paolo says, "but you've pulled together a group of people someone else selected and figured out how to lead them and their differences without so much as a blip on the radar."

"That you've seen anyway," I joke.

"Exactly. All that matters is what the outside has seen and from the outside, it looks like a seamless phalanx of productivity."

I've been drowning in stress—in caterers who had the head count wrong, in needing to redesign the event space to accommodate the various cameras being placed, in logistics and timing—and the fact that no one else has seen or heard any of the problems is miraculous.

Stepping in to lead Lisa's team hasn't been without its trials and tribulations. Our managing style is different and so despite the initial growing pains, I was pleased that everyone adjusted. And once they realized I was here to help them as much as they were helping me, things became even smoother.

"Your team is doing a great job."

"Thank you," I say and then hesitate. "And as for Monica's request."

"Yes." His sigh is how I feel. "I'm doing my best to accommodate at least a few of them, but I feel this is a gross overreach on her part. It's not Tori's team asking, it's her. You're not trying to get on her good side for something, are you?" He chuckles at the joke. "She doesn't have a billionaire son you're trying to win over?"

"You're a real comedian, Paolo."

"I know. I try."

I end the call and move toward the window. Toward the wonderful city and its enticing sounds. It's beautiful here—the city, the people, the culture—but even with all that, I know one I'd love to be looking at even more.

The track.

The grandstands.

The cars.

Lachlan.

The purr of the engines in my chest on race day has been a constant in my life for so long that it's weird to have the television on, to see the cars moving on the track as they test but to not feel their horsepower rumbling through my body.

I'm here, but I feel so very far away.

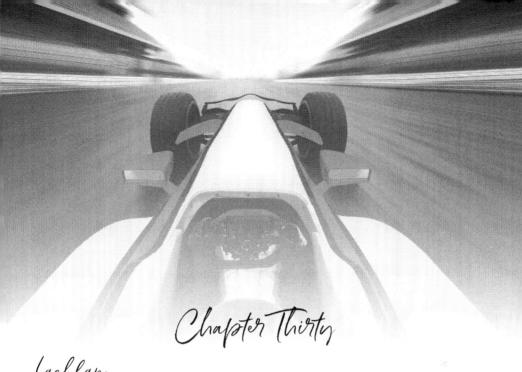

Chapter Thirty

Lachlan

"**Y**OU LOOK EXHAUSTED," SHE SAYS AS SHE WALKS ACROSS THE SPACE and wraps her arms around me.

I never realized how incredible it felt going home to someone after a long day's work.

Interviews. Testing. Debriefing. Team meeting.

"I am, but I'm all better now." And I truly mean that. This, coming home to Blair, is like nothing I've ever experienced. I take in the feel of her body against mine but know it's so much more than that. It's having someone here. A person to wrap their arms around me regardless of whether I test well or give a good interview or have a shitty day. A partner who doesn't care about that because she cares about me more.

I've never had that before, never wanted it, and now, as she's pressed against me and the tension of the day dissipates second by second, I can't help but wish that this was my everyday normal.

However, for now, this whole private vacation rental away from the team hotel is the way to go. I get her, I get quiet, and . . . *I get her.*

"Testing went . . ."

"For shit? Yeah. Definitely a crap day." I love that she follows even when she isn't there.

And it was. A total shit day. Everything that could go wrong went wrong, and that's why being here right now with her is what I need. Normalcy. Honesty. *Her*.

"I was going to say *fucked* but sure, your adjectives work too." She loops her hands around the back of my neck. "You'll get 'em tomorrow. Got all the bad out today."

"Mmm."

"That doesn't sound convincing," she says.

"Tired?" I don't want to think about me or my day. I run my hands up and down the length of her back. *Will I ever stop wanting her?*

"Tired. Overwhelmed. Stressed. Putting out endless fires." She chuckles. "It feels like this is a normal state these days. But once the gala is over, life will go back to normal and I'll miss it."

"Back to normal?" I spin her out by her hand and pull her back into me.

She throws her head back and laughs at the unexpectedness of the action and the sound, the look in her eyes, and the feel of her body as it collides back with mine makes me smile.

"What? Why are you looking at me that way?" she asks with her head tilted up and her lips parted.

Because what did I do before you were in my life?

"I like coming home to you, Tink." I slant my lips over hers and my tongue seeks the access she grants. She tastes of wine and . . . dare I say *peppermint?*

I smile against her lips.

Leaving my peppermints for her is such a childish, silly thing to do and yet . . . when I taste them on her tongue it makes me happy.

"There are definitely no complaints there," she whispers.

"I have a surprise for you."

"For me?"

"Mm-hmm." I hope everything is in place. It isn't exactly the easiest to get things organized when in a different city, spending all day at the track surrounded constantly by people who might overhear my scheming.

And of course, here I am stressed about this little thing while Blair is organizing something a thousand times bigger.

"Follow me?" I ask and link my fingers with hers.

"To where?"

"The answer is supposed to be *sure, Lachlan. I'll go anywhere you lead*." I laugh.

"Sure, Lachlan. I'll go anywhere you lead," she mimics but smiles as her eyes narrow. And they stay narrowed as she tries to figure out where the hell I'm taking her.

But it's not far.

It's across the hall actually.

"Lachlan . . . what are . . ."

"I rented out both places—the whole floor so we could have our privacy," I explain as I unlock the door and push it open for her. "And I wanted to do something nice for you."

I breathe a sigh of relief when I look in the apartment to see the massage table set up, flowers on every possible surface, and candles flickering in the darkened room.

"I don't understand."

"You're under a lot of pressure, a lot of stress, and I wanted to do something to help you relax."

Emotion swims in her eyes as she stares at me. "You're the one who had a tough day. You're the one who deserves—"

"Shh." I put my finger to her lips. "Enough about me. There's always too much about me and not enough about you." I replace my finger with the touch of my lips. "Please don't fight me on this. Leave your clothes on the chair. Slide under the sheet on the table. And I'll have Carlotta come in in a few minutes to start your massage."

"You're serious, aren't you?"

"When it comes to making you feel good? Dead serious."

"Lach." I love my name on her lips. Especially when it's breathless and disbelieving and full of whatever emotion is fleeting through her eyes.

"I know," I whisper against her lips. "I know."

Chapter Thirty-One

Blair

"THAT FEELS LIKE HEAVEN," I MURMUR INTO THE DONUT MY FACE IS pressed into on the massage table.

My body is absolute mush. Carlotta has the hands of an angel, and she has worked every single knot out of my shoulders and back. The way she rubbed my feet and hands. The way she's worked in silence and allowed my mind to wander to a million places.

And yet, it always comes back to one person in particular.

Lachlan Evans.

The man had a shit day and rather than brood or pout or take it out on me, he somehow managed to organize something to make me feel good. To step outside of his own world and care for me.

It's such a drastic change from what I was used to with Rossi that I struggle to accept it.

Well, not really. What person is going to struggle with being massaged into blissful oblivion? No one.

But the thought remains. *He takes care of me.*

"I will be right back," Carlotta says softly. "I need more oil and it's right outside the door."

"Okay. Thank you. I'm not going to complain about more oil," I joke.

The door opens momentarily and then clicks back shut as footsteps head back toward me.

I hear the pump of the oil. The sound of it being shared between two hands. And when the hands hit my lower back . . .

I'm an instant pool of need. A relaxed body. A clear mind. Warmed oil. *His* strong hands. How could I not be?

His lips land between my shoulder blades. His strong hands work firmly over my muscles, the content sounds from deep in my chest simply reflexive.

The man has incredible hands.

And those hands slide down to knead the ample flesh there as his tongue slides a line down my back.

"Lachlan," I moan.

"Shh," he murmurs. "Let me worship you, Blair. Inch by inch. Muscle by muscle. Sensation by sensation."

"But you deserve—"

"Uh-uh," he says, pressing a kiss to the dimples in my lower back. "This is all about you. I had a shit day. I needed time to decompress. You didn't deserve my bad mood, so I thought I'd treat you to this while I did."

His hardened cock hits the side of my thigh—*I guess he's over that bad mood now*—and brings that delicious, sweet ache for him to life.

"You didn't have to do that."

"I wanted to. I needed to." His hands spread my thighs apart. "And now I need you."

I gasp at the wet warmth of his tongue as he slides it between my thighs. As his tongue pushes into me. As his fingers work over my clit.

"Christ." The warmth of his breath hits my skin. "You taste like fucking heaven."

He uses his hands to lift my hips up so that I'm on my knees and then spreads the globes of my ass so he has better access. And access he has as he begins to push his tongue in and out of me, building the pressure like only he can.

The ache spreads from my inner thighs through my muscles and down to my fingers and toes. My breasts feel heavy, and my body burns with the sweetest ache as he works every single nerve ending I have.

"Mine." A slide of his tongue. "This sweet fucking pussy." His fingers dig into the flesh of my hips. "You." A suck on my skin. "Just fucking mine."

I cry out when the wet warmth of his mouth leaves me and then yelp when he pats me just so that those nerves he just seduced are awoken from their sleep-drugged state.

"Lachlan," I moan as the cool air hits me seconds before I feel the head of his cock slide up and down my slit. He leaves it just at my entrance—enough to tease and for me to beg. "*Please.*"

"Just admiring the sight. How fucking drenched you are. How pink you are. How you stretch around me when I do this—"

"Ooohhh." The sound is drawn out as he takes his own sweet time pushing his way into me, inch by glorious inch, until I'm so full I can't take any more.

He feels incredible. It's so goddamn addictive that I want to push back on him and stay where I am all at the same time. I know from experience that both are damn incredible.

"You ready for me to make you feel even better, baby?"

"I don't know if that's possible," I murmur where my face is pressed into the pillow.

"It is. Let me show you." Lachlan begins to move. It's slow at first, the crest of his head hitting every place it needs to hit to have my nerves singing and my body soaring.

It's a sensual build. His hands on my hips. His quiet praise. "There's my girl." A grind against my ass. "Take it all for me." He pulls out so that his cock just pops out. "You want more of that?" Before a slow, taunting press back in. "Nothing has ever felt this good before."

"Lach. Faster."

His chuckle is strained as he adjusts his grip on me. "No. Death by orgasm sounds good about now. I love the way your arse looks like this. The way your thighs are dripping with what I do to you. The way you look over your shoulder to watch me fuck you." He hums. "No. I'm nowhere near done yet."

His words are a seduction all in themselves. And much like how he took care of me tonight with the masseuse, he's taking care of me now. Building me up. Making this last. Letting my body absorb the pleasure he builds. Motion by motion.

When I start to tighten around him, he pauses. He lets the pressure ebb some. Lets that coil unwind a bit. And then he starts the slow torturous ascent all over again.

I whimper from the pleasure. From the need coursing through me. From the bliss he's painstakingly—and at his own expense—created layer by layer.

"I can't—please. I just . . ."

He bends forward so that his cock hits unheard-of depths in me and then laces an open-mouthed kiss between my shoulder blades. "Come for me, Blair. Tighten that pussy around me. Let me feel what I do for you. I'm going to keep fucking you nice and slow like this. My balls are soaked, and my cock is so fucking hard for you. Do you feel that? Do you feel what you do to me? How you make me feel?" I push back on him, needing just one more slide of his cock before I—

"Fuck." I yell the word out as my world crashes around me. It's the most intense, most blissful heat that pulsates and races through and over every part of me. I'm so consumed by it that I'm lost in its haze as Lachlan shatters my bliss with his roar of a growl as he climaxes shortly after.

I'm out of breath.

Unable to think.

Can only feel.

Only want to feel.

And love that as his cock softens inside of me, he wraps his arms around my torso and hugs me against him, my name a refrain on his lips.

"That's one," he whispers so his warm breath heats my skin.

"Mmm."

"Good thing you're nice and relaxed since we need to hit those even numbers."

I chuckle and then shift so that he slides out of me and we're face-to-face. My fingers thread through his hair as I stare at him, my body swamped with so many sensations and my heart overwhelmed with emotions. He made this about me when he could have easily made it about him.

How did I settle for less? That's what I'm used to.

This has just absolutely thrown me when I wasn't sure I could be thrown anymore.

"Lachlan," I murmur for what feels like the hundredth time in the past hour and press my lips to his.

"Hmm?" His eyes flutter open so I can see the flecks of light green in his irises.

"Thank you. This was . . ."

"Perfect." His lips curve up. "Thank you. That's my new favorite way to unwind."

"No complaints here." I run my hand over the rough stubble on his cheek, down the ridiculously strong muscles of his neck, and then to rest over his heart. "I hate that we have to do this. To hide."

He puts his hand up and we touch our fingertips against one another's, both of us looking at that instead of each other. "I agree. One hundred percent."

"How much longer do you think—"

"I don't care about the fallout for me. I care about you and the risk to all you've worked for. The last thing I need is for you to be demoted because you're with me. I can't risk that for you."

"Let me prove myself with the gala. Then maybe I'll talk to Paolo and explain—"

"You shouldn't have to explain who you're with."

"I know. And I make no apologies for it, but I still think we need to play it safe. You don't want Gravitas or Apex to think you're causing problems in the garage, and I love my job."

"The end of the season then. That's how long we have to keep doing this."

"The end of the season," I repeat as I lean forward and kiss the tips of his fingers before looking back at him. "Then we get all of the above."

His smile is shy and owns my heart. "Then we get all of the above—*in public.*"

"Yes. That." I fall silent though and stare at our hands touching, our connection so strong that I know the risk is worth it. He's worth it.

"What are you thinking, Blair?"

"Why?"

"Because you just got that little line between your eyebrows that you get when you think too hard."

I hate that line. I wish I didn't have it. But he's right.

"Talk to me, Carmichael."

My smile softens. There's no other way to say it than to just say it. "I'm falling for you, Lachlan Evans."

"Then you must be looking down where I'm on the floor because I already fell a damn long time ago."

Chapter Thirty-Two

Blair

"**B**LAIR."

"Oliver? What . . . is everything okay?" I set down my coffee, shocked at hearing the sound of his voice.

"No. Yes." He snorts. "Fuck if I know."

"What does that mean?"

Silence weighs heavy on the line and my heart leaps into my throat. He's still my Oliver Rossi and I know him well enough to know how much it took for him to make this call.

I glance at the clock. From my texts, Lach got to the track early today because of a meeting with his agent. Did something happen that I don't know about? Contract renewal? Missed meeting? Why is Rossi calling me right now?

"I miss you. Like"—he sighs heavily—"talking to you. Joking with you. Just you."

"I miss our friendship too."

He barks out a laugh that's laced with sarcasm. "Way to keep it in the friend zone."

"I don't know what you want me to say to that," I say gently. Because I don't.

"Nothing. Look, I don't know why I called. I'll go—"

"No. Please. Talk to me." And I mean that. I still care about him. "Please?"

"Blair," he says so quietly I almost don't hear it. And there's only one thing worse than hurting someone you love—hearing the hurt in the voice of that person. Because that means they know you hurt them too. That means they're hurting.

"I'm here."

"Everything is up in the air. I used to have two constants—you and my ride—and right now I don't have the first and the second is unknown so it's just . . . unsettling."

"I'm still here. The ride will happen. You're too talented for it not to. You—"

"Rossi," a sleep-drugged feminine voice says coyly. "Come back to bed."

Oh.

Whoa.

Okay.

Talk about putting things into perspective. For a man who swore I'd be crawling back to him like a lap dog, he just showed me exactly how much he respected me. *Or rather disrespected me.*

If any part of me thought he was pining for me or that the whole melancholy exchange at the patisserie a few weeks back was because he wanted me back, what I just heard demonstrates how wrong those thoughts were.

And worse, I question all the other times we've been on a break in the past. Is this what happened then? Did he use someone else to get over me? Or maybe not even get over me. Maybe it's entitlement on his part that he's always felt. An entitlement that said the rules we had only applied to me and not him.

I'm beginning to think that's the case.

And more than that, I know for a fact that Rossi and I will never be a couple again. Especially not after being with and experiencing someone who puts me first. Who tries to take care of my needs, despite being a world-famous driver with people who adore and obsess over him.

Lachlan derives pleasure in putting me first, not in the pampering of his ego.

"Um. It sounds like you're busy. I'll let you go."

"Yep." He clears his throat. "Yeah."

"I'm here if you ever need to talk."

"Nah. I'm good."

"Well, good luck in quali today."

He pauses. "Goodbye, Blair."

I sit and stare out the window at the streets below for a long time after he ends the call.

"Everything is up in the air. I used to have two constants—you and my ride—and right now I don't have the first and the second is unknown so it's just . . . unsettling."

Rossi is struggling. Yes, he's struggling because I broke it off with him, but it's the consequences of his own actions. He didn't value me as he should have.

Because of that, I hear him, I feel for him, but not enough to stop and coddle him. He needs to figure his own shit out.

And meanwhile, I'll be putting myself first in a relationship where someone else does the same.

"Then you must be looking down where I'm on the floor because I already fell a damn long time ago."

I'm falling in love with the man who states he's already there.

It's the weirdest, most wonderful, most satisfying feeling.

I'm happy. Truly happy in a way I haven't been in as long as I can remember.

And I deserve to feel that way.

Chapter Thirty-Three

Blair

"WHY DO YOU CONTINUALLY SHOW ME THINGS I DIDN'T THINK I needed?" I say as we stroll down the back alley behind the restaurant.

Lachlan's hat is low on his head, his sunglasses are on despite it being evening, and his collar is popped to hide his profile.

"I was going stir-crazy and thought you might like to get out."

"I was and I did. Thank you."

I link my fingers with his, grateful that he arranged a private rooftop dinner for just the two of us.

"Cosiette is out of town," he says of his friend's villa on the outskirts of town where we just spent the evening. "He always offers his place to me for whatever reason and so this time I accepted it. I thought it was just what we needed. To be out . . . but not be out."

"It was perfect."

He stops and pulls me against him in a soul-searing kiss that leaves me dizzy.

"Now to get you back to your place before anyone sees us," he says and then brushes a more tender, less hurried kiss against my lips.

"The sunglasses are throwing me," I tease.

"They are a bit much." He angles his head to the side. "And probably draw more attention to me than not."

"Well, it is a bit strange to have sunglasses on at one in the morning." I lift them up so I can see his eyes. "And it's a shame to hide these gorgeous eyes from me."

"There's nothing I hide from you." He links our fingers again and we begin walking back toward my place.

The streets are littered with people for this time of the "morning," but everyone is busy with their own conversations or on the phone and aren't looking our way.

It's the freest we've been in public since this whole thing started between us two months ago. It gives me the sweetest glimpse of what is in our future, and I couldn't be more excited for it.

"Hey, Lach?" I murmur.

"Hmm?" He brings our linked hands to his lips and presses a kiss to the backside of my hand.

"Thanks for taking me out to play."

He chuckles. "Playing with you is my best kind of fun."

"That sounds dirty."

"I am dirty."

"Guess what?" I ask, preparing myself for the race I'm about to gladly lose.

"What?"

"Tag. You're it." I take off down the street, running like a madwoman. A woman who knows she is no match for a man who does daily cardio and lifts weights without ever breaking a sweat. But it's my own homage to what started this. The night on the golf course. Our first kiss. The start of twenty-one days and then . . . all of the above.

I revel in the few seconds of advantage I have before his footsteps sound behind me. Lachlan grabs me from behind and swings me around in a circle as we both cry out in laughter.

I'm dizzy from the action, from the way he makes me feel, and from the moment.

And when I spin back around so that we're body to body, face-to-face, I notice his hat has fallen off with our swinging before I take advantage of our breathless moment and kiss him again.

Our kiss dissolves into laughter as we both break to catch our breaths.

And it's then that I look up and directly into the eyes of Paolo, standing about twenty feet away.

He looks from me to Lachlan and then back to me again. The set to his jaw matches the intensity in his eyes as we stare at each other.

Oh. Shit.

I stand there in a suspended state of disbelief. One where my two worlds collide. Two worlds that now may implode.

"Um. Paolo." But as soon as I utter the words, he just gives the slightest shake of his head before turning on his heel and walking the other way.

My heart drops into my stomach. Instinct has me wanting to rush after him, needing to explain, and feeling like I need to right everything about this.

"Don't." Lachlan holds on to my arm as I start to go after him. I try to shrug out of his grip as every part of me riots inside. "I know you want to, but chasing after him will just make it worse. Give it a day. I know it will kill you but let him sort through things."

Tears burn in my eyes. "You don't understand," I murmur as he stoops down to pick up his hat and puts it back on his head.

He turns me to face him, his eyes clear. "I don't pretend to understand, but I know it'll work out. You're working your arse off on an incredible event. It's going to go flawlessly. And that is all you need to do to prove your worth. Who you spend your time with in private doesn't matter."

I worry my bottom lip between my teeth and stare at the empty space where my boss was.

Chapter Thirty-Four

Blair

"**P**AOLO."

My boss glances up from his seat behind his desk and meets my eyes before looking back down at his work like I didn't speak at all.

An impromptu trip to our main office in the UK was the last thing I'd expected to be doing today, but after a day of stressing about this, and Paolo not returning my calls, I knew this was the place I needed to be.

But now that I'm face-to-face with him, the courage I'd worked up on the way here has waned.

Big time.

Despite that fact though, I step into his office and shut the door at my back. "We need to talk about it."

"You lied to me," he says and then lifts his head to finally meet my eyes. The disappointment in them guts me.

But I didn't lie to him.

I didn't say a freaking word, and I shouldn't have to. There is no rule that says I have to tell my boss who I'm dating or if I broke up with someone. None whatsoever. In fact, I think that's a broad overstep of his purview. I understand that I need to keep things on the down-low, but this is . . . this is just wrong.

"It shouldn't matter who I date, Paolo. My job isn't affected by it."

"You knew I put my neck on the line for you on this. I explained the why behind it, and the gala has turned into the biggest event we've ever had and now—"

"And now, nothing."

"Nothing except the supposition of impropriety."

"Paolo." I open my mouth and then close it and then sigh heavily. "This isn't fair. I mean . . . if I were a male, would we be having this same conversation?" I lift an eyebrow. "I don't think so. I didn't lie to you. And who I spend my time with is my business. I kept my relationship with Rossi on the down-low for years. Even our breakup didn't make any tabloids, did it? So, I'll continue to be wise and circumspect."

"There's a lot on the line here."

"As you've mentioned numerous times before and so I'm more than aware of it."

He clasps his hands on his desk and leans back in his chair. His stare is like a laser. "This better not become a problem."

"It won't."

"Says the woman whose ex and new man are on the same goddamn team. The same garage where rumors leak daily about the tension between the two drivers, even though no one can figure out why. The tension that just might cause one of them to lose a contract."

Am I that out of touch, that I'm used to Rossi's rumors from the past, that in la-la land with Lachlan that I didn't know this?

"No one knows about me and Lachlan besides you," I say softly. "So any rumors about tension between the two of them aren't over me."

He snorts. "I never pegged you for being that naïve, Blair."

His rebuke stings and I struggle to bite back my response, but I manage to.

"Then there's Monica Chamalet making demands of you when we both know she's the private advisor over at Gravitas. A team who is looking actively at both of the drivers you're affiliated with for next year."

"One doesn't have anything to do with the other."

"No? You may think that. I may think that. But from the outside looking in, if it's ever found out, it looks like you're trying to cave to her demands to get your new boyfriend a big ol' contract. And that is exactly why we don't allow our employees to date drivers."

"That's an unfair statement."

"It might be. It might not be. But fair or unfair, all that matters is perception, and we both know that people are obsessed with these drivers and scandal definitely sells better. Did you ever think of that?"

No.

Yes.

Oh. My. God.

"No one will know," I repeat.

"And yet you were so careful that I found you on an off Wednesday night when I just happened to come into Nice and have dinner with an associate. But sure, no one will find out."

My entire body vibrates with the adrenaline of being put on the spot. Of having to face my boss and explain myself. Of fearing I might lose my job or never get the chance to plan another event again.

My hands sweat. My cheeks heat. My pulse races.

"My personal life will not interfere."

"I don't want to have to discuss this topic again until after the gala. I know you've busted your ass to get here, but I have twenty-three years under my belt. The last thing I want is my service here with the company tainted because I put you in charge, and you're giving favors to a spoiled heiress to secure your boyfriend a contract."

"Whoa. That's a long reach there. Have I ever used my position or the person's I'm seeing to gain something? No. Do I have anything to do with contract negotiations? Again, no. Have I tried to mitigate Monica's ridiculous requests over and over so that we don't have to comply while seeming gracious for the Tori Michelle performance? Yes. So if you are questioning any of those three things, then it's clear you undervalue what I've contributed to our department and there's nothing more for me to say."

"I don't undervalue you at all. In fact, I want the world for you and don't want any of this other stuff to taint it. We have the world watching us, Blair. A world of rabid F1 fans who will do or say anything to support their driver. We need clear-cut lines that we don't cross. That's all I'm saying."

"No one will know about Lachlan and me until after the gala. That's the best I can give you. My private life is just that—private. And while I understand all that you're saying and the assumptions that could be made, my work stands on its own."

"Great. Glad we cleared that up. You can see yourself out," he says and looks back down at the work in front of him, effectively dismissing me.

I stand there for a few seconds before turning on my heel and walking out, hating that as a woman, I'm being judged on who I'm dating and not the worthiness of my work.

At least that's what it feels like right now.

Chapter Thirty-Five

Lachlan

SHE LOOKS EXHAUSTED.

And defeated.

Her meeting with Paolo went as well as can be expected. I'm proud of her for standing her ground, and yet it's obvious it's taken its toll on her.

"You're here," she says when she sees me sitting in her flat waiting for her. How could I not be when she's being forced to go to battle because of me?

"I'm here." I hold my arms out and she crawls into them, snuggling up beside me on the couch.

I hate this for her.

I hate everything about it. And I can't fix a goddamn thing about it.

If I hadn't pursued her . . .

Then we wouldn't have this right now. We wouldn't have each other.

I breathe her in and close my eyes as she settles in—her head on my chest, her hand over my heart, the warmth of her breath against my shirt.

"I love you," I murmur into the top of her head.

The one emotion I've never felt for another person outside of my family. I don't expect her to say it back, in fact I'm glad she doesn't. Her silence says she's been through the wringer over the past forty-eight hours and my silent support—my quiet love—is exactly what she needs to know she's cared for.

I love you.

They're the easiest three words I've ever had the pleasure of saying.

Three words that sound so little but that say so goddamn much.

I should worry that it's too soon. That I'm pushing this too hard. That she's not ready.

But I don't.

It's just Blair. It's just me. It's over the limit and beyond the pale, and everything about it feels right.

She slides her hand up to my cheek as she lifts her head to look at me. I can see the same emotion swimming in her eyes that owns me every time I look at her. The same emotion I've never felt for another person.

When she brushes her lips against mine, when her tongue touches ever so gently with mine, I know I've never meant those three words more.

We move in hurried silence. Our pants. Our shirts. Anything to feel the reassurance of each other's touch to our skin. Of the certainty in our emotions. In the need to connect.

I want my kisses to erase how hard it was for her to stand up for herself.

I want her touch to erase how helpless I feel not being able to stand up for her myself.

We lose ourselves in the tenderness of brushed lips. In the slow simmer of feathered touches. In the notion that this is all we need. Her. Me. Us.

And as I slip into her, as I hear her rapturous murmur of pleasure, I know it's us against the world.

And I welcome the fight.

For her, I'd do anything.

Chapter Thirty-Six

Lachlan

"Okay. Just so I'm clear, both teams are setting to offer," I say and glance over to my packed bags at the door. My flight for AMS leaves shortly.

"Correct. The what or the how is still up in the air," Chandler says.

Chandler and I have been on the phone for nearly five minutes, and really, there's nothing more to add. I need to do my job, perform to the best of my ability, and he'll do what he can. He's fully aware of the irony that I'm being expected to perform for Apex with their car that is underperforming. And he probably expects my next question too. "Any news on Rossi?"

"No. You know I've had my feelers out on this but from what I hear, he's in the same boat. Everyone is waiting to see what the next few races hold."

"Same boat? Got it. I'm competing against my own teammate. There's no cause for any drama there."

"Or maybe that's just it."

"What's that supposed to mean?"

"Oh, you know the rumors, Lach. Teams adding more drama to the season to make the sport more interesting. The circuit being fixed so there's always something new to look at versus the same drivers winning the same races."

I've heard the rumors, but it doesn't make it any less absurd.

"Fixed. Right." I roll my eyes. As if they could fix me sleeping with my teammate's ex-girlfriend and then falling for her. "All I know is that Rossi despises Gravitas with a passion, so that's in my favor, is it not?"

"Logic says yes . . . but you and I both know there are only twenty seats and at the end of the day, all of you would eat crow if that meant getting a seat, regardless of whether you like the team or not."

"Are you implying we're shallow here, Chandler?" I chuckle. It's good to stir my agent every now and again.

"Not shallow. Just realistic."

We both laugh.

I scrub a hand through my hair and sigh. "I know. I know." Isn't that part of the reason I'm willing to play this fake-dating game with Zola? To try and get in the good graces of Monica who will in turn tell Gravitas to pull the string on signing me?

My phone beeps in my ear and I pull it down to see that it's Blair on the other line.

"I'm just growing impatient."

"I know," Chandler says. I know he knows but it doesn't make it any easier. "But we've been here before. I'm trying to do my job so that we're not here again for a few more years."

"I know you are."

"Just hold on for a few more races. It'll be worth it all in the end."

"Okay. Yeah. I know." I lean my arse against my counter and hate that at Blair's place there are pieces of me everywhere but, here at mine, there isn't a trace of her.

I want her here. I want her in my space. I want a normal life where I'm not hiding her.

We end the call and before I can even dial her again, she calls.

"Hi. What's up? Sorry. I was on the phone with Chandler."

"Any news?" she asks, well aware of the ongoing contract negotiations.

"Nothing to report, no."

"I have good news."

"Oh?"

"Monica requested that I be at the Dutch Grand Prix and that we meet to go over the gala."

"I'm not even going to ask why she's able to pull rank like that but I'm glad she can. That means I get to see you. Every day for the next few days."

"You get to see me from afar." She laughs. "There will be no—"

"Sneaking off into a quiet corner for a quickie?"

"No."

"Sneaking you into my hotel room in a laundry bin?"

"Nope." She laughs. "How about dirty talking as I sit across the lobby from you, so no one knows?"

"I mean, beggars can't be choosers, but if that's all I get then I'll need to think of a way to break some more rules so I can get more."

"There will be no rule-breaking, Lachlan Evans."

"No? I thought that was what you liked." I groan like a petulant child. "Are you telling me I can look but I can't touch?"

"I'm telling you that we're in the same hotel this time as your team and so, Paolo will undoubtedly keep an eagle eye on me, waiting for me to fuck up."

"The man probably had an aneurism when Monica called and demanded you be there."

"I'm sure he did. But that's why we need to keep our distance so that I can prove him wrong."

"This is going to hurt. I'm not going to lie," I tease.

"Well," she says, her voice lowering to that seductive rasp that suddenly has my balls grow heavy with ache. "I may have just picked up a very lacy, very sexy something or other to wear to help you celebrate after that fantastic race that I know you're going to have."

"Oh, really?"

"Mm-hmm."

"How lacy and how sexy?"

Her laugh is as seductive as her words. "Anticipation is foreplay to pleasure, Evans."

Jesus. I am one lucky man.

Chapter Thirty-Seven

Lachlan

"**S**AVE ME."

"Zola." I chuckle. "Always dramatic."

"But can you blame me? My mother is breathing down my neck saying I have to give Baron a few more chances. I don't want to give him more chances. I want him to—"

"I can't blame you. No." I feel sorry for you.

"Then you'll go with me to the dinner?" she asks like I know exactly what she's talking about.

"Your mum is beginning to think this is a real thing."

"Isn't that the point?" she asks.

"Yes, but . . . when she finds out it isn't . . ."

"When she finds out it isn't—*nothing*. She loves you. She's pushing for you to be on the team. Just let it all fall into place and then we'll figure it out."

"Zola. The last thing I want is—"

"A contract?" she laughs. "Come on, Lach. With my dating history, it's perfectly reasonable for me to fall in like with someone one minute and then out of it the next. That's exactly what will happen. Let's get through the gala and then—"

"The gala?" She never said anything about the gala.

"Yes. Pretty please?" she says in that deceptively timid but *I'm going to convince you* way she has.

"What if I already have a date?"

"You don't. You're keeping the girl you're head over heels with a secret, so I know you don't have one."

I open my mouth and then close it. She's right. And I hate that she fucking is. My heavy sigh fills the line.

"That means it's a yes. You're the absolute best, Evans. I'd kiss you for it, but your girlfriend has already been tolerant enough of me borrowing you, so I won't push my luck."

"I wouldn't. She has claws," I tease.

"I'm sure you enjoy her scratches." She chuckles. "It's always the quiet ones who are the freaks behind closed doors."

"Whatever," I say, but I laugh.

"Which is why you're saving me from Baron von Steubing. *Yuck.*"

"I'm going now, Zola."

"You know you love me."

"Love is a strong word," I tease.

"Well, you've got two more dates to fall out of it with me. So that should be easy for you."

When she ends the call, I simply shake my head. The woman is a force to be reckoned with. No doubt.

No woman should have their worth tied to a man. That's why I supported Blair so much when she went to talk to Paolo. And that's why I'll go on these two last dates with Zola.

It's the least I can do considering what opportunities might arise for me.

Chapter Thirty-Eight

Lachlan

"FOR THE RECORD, TINK, I'M TRYING MY DAMNEDEST TO RESPECT your job and keep my distance, but when you're two floors below me, your dirty mouth and my hand on my cock isn't doing it for me anymore."

These phone calls are the best and worst kind of torture.

"I know." Her laugh is sultry.

"How'd the meeting go?"

"Good. Par for the course. Monica made more demands and I wondered how in the hell I'm going to stay under budget while trying to fulfill them. But then I think, Tori is performing for free. Like . . . Monica did that. So why can't I make at least a few of those demands come to fruition for her?" She groans in frustration. "Then there's the Paolo angle and his side-eye glances every time I try to get his approval to fulfill one of these requests. Like if I say yes to caviar, Monica's going to give you a contract, when she doesn't even know we're together in the first place. It just feels like one convoluted mis-step of misunderstanding away from devolving into total anarchy and that's never a good feeling."

"You and I know that it's going to be flawless and incredible."

"I appreciate the thought." She clears her throat. "But—ugh. Not again."

"What?" I ask.

"Someone's at my door. I think it's Rossi."

"What do you mean *not again?*"

"I mean he's drunk, and this is the fourth time he's—"

"Keep me on the line," I order and am already throwing on my sweats and a shirt to head down to her room. So much for some phone sex.

I'll take care of this shit real quick. Then we'll get back to the regularly scheduled program.

"Oliver," she says through the phone. "I can't do this."

"I just wanna talk," my teammate slurs.

I'm already in the stairwell going down the first flight.

"No, you don't. You want to fight and we're past fighting."

"But you're my Blair and now you're not and—"

Down the second flight.

"Please. Stop. You're making this harder than it needs to be."

"I love you. Don't you know that?"

"You love me and yet you're sleeping with God knows who every time you call me."

I'm pushing open the door and I can see him standing in the hallway blocking her door. Their voices are now in my ear and floating in the hall around me.

"Rossi," I shout down the hallway. Both of them give me a double take as I jog toward them.

"What are you doing here?" he says slowly, his eyes blinking and bloodshot.

"It's our hotel. Why wouldn't I be here?"

"But not on this floor," he says, and I'm hoping he's too drunk to keep up this line of questioning.

"Blair. Hi," I say as she narrows her eyes at me. I'm not sure if that's because she's pissed I'm interfering or happy that I am.

I'm here.

Doesn't matter now.

"Rossi." He keeps looking at Blair. "Oliver," I say, and that startles him. He looks back at me. "Let's go have a drink together."

"You? A drink with me? On a school night?" He laughs at his own joke. "I'm sure the Apex powers that be would be thrilled with that."

"No one controls us," I say to feed into his loner bullshit while taking his arm and pulling it around my shoulder. "C'mon. Leave Blair alone. Let's go have a drink."

"You sure?" he asks.

He's going to be in bad shape tomorrow. Never a good look during race week. And an even rarer one at that.

"I'm sure."

It doesn't take us long to make our way to the bar down the street from the hotel. It's a hole in the wall I've been to before. It has dark lighting and a *keep-to-yourself* attitude, and that's exactly what we need right now.

That and maybe the dim lighting and his inebriation will allow me to mask my lies even more.

We keep our hats low over our brows and our heads down toward the floor as we walk in and toward a table in the back. It doesn't matter though. The people in this bar want nothing to do with anyone other than to be left alone so they can drown their sorrows.

Seems like a perfect place for Rossi right now.

We sit in silence as the waitress takes our drink orders. It's clear she's anxious to be off shift or is more concerned with trying to impress a guy at the bar by the way she barely even looks our way when taking our orders.

It's perfect.

"So," I say once drinks are in front of us, "want to tell me what that was all about?"

"No." He takes a long drink and the fact that the burn doesn't faze him one bit tells me how far gone he is.

"No?"

"What's it to you?" he snaps. Clearly the jovial guy from moments ago is now gone.

"I'm just trying to figure out why you're at Blair's door drunk off your arse when I think I've seen a different woman leave your hotel room every night we've been here."

"Fuck off. Don't you have something else to do other than butt in, huh, Evans?"

"Butt in? We share a hotel room wall. You're not exactly quiet and the women you choose seem to be all for show if the screaming is any indication."

"Or I'm just that good."

"Yeah. Right. That's exactly it." I take a sip. "The tough-man shit gets old, Oliver."

"So does the holier-than-thou shit." He sniffs. "And stop calling me *Oliver*."

"Look. I'm trying to be a friend but it's getting harder and harder to try when you're a dick, *Oliver*." Fuck it. I threw that one in for good measure.

"Perfect. At least I'm successful at something."

"Fine. Whatever." I scoot back my chair and go to leave.

"Evans. Wait."

I sigh and drop my head down for a beat before meeting his eyes. "What?" Disdain paints the edges of my tone.

"I miss her."

I snort and take a seat. "You can miss her all you want but that doesn't mean you fucking deserve her."

"You don't know what I deserve."

"You're right. I don't. Let me rephrase. She deserves better than you."

The *fuck you* is on the tip of his tongue. I can see it. He knows I can see it. But he sighs instead of saying it. "And you know this how?"

"Because she's a great person."

"I'll repeat my question, and you know this how?"

"I don't. It's an assumption." I pause and make myself redirect because fuck, did I step in that one. "No woman is going to be satisfied with being fourth or fifth on your list of priorities."

"Who said she was?"

I level him with a dubious look. "Having racing come first is a given, but it seems to me that you put partying, flirting with other women, what-the-fuck-else-ever in front of her."

"Total bullshit."

I shrug. "You can say the words but deep down you know it's the truth."

"Like you could do any better. There's a reason you don't have a permanent woman."

"This isn't about me."

"Keep dreaming, Evans," he slurs. "A woman like Blair would never even look at you twice."

My smile is tight, the *fuck you* I kept in now loaded on my tongue. "You need to leave her alone."

He throws his head back and laughs and I wince. Can't keep to ourselves when he keeps drawing attention. "And you need to keep your opinions to yourself."

"She's not going to take you back." *She's mine.* God, how I want to say those words.

"Like you fucking know." He snorts, and then fuck me. He looks right at me, eyes boring into mine. "*Right?*"

I lift my drink to my lips, our eyes meeting over the rim of the glass. "Right."

A chill falls over the table and, even though he's drunk, I can see his wheels turning and don't exactly want them to click into place right here and right now.

"She probably just needs space," I say. "Isn't that what all women say?"

"Something is different this time around," he murmurs more to himself than to me. "Just feels fucking different."

"Probably because you let her go without a fight," I muse, my eyes on my drink and not on him. "At least that's how it seems. But . . . then again, it also doesn't seem like she wants to be fought for. She's not in the paddock. She's not accidentally walking past the garage. She's nowhere."

"And you've noticed this why?" He narrows his eyes at me.

"I notice everything."

"Of course you fucking do." He shakes his head and tosses back the rest of his drink before lifting his finger to the server for another.

Looks like I'm in for a long fucking night.

But if it keeps this arsehole away from the woman I love, then that's the sacrifice I'm willing to make.

Chapter Thirty-Nine

Blair

"BLAIR. WAIT UP."

Rossi's voice rings across the paddock and everything about me falters at the sound of it—my expression, my footsteps, my breath. I steel myself for seeing him. For this conversation, one that hopefully goes better than the other night when Lachlan had to drag him away from my room.

Do I miss my best friend? Yep. Still do. But I haven't exactly loved his behavior as of late. The drunken calls, the passive-aggressive texts. Rossi acting like a spoiled brat isn't exactly a new revelation to me—but acting like that *about* us is.

More than anything, it shows that I had a specific role in his life. That I was his champion for all things public and private. But now with our relationship over, I am no longer obligated to be anything when it comes to him.

Do I want to tell him I've moved on? Definitely.

Can I tell him a damn thing? Nope. Sure can't.

I take a fortifying breath and brace myself for whatever this conversation might bring.

"You're back here. At this race," he says more like a question than a statement.

"I am. I had meetings with . . . some people."

"Some people?" He lifts his eyebrows. "That's where we're at now? You're not talking to me?"

"I am talking to you, Oliver. I'm not quite sure which version of you I'm going to get though. Nice friend, Oliver. Or drunk prick banging on my door, Rossi."

"Jesus. Seriously?" He laughs like it's all a joke but, when he meets my eyes, he realizes that I'm pissed about the other night. Even over the noise of the paddock, I can hear his sigh. "Look. I'm sorry. I just . . . I was having a bad night."

"What? One of your one-nighters bailed before the good times got rolling?"

"Hey. That's not—"

"It is fair. So long as you're as understanding when I take the next step," I say. "I'm happy for you. I'm glad you're moving on. All I ask from you is the same courtesy when I do so."

"That's not going to be easy."

"And you think it's easy for me?" I stare at him with my jaw clenched and disbelief in my expression. "I'm done with the two sets of rules for us. What's good for you is just as good for me. Just because I broke up with you, doesn't mean I don't love the person you are. It also doesn't mean I enjoy watching you whore yourself out."

"Like you said, you broke up with me." His tone changes. The defensive stance is clear in his voice.

"I did. And I think it was the right decision," I say and hate the stiffening of his body. That stiffening means he was holding out hope for a reconciliation. Shit. "Our relationship ran its course, Oliver. Nothing more. Nothing less."

He pauses for a beat, looking down before meeting my eyes. "It kind of sucks," he whispers.

"It does. I know." I reach out and grab his hand. *I still love you.* Those words are on my tongue, but I know he'll think they mean more than the platonic way in which I mean them, so I bite them back. "We'll get to a place where we're okay. I promise."

"You promise?" he asks and reminds me so much of the boy I fell for all those years ago.

"I do."

"Come here," he says and pulls me into a hug. My hesitation is brief and telling because when I'm folded in his arms, I realize it's such a different feeling than when I'm with Lachlan. With Lach I feel safe, secure, desired, understood, and excited. With Rossi I just feel . . . like an uncertain teenager waiting for the next shoe to drop.

How did I never notice it before?

"I missed you," he murmurs and this time when he squeezes me, there's a crinkling noise. He laughs. "What the heck is that?"

"I don't know. Nothing."

But before he lets me go, he feels inside my jacket pocket and pulls out two wrapped peppermints and two empty wrappers.

The ones that Lachlan left on my desk as a silent acknowledgement that he's happy I'm here at the race.

I see the minute awareness hits Rossi.

What they are.

Who they're from.

Why I might have them.

He holds the four items in his hand, his eyes blinking rapidly as if it will help him process the thoughts slowly connecting in his mind.

And when he looks up at me, when he meets my eyes, there's nothing I can say or do to erase the hurt etched in the lines of his features.

"Why are his fucking stupid candies in your pocket, Blair?"

I have nothing. What can I say to that?

"Evans?" he asks. *Oh shit.* "You're what? Fucking *him*? Him? The boring-as-shit Australian?"

"Rossi," I whisper his name as I see the shock radiating through his expression. "He's my friend," I lie.

"You're a shit liar. Always have been."

That expression shifts to anger.

To something I don't think I've ever seen in him before.

"Oliver. We—"

"Fuck this. Just fucking fuck this."

He backs away, head shaking, cheeks red. *I've never seen him like this.*

"Please."

"You want *the prick* Rossi? You got him, sweetheart. You fucking got him."

"Don't be that way . . ." I shout after him as he turns on his heel. But I can't chase after him. Not when I see Paolo standing across the path, arms over his chest, looking concerned.

Fuck.

Not when what I just broke, I'm not sure I'll ever be able to fix.

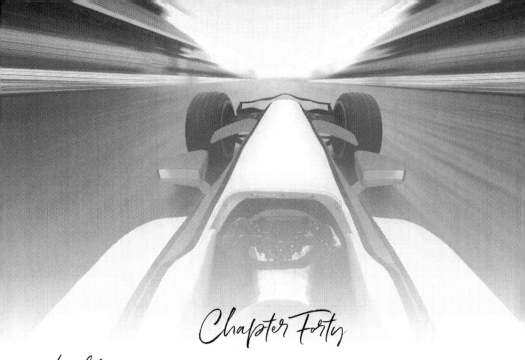

Chapter Forty

Lachlan

"YOU MOTHERFUCKER."

Rossi comes at me out of nowhere. His growl echoes around the garage and luckily for us, everyone is out at an FIA meeting about track issues and it's just me and a few other team members milling about.

Milling about but still there.

And now Rossi.

His words catch me off guard, but not enough that I'm prepared for him to pin me against the wall. And nowhere near enough that I don't already have a feeling what this is about.

He knows.

He fucking knows.

Shit.

Shit.

Double shit.

"You lowlife, cheating, stealing motherfucker," he repeats as he presses his forearm against my chest.

Anger thrives in his every feature. The set of his lips. The squint of his eyes. The pressure on my chest.

"Take your bullshit out of my garage," I growl right back.

"My bullshit?" he asks, his voice raising with each and every syllable. "My fucking bullshit? Playing the goddamn valiant friend when you're nothing but a two-faced motherfucker who steals—"

"*That's enough,*" Henry shouts from the outskirts of the garage. He strides over to us faster than I can draw in a breath. "That's fucking enough. Gio is ten feet away from this garage and if you don't want a contract—*either of you*—keep your fucking shit up."

Rossi grits his teeth, his breath labored, and his fury eating up the oxygen around us.

"You got a problem? Want to kick each other's asses? Do it outside of my garage," Henry continues.

And for the slightest moment, I think Rossi's going to throw a punch. His free hand is fisted and I can see his arm tighten up, but when Henry puts his hand on Rossi's shoulder and yanks him backward, I know he won't.

Instead, Rossi just glares at me.

"I wish the two of you had this much fight in you on the track," Henry spits out. "Then maybe we'd win a fucking race, huh?"

Rossi mutters something about *fucking piece of shit* but it's lost in his grit of anger.

"Then maybe we'd get somewhere," Henry continues before turning to Rossi and pointing outside of my garage. "Get to your own garage. Get suited up. Get ready to qualify."

Rossi grumbles a bit more as my heart decelerates and I wonder how the fuck he found out.

Henry has one finger held up to me to stay where I am as he looks over his shoulder to make sure Rossi has gotten out. Everyone else in the garage averts their eyes as he looks around and back to me.

"Want to tell me what the fuck that was all about?" he demands, his shoulders squaring and his own anger obvious. "Because it seems I'm having to ask that a lot of you lately." And as if on fucking cue, just over his shoulder, I see my father step into the garage.

Smart and more than astute, he sizes up the situation in a few seconds. The way he crosses his arms over his chest and lifts his eyebrows says as much.

I can't deal with him right now. With his shit. With knowing I'll have disappointed him too.

I clear my throat. "It was nothing."

"Nothing?" Henry takes a step closer.

"It's personal. Off the track shit. It has nothing to do with this garage or our team."

He chuckles and it holds no amusement. "Clearly it does. You fucking his girl? You kill his dog? You take his prized stuffed animal? What? Because this team's already broken down enough with all our asses on the line and that"—he points to the wall where Rossi just had me pressed against—"says it's fucking imploding."

I grit my teeth and straighten my own shoulders. "Just because Rossi can't control his emotions doesn't mean I can't," I say and shake my head like I'm mad at being accused of the shit that's churning in my gut. "We can continue this later if you feel the need to. If not, I need to get ready for qualifying."

And without another word, I turn and head for my private driver's room.

"Lachlan," my dad calls out.

But I keep walking.

I meant what I said.

I need to clear my fucking head. Get it where it needs to be. Get in the zone.

Once I close the door at my back to block out his footsteps behind me, I lean back against it and squeeze my eyes shut.

What the actual fuck.

But when I grab my phone to call Blair, to see how the fuck Rossi found out, I remember there's zero service where our team suite is located this race.

None.

And so I'm figuratively and literally left in the dark.

Rossi knows.

The only question left is how I'm going to protect Blair and her job from the fallout.

Chapter Forty-One

Blair

THEY DRIVE LIKE MADMEN.

Like men racing with something to prove.

Like lovers trying to win my favor by claiming the best grid position for the day.

None of it—their high finishes, the team is ecstatic that they finally finished with second-row grid positions, that this might be a turning point in their season—makes me feel any better.

Not in the least.

Instead, I stood in the Formula 1 suite with my heart in my throat and a ball of nerves in my stomach, watching the day unfold lap by lap on the telecast.

The frantic texts I sent to Lachlan hours ago went unanswered.

Clearly, he knows by now that Rossi knows about us. That's a given.

Fuck. Just fuck.

They're doing what they do best. Racing. Wowing the crowds. Being the incredible drivers, I know them to be.

But by the optics from the cameras panning over the garage and the drivers themselves, there was a solemnity in the Apex garage.

Rossi has had his sunglasses on the whole time and his jaw is set in that *don't fuck with me* attitude he has.

Lachlan's usual smile is missing. He keeps his head down and doesn't joke with the cameraman like normal.

They both had their best day of the season so far—but none of that matters.

The damn mint wrappers.

The ones I thought were so cute—my constant reminder that Lachlan had made an effort to see me—were also what made Rossi see us.

The irony isn't lost on me.

To remember me by.

Guess that didn't turn out as well as we thought.

I stress over it as I head back to the hotel. Their work is far from done at the track, but right now it's the last place I want to be.

I keep seeing Rossi's face. I keep hearing the hurt in his voice.

I knew he would take it hard . . . and yet that doesn't make this any easier for me to process.

Afraid I'll miss a second of it, but glad I'm alone in my hotel room, I turn the telecast on.

"Well, it was clear that there was some kind of unspoken tension in the Apex garage today," Will, one of the announcers, says.

"Clear indeed, but maybe they need that more often because it's the first time all year they have two drivers starting in the second row," Francisco, his co-anchor, says.

"Agreed. It was a special day for the blue team. A lot of intensity and silence but at the end of the day, they pulled through."

"A possible disagreement over contracts?" Francisco asks.

"There's that constant weight on their shoulders since neither current driver has signed for next year yet . . . but if that's the case, then both Oliver Rossi and Lachlan Evans put on a show that makes them desirable for all open contract spots."

"You have a point there. I guess we'll just have to see what tomorrow brings. At the end of the day, it's what happens on race day that matters."

"Agreed, Francisco. Agreed."

I tune out as the analysts move on to discussing Team Moretti and their incredible run over the past few races.

And I sit at the window and stare out at a city beyond, but not really seeing it.

It's well after five o'clock when I pick up my phone to call Lachlan. He doesn't answer until the fourth ring.

"Hey," he says softly, and the sound of his voice has the tears immediately flooding my eyes.

"Hi."

Silence hangs on the connection, the weight of the day so heavy it's almost as if both of us are afraid to talk.

"Congratulations on P3," I finally say.

"Yep. Well, I either just fucked up my contract for next year or solidified it. I don't know which one."

"Lach—"

"I can't do this right now, Blair. I appreciate that you need to talk, to explain—and I hate that I'm unable to give that to you—but I can't offer you the undivided attention you deserve right now. The last thing you need is my shitty mood taken out on you. I'm sorry you were hurt today. I'm sorry you're probably still hurting, because you're a good human and that's how good humans react . . . but I have a lot on my plate and need some time to decompress."

I want to be hurt by his words, but I refuse to be. The fact he even uttered something like that when I'm so used to being shut out is enough for me. Has to be. He's being far more gracious than Rossi ever could have been. *And I respect him more for it.*

"I understand," I murmur.

"Thank you for giving me that grace. It's just been a shit day, I have a ton riding on tomorrow, and I need to get my head in the right place."

"Okay." I clear my throat, my heart grieving that I put him in this position. That I can't comfort him and just hold his hand while we lie side by side together. "Good luck tomorrow."

"Thanks. Good night."

"Good night. I love you, Lachlan." I wondered when the right time to finally express to him how I feel would be, but I know it's now. Undoubtedly. It's right now. "*I love you,*" I repeat. He needs to know that he is loved.

His breath stutters across the line and something about it—about knowing how much hearing those words affect him—makes me smile.

"I love you too, Tink. All of the above."

"All of the above."

I sit with my phone clutched in my hand for the longest time. The last thing I want to do tonight is go to an event with Monica.

Where I have to plaster on a smile and listen to her worry about which millionaire will be the best for her daughter.

Where I have to pretend that an heiress's ego and being right is so much more important than the chaos going on in my personal life.

Where I have to pretend that I didn't crush Rossi today.

And where I have to pretend that both of the men I love—one romantically and one platonically—don't feel like they're about to do battle tomorrow . . . with me as the source of their distraction.

Chapter Forty-Two

Lachlan

"FIVE LAPS TO GO, LACHLAN. FIVE LAPS," HENRY SAYS IN MY EAR.

"Position?"

"Currently P3. Good job. Stay strong."

"And Rossi?"

"P4. Right behind by five tenths of a second."

Hold on, baby. Hold on.

I take the turns. The straights. Every single kilometer I drive with a precision like I've never had before.

Four laps to go.

I'm looking ahead at Bustos's taillights. At staying close enough but not pushing the engine so hard it blows. And that's where my concentration is. On Bustos. On my car.

So I'm startled when I look in my mirror and see Rossi there. Like right fucking there.

"Henry?" I ask. "Are we free fighting or are we . . ." I need to know if Rossi is really racing me—and if that's the case then why the fuck didn't my team tell me?—or if he's supposed to protect me from the fifth-place driver.

"We're having radio issues. Rossi's isn't working."

I don't buy that for a fucking second.

Not with how he was today with me in the pre-race activities. Not with how he won't even talk to me. Not with him just being Rossi.

His radio isn't working because he doesn't want to be told to stand down. Because he wants to prove that he's better than me.

Well, fuck him. I don't race at all costs, and it seems he wants to.

Team.

Teammate.

Crew.

"So that means we're racing," I say more to myself than to Henry.

I welcome the fucking challenge.

I pick up my pace, hurtling down the straight at the best speed I've clocked all day. He edges up beside me and I fight him off. We slow in the corner and I keep the advantage.

But our cars are about even in performance today. Mine has the edge but he has the recklessness. There's no telling how this will end up.

Bring. It. On.

We race each other through the next lap. Me fending. Him charging. You're taught to race the track, not the driver.

This is a clear case of him racing against me.

Of him taking me on.

My hands vibrate and my jaw clenches as we battle. We both need this finish. We both need this for our ego.

And then I'm flying.

My car lifts off the ground and I'm flying parallel to it. I'm weightless. Helpless. Without any time to think. Any time to react other than to take my hands off the wheel.

The car touches down in the gravel. It spins and spins before it slows. I brace for impact but fortunately for me it slows enough that the impact isn't as brutal as I anticipated.

"Fuck!" I shout, well aware people are listening—but not really giving a fuck.

"Are you okay, Lachlan?" Henry asks.

"He fucking took me out, Henry." I disconnect my steering wheel and throw it on the hood. "Took me out on purpose." I unbuckle and exit from the car. "Took me out for his own goddamn good." I'm out of the car and jogging down the outside of the track toward the garages.

Motherfucker.

Mother. Fucker.

"Rossi is wrecked too, Lachlan," Henry says in that calm even voice of his.

"Good. He should be," I shout as I unbuckle my helmet and hit the garage.

Just about the same time Rossi does.

"Seems that's racing," Rossi says the minute he sees me. And smirks.

He wants a fight.

He's about to get one.

I lower my shoulder and ram him into the wall. Oof. It's all I hear exhaling from his lungs followed by a gasp from those around us.

"You want to fucking try to kill me?" I shout in his face, my forearm at his throat. "You have to do a much better job than that."

"Fuck you," he grits out.

"Gladly. Because I win, Rossi. You weren't man enough to keep her, but I am. So fuck. You."

Commotion.

It's all around us.

Hands on us. Shouts at us.

And the next thing I know we're being shoved into a conference room, just Rossi and me, and the door is shut at our backs to close out any and all eyes and ears.

"You two figure your shit out and figure it out now. The FIA is going to be down our throats by the race's end no doubt imposing penalties for impeding, Rossi, so you better figure out what the fuck that was back there. If it was what I think it was, you might never sit behind a wheel again."

"The throttle stuck. The electronics failed. No radio. No gauges. Not sure what you mean."

The look Henry gives Rossi rivals mine. The difference is, Henry can believe his bullshit if he wants to. I lived with the consequences of it and don't believe a fucking word of it.

"Like I said, our whole team will suffer because of whatever FIA hands down." He points to Rossi and then to me. "Don't leave here until you're sorted."

He slams the door at his back and Rossi turns on me, seething, as we stand ten feet apart, circling like wolves before a fight.

"I fucking hate you," he grits out.

"Good. Glad to hear it." I toss my gloves on the table. "You're reckless and dangerous, and you just fucking took me out because it bruises your ego that she chose me. That's on you, not me."

"You took her from me," he spits out.

"You lost her yourself, but you're so goddamn arrogant that you can't fathom that, can you? Oliver Rossi isn't a god. He's a great driver but he's a shit person."

"Like I give a flying fuck what you think. Just you wait," he says and steps up to me so that we're a swing away from each other. "I'm going to ruin you. Your reputation."

"Looks like you already just ruined yours."

"That you're a cheater."

"Taking your teammate out on global television."

"That you fucked over your teammate."

"Reckless. Dangerous. Out of control," I spit out as the anger grows. Multiplies. As the adrenaline surges from what just could have happened.

"I'm going to go out there and let the entire world know that Golden Boy Evans fucked me over with her—"

I'm at him again in a second. He throws a punch that connects before I can pin him against the wall. Before I can throw my own.

And it's a good fucking punch, but I take it. I wear it. Because what I have to say is ten times more important.

"Do you still love her?" I ask.

"Not your fucking business."

"But it is. Because if you love her, you won't say a goddamn word. Her job, everything she's worked for is on the line . . . and while you were too self-centered to notice that before, maybe you'll acknowledge it now. If you love her like you say you do, then you'll keep your fucking mouth shut so she doesn't lose the job she loves."

"That's asking a fucking lot."

"No. It's me asking you to be the man she *still* thinks you are. The one you've yet to prove to me that you are. The one you never were when the two of you were together."

I barge out of the conference room.

I push past every person wanting to talk to me.

And I head straight for the showers where I can stand under the stream of water and let the adrenaline of the crash wrack my body.

Where I can get control of myself. Because that wasn't me. That fury. That desire to hurt another human.

But why the fuck did he do that? Risk that? We could have both been killed. What. The. Fuck.

I crank the shower even hotter.

If he hurts Blair? If he ruins her career . . .

Holding back won't be an option.

Fuck.

How could he be so fucking reckless?

Could have killed me.

Others.

I turn the water off, wrap a towel around my waist, and step into my driver's room. *Of course he's here.*

"I don't want to talk about it right now, Dad," I mutter and turn my back to him. The last thing I need to see is the disappointment in his eyes. I can already feel it.

"You don't need to talk. I do."

"Good. Great." I roll my shoulders, the ache in my neck from the collision starting to present itself.

"I knew you had eyes for her. It was obvious to me. But I never thought you'd risk your career over it."

"Risk my career?" I snort.

"Yes. Risk it. Because that's just what you've done and if you think no one in that garage is going to talk about what they just heard or saw between the two Apex drivers, then you're as naïve as you are pussy-whipped."

I whirl around. If he was trying to get my attention, he sure as fuck just did. "My life. My business."

"You need to shut it down, Lach, and focus on your career."

"Unbelievable. Of all people—"

He holds his hand up to stop me. "I'm not telling you not to pursue it. I'm not telling you not to even love her. I'm telling you that you've worked your whole fucking life for this moment, and this is the one time you need to be selfish. That you need to think of you. That you need to keep the seas fucking calm so you can make the press because you just signed a big contract and not because you stole your teammate's girlfriend."

"I didn't steal her."

He nods and I hate that I wonder if he believes me or not. "If this Blair is your person, she'll wait. She'll know that this is the wisest course of action for your career right now."

His words burn in my chest. Not seeing Blair? That's not a fucking option.

"I know you're already rejecting what I've said, but I'm telling you that you need to hear me. That you need to listen to me. Fifteen years' worth of preparing for this career and you're risking that to throw it all away for a woman?"

"Dad." The word is hoarse. She's not just a woman. She's Blair. She's . . . fucking everything.

She's my all of the above.

"I know, mate. But if she's who you think she is, she'll understand. She will. And if she doesn't, then she's not worth being with you." He gives a definitive nod before stepping out of my driver's room and shutting the door behind him.

Fuck.

I'm back to being fifteen and forced to question anything and everything.

Just fuck.

I shout the word over and over in my head.

As I get dressed in my Apex gear.

As I check my phone one more time for texts I no doubt know she sent but that I never received.

As I consider my dad's advice. The truth to his words. The punch to the gut they make me feel.

It's going to be a long fucking post-race.

Not just with the media.

But with Gio and our team.

With my thoughts.

And then, no doubt, the FIA. *I did nothing wrong so I'm not worried about what they'll find when it comes to my actions. I didn't contravene any rules.*

But . . .

Petty never looks good on anyone, and Rossi just made sure of that for the both of us.

Chapter Forty-Three

Blair

H E COMES TO ME THAT NIGHT. TO MY PLACE.

Other than the two texts he sent me saying "I'm all right" and "Rossi won't say a word," I haven't heard from him.

He comes straight from the private jet, opens the door, and crawls into bed with me.

"Lach—"

"Shh. No talking." He wraps his arms around me and rests his head on my chest. "I just need this. Need you. Need us. Please?"

I run my fingers through his hair and for the first time since I saw his car flying through the air, since I felt like a part of my soul was twisted like the metal of his car, I feel like I can breathe.

Sure, I saw him on the telecast. The interviews with the talking heads. Heard him recount how he felt about the accident. Heard his stoic, team-oriented response to the FIA imposing a fine against Rossi for impeding him.

But seeing him on the television and feeling him in my arms are two very different things.

This—his warm skin, the beat of his heart against mine, the sight of his crooked smile—reaffirms what I knew to be true. That he is okay.

"I'm here." They're the words I need to say, and I want him to hear.

Rossi went after him because of me. This is my fault.

"Take what you need from me," I whisper as I bring each one of his fingers to my lips and kiss them.

I love you.

"I'm all yours." I lean forward and brush my lips to his.

I think I was made to love you.

We move in the darkness. A synchronized dance we know so well by heart now. We explore each other's flesh not because we're figuring out what pleases each other, but rather because we know.

He kisses the spot just below my ear. My fingers dance over his lower abdomen. He cups my breasts and rolls my nipples between his thumbs and forefingers. I lace kisses down the line of his jaw.

We lavish attention in the shadows much like we've lived this relationship. Without many words but with the reassurance of touch. With the affirmation of moans. With the press of our lips to one another's as the only currency we need to interact.

I spread my thighs. I guide his cock to my core. He pushes into me in a motion we know so well but that feels new and different each and every time.

And this time does feel different.

I sense a solemnity to us. A gratitude that he's here, that he's whole and healthy and loving me. And at the same time, with some kind of quiet resignation of what happened on his part.

He moves inside of me just like he always has—attentively, sensually, generously—and yet I can't help but feel like something is amiss. Like he's been pushed too far with the circumstances today and it's making him question everything.

In normal circumstances, it's something I'd be able to understand. To process.

But right now, with me sharing every part of me and then some, it's the most bizarre mix of seductive, confusing, and desperate.

"Look at me, Lach," I say as he begins to use me for himself. In deep, hard thrusts that bottom out within me. With a feral greed that's both attractive and sexy. With a possessiveness that's heady and arousing.

But he doesn't look at me. He just fucks me like he's angry. Like he's saying goodbye. Like this is the last time we'll be together.

And when he comes, when I wrap my hands around his neck and thread my fingers through his hair, when I murmur, *I love you* against his bare shoulder, there's an emptiness when there should be contentment.

There's confusion when there should be certainty.

I chalk it up to his emotions being all over the place after the day he's had.

But when I wake up in the morning and the bed is empty beside me, there's fear that I've never felt before.

And an acceptance that I needed to give him space to process it.

And then I call the one person I know will comfort me how I need it.

"Sky, I need you," I say as she answers. And then I cry.

Chapter Forty-Four

Blair

> Monica: See? My matchmaking skills have worked. Look how fabulous they look together.

I STARE AT THE PICTURE IN THE TEXT AND DO A DOUBLE TAKE. I WAS expecting a picture of Zola and Baron, not Lachlan and Zola.

Unfounded jealousy runs like wildfire through my veins.

I know what's going on between Zola and Lachlan. I told him it was fine. But one, Monica is delusional that all of a sudden, she's trying to take credit for setting them up and two, Lachlan has been quiet for the past two days. Withdrawn. Contemplative when I've spoken to him. So seeing him like this—in a tux, smiling with Zola—at an event he told me about weeks ago, leaves a bitter taste in my mouth.

But I'm well aware it's the unsettled ground that I'm concerned Lachlan and I are on right now that's causing all these shitty feelings to bubble up. Insecurity. Uncertainty. Jealousy.

It's like he's not mine when in fact, he is.

But as the seconds tick away to minutes.

And the minutes turn into an hour, I can't help but relive the other night after the race. When we made love. When he was gone the next morning. When he left without saying goodbye.

Professionally, everything's on the line right now. His future in the sport.

The legacy he'll leave behind when he leaves it. And because of me, he and Rossi are at odds. Because of me, he might have risked it all.

Is that why he's been so quiet? Why he's taking space without asking for it? Is he thinking he has to choose between me and his career right now and can't have both with Rossi as his current teammate?

The questions don't stop. The problems and doubts seem to magnify. And as easy as it would be to drop him a text and ask the question, I don't.

I'm afraid to.

Afraid of the answer.

I was so sure of us a few days ago and now, I feel so up in the air.

But then at midnight, I'm confused as he shuts the door behind him. Without a word, he slowly begins to remove his layers of clothes that disguise him. The oversized hoodie that's pulled over his baseball cap. The medical mask that covers his nose and mouth like he's sick and protecting others from germs.

And when he sheds them all, I'm hit squarely in the gut by the sight of him. He's dressed in a tuxedo. Sexy as hell and mouthwateringly attractive.

"*Lachlan?*" Surprise peppers my tone and relief floods every bone in my body.

"You sound surprised to see me." He angles his head and studies me.

"I—I wasn't sure—after the other night—I didn't know . . ."

He crosses the room to me and kisses me tenderly on the lips. I almost choke on a sob. "Shh. I'm here," he murmurs. "I'm right here."

"I thought you'd left. I thought you'd—I don't know what I thought." Every crazy theory that went through my head over the past few days suddenly feels ridiculously silly.

I was trying to let him figure out whatever it was he needed to figure out and that only served to work myself up in a frenzy. And now he's here.

I feel stupid but I can't control my emotions or the tears that keep threatening.

He leans back and frames my face so I'm forced to look in his eyes. "Blair. Shh. I'm sorry. I . . . I had a lot to think about. To question myself over. I shouldn't have taken the space and not explained it to you, but the race and the aftermath weighed on me."

"Let me be here for you."

"You were. You are. Don't you get that? It doesn't matter if I'm beside you or halfway across the world, I know you are."

"I'm sorry this all happened because of me."

"Don't you dare." He presses another kiss to my lips. "If it hadn't happened, that means I wouldn't have you. Have this." He sighs. "But you were right. Shit got out of hand. Rossi finding out. Paolo finding out. The stakes are too high and I just . . . I just needed time to think."

"Okay. And?"

"And you're my all of the above." He smiles shyly. "When all this is gone, you still will be."

"We lay low. Until the gala is over. Until you get a new contract."

"We fly under the radar—"

"Or fly backward like a hummingbird," I say softly.

"Or fly backward like a hummingbird." His smile widens. "I'm sorry I didn't communicate what I needed better."

"It's okay."

"No, it's not okay. You're mine, that's what you are. Every single part of you is mine, and I can't wait to be able to tell the world. Don't you get that? This mind. This heart. This body." He growls the last word out. "Baby, you are mine."

"That doesn't help when Monica sends me texts of you and Zola or you leave my place without a word. Do you know what it's like to feel like you're going crazy?" I chuckle self-deprecatingly, close my eyes, and sigh before scrubbing my hands over my face.

"I do. I feel it every time I think of you. Every time I want you."

"I'm sorry. My emotions are all over the place. Between the stress of the gala and then the accident and knowing it's because of me—"

He presses a finger to my lips. "Rossi did that because of his issues. He was reckless and dangerous and could have caused a massive accident. *That's not on you.*" I shake my head. I still can't believe Rossi did what he did. He could have taken lives. He should lose his seat.

"But still—"

"No *but stills.*"

"I'm just tired is all. Tired and overwhelmed and—"

"And I have the perfect cure for that."

I lift a lone eyebrow. "Of course you do. Sex, *right?*"

"A few orgasms wouldn't hurt, but no, that's not what I was thinking."

"You're being cryptic."

"And you are overwhelmed and need a break."

"Lach?"

"You have a flight scheduled for Friday night."

"To?"

"Home. Your parents keep telling you to come home and maybe that's what you need. A reset. Some time for yourself before the big gala. Some time to be with your family, just a few days—enough time to enjoy but not too much to get sick of them."

"Lachlan. That's . . ." *Just what I needed.* My heart melts in a puddle at his feet. "The perfect way to get me out of the way so you have more time with Zola," I tease. My smile is wide, and my heart suddenly feels lighter.

"That's exactly my plan. A Zola-fest of a weekend," he says as I stand up between his thighs and slide my hands around his neck.

"Thank you," I whisper and then kiss him. "You are always so thoughtful." Another kiss. "So considerate." This one a little more intense than the last. "So very mine."

His lips spread into a smile against my lips. "It feels good to say it, doesn't it?"

"So very mine."

Chapter Forty-Five

Lachlan

"TALK TO US," CRUZ NAVARRO SAYS AS HE SITS ACROSS FROM ME AT the bar.

"I'm not saying shit," I say and toss a poker chip on the table we're sitting at. "I call."

"If you're not saying shit then it *is* serious," Spencer Riggs says.

I lift my middle finger to the whole table. There are six of us drivers here at our monthly—or at least we say it's monthly, but it never is during the season—poker game. We're in a private room somewhere in the back of the Casino de Monte-Carlo. The same room, the same server, the same dealer as always.

People who act like we're nobody. Just how we like it.

And people who know if they keep their mouths shut about us being here, their tip will be ridiculous. *And that we'll continue to come back.*

This is the most normal we get to be. And it's always a fucking good time.

"Okay, so you aren't talking about your woman—*for now*—so let's talk about the other topic we're all avoiding," Navarro says.

I lift my eyebrows and play dumb. "The weather?"

Laughs bark out around the table. "Funny," Riggs says. "And Navarro, he may be avoiding it, but we aren't."

"Rossi," Finnegan says.

"Rossi," I murmur and bring a drink to my lips.

"Is it true?" Riggs asks.

"Is what true?" *Fuck. Maybe going drinking with the guys wasn't the best idea. Lies and alcohol don't always mix.*

"The part where he blamed the accident on the car when it looked a hell of a lot like it wasn't the car," Laurent states.

"The FIA fined him for impeding," Finnegan says.

"They did," I muse, not wanting to impart any opinion here. If I give one, then I have to explain why Rossi pulled the bullshit stunt he did.

Bullshit stunt? More like reckless driving that we're both so fucking lucky we walked away unscathed from.

Were there problems with his car? I have to believe the authorities—that yes, there were. That yes, he had issues. Do I have to wholeheartedly believe there wasn't malice or intent that played a part? The further away from the incident, the more I question that.

Would he really let emotions take over? Would he really risk his ride for next year? Would he really risk killing either or both of us?

I know that I wouldn't. But would he?

Then I remember the jolt of being hit. I feel the dizzying spin across the gravel, and I question myself for trying to reason against the evidence.

Wrecking is racing, but . . .

"What did Johann say about it?" McElroy asks.

I purse my lips and nod. "That it was bullshit. That it's twice this year in a very short fucking period that both of the Apex cars have touched and are out of the race. That too much money is being wasted and not enough answers are being provided." I shrug. "As far as what they've said to Rossi, I don't have a fucking clue, but there have been several meetings behind closed doors that I'm not privy to."

"And your thoughts on all of it?" Riggs asks.

"I think a lot of shit went down," I say carefully. Do I want to share with them everything? Fuck yes, it would be great to get it off my chest. But one random comment from one of the guys to another person and then there's a headline story in the media. People are digging into our pasts. Blair is identified and thrown to the wolves. It's not worth the fucking risk. I bite back all the words I want to say. "The FIA looked at it. They made their decision. And whether I think it's right or wrong, it's what it is."

"Neutral as fuck. Really?" Navarro asks. "That's all you're going to give us?"

I glance around at the eyes of all my friends. "You all have rides next year. I don't, so fuck yes, I'm going to be neutral as fuck. Wouldn't you be?"

Quiet murmurs arise as another hand is being dealt. They know how it feels to be on the bubble. They know how not having a contract causes uncertainty to own you and allows doubt to creep in. Doubt over if you really are as good of a driver as everyone thought you were. As you thought you were.

"So," Laurent says as he groans when he sees his cards and tosses them back to the dealer, folding, "then we're back to the woman." Everyone laughs. "You have to give us something. Who is she? Where'd you find her?"

I throw two cards into the pile and get two new ones. Shit. That didn't help my hand any. "Come on, guys, I don't kiss and tell," I say.

"God, you're so full of shit," McElroy says and throws his cards in and folds his hand. "When you slept with that model for however long it was, we all knew."

"Then there was the actress from Bordeaux. God, she was smoking hot," Finnegan says and takes a sip of his drink. "We all knew about her even though you said there wasn't shit happening."

They were my past. And none of them were as hot as Blair—my future.

"But this one," Riggs says. "There's something different about this one."

"Because I'm not telling you guys shit so there's something different?" I toss in poker chips for my ante. "Are your sex lives so boring you need to know more about mine?"

I get middle fingers from three of the five sitting around me.

"Nice deflection, asshole," Laurent teases.

"He's in *lurve*," Cruz says, drawing the word out ridiculously, and then motions to the pile of poker chips in the center of the table. "I bet this whole pot that that's what's going on here."

"Like you would know," I scoff.

He raises his eyebrows.

Shit. He does know. I forgot. The man is madly in love with his fiancée. "How fast we're all falling when we all swore we'd stay single forever," I joke.

"Not I," says Laurent, hand in the air and scooting back from the table. "I am having too much fun playing the field. Different women in different cities." He does the chef's kiss motion. "Not happening for a long-ass time."

Riggs leans back in his chair and eyes me over the rim of his glass, the platinum band on his left finger blaringly obvious to the rest of us. Proof that we do fall. "Hey, Lach? Don't look now but you just said *how fast we fall* and we all caught it." He pushes all his chips into the center of the table. "I'm all in. Are you?"

Motherfucker.

I nod my head and chuckle. "I've been all in. That's the only way to be."

Chapter Forty-Six

Blair

"I T'S BEEN GREAT HAVING YOU HOME," MY MOM SAYS AS WE SIT ON THE porch swing. The one constant that has moved with us from house to house during deployments.

But it's been here for the last ten years. Italy has become the Carmichael's second home, and it's always good to come back to it.

The breeze moves it gently and if I close my eyes, I can remember back to when I was a kid, and we'd have our heart-to-hearts on it regardless of the location.

Many nights we'd swing as the sun set or the crickets chirped, and I'd tell her about everything that was bugging me. This was our spot.

Apparently, it still is.

And that makes me smile even more because Lachlan was right. This is what I needed.

"It's good to be here."

"I know the house can be chaotic. I just hope you were able to get some time to relax and unwind."

"I did. I have been. It worked out perfectly—me flying out Friday night and going back today." The forty-eight hours home have been a godsend and, while the time might have been better spent double-checking all the details for the gala next week, that is what my staff is for. That is why I trust them.

And this time is what I needed for me. To have a short reprieve so that I can put my best foot forward with the massive undertaking that's coming to fruition in the next couple of days. "It was . . . nice. And it doesn't feel chaotic when I'm here. It just feels like home."

She slides an arm around me and pulls me closer as I rest my head on her shoulder.

"Good. I'm glad. No matter where you are in the world, wherever we are there will always be a home for you to come back to." She presses a kiss to the top of my head as I breathe in her perfume. "And I'm so impressed with you. The gala sounds like it's going to be spectacular."

"I can hope."

"I'm sure there will be a few snafus that happen, but isn't that how life is?"

"Hopefully they're nothing major."

"And if they are, I'm sure you'll handle them just fine." She rests her cheek against the top of my head. "Just think. It'll be over in a week and you'll find another incredible project to work on."

"That's true." And what is that next project? Where will the gala and its success—because it will be successful—steer me? But with the moments dwindling before I need to leave, I can't avoid the proverbial elephant in the room. "You haven't asked about Rossi," I say.

"I don't have to. You'll tell me if you want to tell me and if you don't, it's clear you're already over the moon about someone else, so we'll leave it at that."

I stiffen beside her and then laugh. "What makes you say that?" The weekend has been too short for me to get into the Lachlan aspect with her, so I haven't said anything.

"Blair Grace Carmichael. If you think I don't know what it looks like when my daughter is smitten, then you'd be sadly mistaken."

"Smitten?" I laugh the word out.

"Yes. Smitten. Sneaking off to have hushed phone calls. Goofy smiles when you receive a text. That lightheartedness about you. I mean, it's written all over you."

My sigh is my answer. "Maybe."

"Well, you'll tell me about it in time if you want to." She pats my leg. "The hardest and best part about letting your babies grow up is knowing that they'll share when they want to. And if they do, you as a mother best be listening."

"Olive juice, Mom."

"Olive juice, sweetheart."

We sit for a while longer, just enjoying each other's company. "Where'd Dad go, anyway? It's way too quiet for a Carmichael house."

She chuckles. "He took everyone out for ice cream so you and I could have some alone time. That's something you didn't always get, so I wanted to make sure you knew how important it was to us that you got that when you come back home."

"Thank you."

"No need to thank me."

"No, there is." I grab her hand and squeeze. "You and Dad raised me to believe in myself. To have strength in my convictions and trust my gut. But . . . I got lost there for a little bit. So lost that I didn't realize I'd handed that power over to Rossi. That I'd taken a back seat and forgotten all those things you'd instilled in me. Things with Rossi weren't bad, but they weren't good either. And I'd put up with that. Accepted that . . . until I befriended someone who showed me more about love with his words and his actions. I hadn't seen it until then."

"Skylar's been saying it all along."

"I know she has, but sometimes the people you know the longest become the white noise. It's only someone new who can make the static sound like music."

"And this new man of yours made you hear the music?"

I nod and smile, thinking about Lachlan. About the lessons I've realized I learned from my relationship with Rossi. And about how Lachlan truly made me hear a different tune.

"He did. He still does. But I never would have been able to hear that music if it weren't because you and Dad believed in me to begin with. You gave me a strong foundation, you continue to reinforce it and for that, I'll forever be grateful."

Chapter Forty-Seven

Lachlan

"**S**O YOU'RE TELLING ME THE DEAL IS ALMOST DONE?" I ASK Chandler—or actually I pant out to Chandler—since I'm on kilometer seven of my 10K run. I'm feeling it today. Poker night with the boys turned into drinks at Cruz's last night.

Too much excess on this body that's supposed to be a well-oiled machine. "It's almost done."

My shoulders sag and my head falls back as I stare at the sky. Tears well in my eyes. "Thank fuck."

"I'm trying to get you that top pick, Lach. Gravitas could be next level for you. Especially with talk about new ownership possibly coming in. An influx of marketing and cash."

Excitement races through me. So does relief.

Apex was where I'd wanted to stay originally, but truth be told, I've become disillusioned with them. Between their delay in pulling the trigger with me on a contract and their continued pacification of Rossi, I'm thrilled to get a chance at Gravitas.

New doesn't always mean better. It presents new challenges—learning a new team, new ways they do things, unforeseen risks—and yet, Gravitas is clearly showing to be the superior team of the two right now.

It seems Zola was right. Our association was good for me. Her mother thinking we were together had her calling in some favors—or more like influencing minds and opinions.

We scratched each other's backs but frankly, I think Zola got the short end of the stick in this deal.

I definitely owe her one—whatever that may be.

I replay Chandler's words in my mind. A three-year contract for a ridiculous amount of money. I mean, I'd be a dumbarse to turn it down and stay with a team who might be offering similar figures but doesn't seem to value me as much.

It's a no-brainer.

"I'm excited." I swear the stress dissipates with each passing second. "Can I sign the contract? Can I announce it? I want to break the news in my own terms rather than have it leaked to the press."

"In other words, you want to say *fuck you* to Rossi."

"No. It's not like that."

"It's not? Because the fucker tried to put you in a wall. It's him you have to be grateful for this contract." He clears his throat. "I'm pretty sure they were gunning for Rossi to sign but that stunt showed that he was a liability."

"Way to boost my ego," I say sarcastically.

"I don't sugarcoat. You know that."

"So when can we sign?"

"We're ironing out the last details in the contract. Early next week is what it looks like right now."

I make a mental note of it. The gala is Sunday. Sign the contract within a few days after. Then have a kick-arse race the following Sunday.

Once that's all done, no more hiding.

Hell. It looks like it's shaping up to be a perfect week.

Now if Blair will just come home, then all will be right with the world.

Chapter Forty-Eight

Blair

THE VALLEY IS LAID OUT BEFORE ME. IT'S VARYING SHADES OF GREEN with an occasional house sprinkled in.

A fairy tale.

That's what I used to call this valley. A place I could imagine a fairy tale taking place. One I'd create in my own imagination full of love and family and a prince of my dreams.

One I used to imagine as Oliver Rossi.

Funny how you grow up and things change.

Even funnier how you resist those changes so damn hard and then in the blink of an eye realized they were exactly what was needed.

Lachlan. The composer of my own personal music.

I miss him.

I love him. Like truly, deeply love him in a way I didn't know was possible. In a way they do in fairy tales.

All of the above.

I smile softly as the breeze picks up and gently tickles through my hair.

"We spent a lot of time out here on this damn rock."

I startle at the sound of Rossi's voice and even more that he's here. That he's back home. I turn to see him walking toward me, the shock still settling in. "What are you doing here? I don't understand."

238 | K. BROMBERG

A parental ambush.

But . . . the thought dissipates just as quickly. My parents wouldn't interfere. Ever. My conversation with my mom said just as much, and I hate that that was my first thought.

"I came home for a day to visit an old teammate from my karting days. He's in the hospital. Hospice."

"Oliver. I'm so sorry to hear that."

He shakes his head and waves a hand at me like he doesn't want it to derail this discussion. "On the way back to the airport, I stopped by to say hi to your parents. They always were good to me, but I could tell by the look on their faces that something was up. They were surprised to see me. Then they said you were here too . . . small world, huh?"

"Very." I struggle with how to feel. Here he's talking to me like he's running into an old friend while I'm still trying to process what he did to Lachlan.

I don't care what the FIA says. I know Rossi. I know his temper. I know what I *think* happened.

"I knew I'd find you here."

"Good. Great."

"You're mad."

My laugh is anything but amused. "Mad doesn't begin to describe how I feel seeing you."

"Look." He hangs his head. "I'm here to try and make things right. To put things to bed. To just . . . close this door so I can move on."

"Does that moving on include crashing into say . . . anyone I might date that you don't like?"

"That's not fair."

"Not fair?" I screech. "You could have fucking killed the both of you. Are you insane?"

His jaw clenches and I can see him bite back every bit of temper he has—and for Rossi, I know that's not exactly the easiest thing to do. "At this point, it doesn't matter what I say or what the FIA determined, you're going to believe whatever it is you want to believe, aren't you?"

"That's a cop-out answer if ever I've heard one. Can't be accused of anything if you don't commit to anything, right?"

"I deserve that," he says stoically, the muscles in his jaw pulsing.

"You deserve a lot more than that."

"Blair. Please."

I stare at him, my heart racing and head hurting, emotions in a constant eddy.

"Can I sit down next to you?" he asks, motioning to the rock.

I glance down at the rock and then back up to him. *No. Yes.*

But we need to get this over with before anyone actually gets hurt. "I can't forgive you for what you did."

He nods, that's the only answer he gives me. "May I?"

I struggle internally. I know that Lachlan has said to let it go, has made his own peace with the incident in his own way, but that doesn't fucking mean I'm as easygoing or as forgiving as he is. The struggle is real for me. "That depends," I finally say. "Am I getting Rossi or am I getting Oliver?"

"You're getting the man who doesn't know how the fuck to feel when it comes to what went down."

So Rossi. Got it. Then I'll give him Blair Fucking Carmichael.

"What went down? You mean the part where I hung on as long as I possibly could to you, but you aren't one to be hung on to? Or the part where you treated me like less than because feeding your ego was more important than maintaining your relationship? Or how about the part where you belittled me and the things that were important to me because you just couldn't find any fucks to give about anyone or anything but yourself? You mean those parts?"

He blows out a long, steady breath, and then takes a seat beside me without asking this time. "How about the part where you cheated on me?"

"First of all, I didn't cheat on you and second, should I ask you the same question? Because don't ask questions you can't answer yourself." He looks over and meets my eyes but doesn't speak. "I never cheated on you, Oliver. And I never lied to you. We just simply grew up and grew apart."

"And if I would have fought for you? Would it have made a difference?" he asks.

"Maybe. For a little while, but truth be told, Oliver, I don't like the way you fight if fighting involves wrecking your cars and putting everyone at risk."

"Blair—"

I hold up my hand to stop him. "You don't want this. Maybe as a teen you did, maybe you like the idea of it, of having someone who knows the real you and the real life that you left behind here when you went off to become an elite F1 driver, but not anymore. You aren't ready for a serious girlfriend."

"Glad you know what I want."

I study him. "I know you better than anyone so, yes, I do know. And

. . . it wasn't me anymore." I draw in a long, deep breath and try to figure out how we got here. "I've never been angrier at you in my life."

"We've known each other ten years and you've never been angrier at me than when you think I tried to crash into Evans. Wow. That says a lot."

"You could have killed both of you." I swallow over the lump of fear that thought creates. "And yes, while I'm not in love with you, Oliver, I'll always love you in some capacity. I do care about you and what happens to you. But my love for you doesn't give you the right to ruin what I have simply because it's not yours anymore."

He stares out at the valley below, the silence stretching between us. It gives me time to calm down. "I'm sorry," he says softly. "For a lot of things."

I know how hard that is for him to say. Just as I know I have to say something as well. "Thank you for keeping my secret. That would have been hard for you, but I appreciate that you respect me and my love for my job enough that you didn't put me or Lachlan on blast in the media."

"I thought about it."

"I'm sure you did." Rossi wouldn't be Rossi if he hadn't.

He hangs his head for a beat, staring at a rock he's picked up and is playing with. "The past few weeks have been . . . rough. Eye-opening. A bunch of shit I don't want to deal with but was forced to. The FIA. Reprimand meetings with Johann and Apex. The fallout with my contract talks. The media shitstorm." He pauses and his voice softens. "And realizing you were actually not mine anymore."

I want to believe the events of the past few weeks have changed him for the better, but I'm skeptical. Words are easy to say. Actions are the proof I need.

"I've learned some things from it. I've said fuck off to a lot of other things, but the one truth is I wasn't the man you deserved."

Wow. That was unexpected. Those six words were nowhere on my radar.

"Oliver—"

"No. Let me get it out. Let me get it out and then I can go back to being the asshole Rossi, which is a way more comfortable place for me."

"Okay. I'll be quiet."

"I don't deserve you. I never did. Not you. Not your patience. Not your friendship. Not your love. I took you for granted—for a long time—and I owe you a huge apology for that."

"Jesus, Oliver. You really know how to take a girl by surprise."

"Don't get used to it."

"I won't, just like I won't apologize that Lachlan loves me better than you did."

He chokes on his next breath. "Love, Blair? Really? Can't you let my body get cold before you move on?"

"You didn't mine."

"Yeah, but the women I slept with were placeholders until you came back to me."

Ouch. "That's even worse. Is that supposed to make me feel better?"

"Was your comment supposed to make me?" he asks, eyebrows raised.

Touché.

"No."

"The truth often hurts as I've come to understand these past few weeks." He swallows forcibly. "I don't like this man anymore, Blair. The one you fell in love with. It's so much easier to be the man I am now. The one who people steer clear of. The one people talk about. The one who doesn't get hurt."

It's a suit of armor.

One that I just proved to him he needed.

"It wasn't supposed to happen," I explain. "The Lachlan thing. It just did and then we were like *oh, shit* . . . and it just happened."

He nods but doesn't look at me. "I'm sorry I couldn't be who you needed me to be."

"Please don't apologize for who you are."

"It'll take me some time, but I'll get used to the idea of you being someone else's. Not for a long time, maybe, but eventually."

I hesitate at first but then rest my head on his shoulder—much like I used to in this exact spot for so many years. I feel like I'm betraying all the emotions I've been holding in over the past few weeks. The hurt. The anger. The disbelief. The betrayal. The fear. But at the same time, this is Oliver. The boy I used to know, the one that some part of me will always love, and somehow, we have to take steps to get back to where we can be good. Baby steps, but steps, nonetheless.

It will never be the same between us again, but it can be more settled.

Is that what I feel? Like this might be settled and I can have my friend back eventually?

"You know when we were teenagers, we'd sit here for hours. We'd—"

"Make out."

"Yes. Of course that's what you'd remember"—I nudge him—"but you'd talk endlessly about driving and what it would be like when you made it to Formula 1 and I'd sit here and daydream about being able to fly."

"Fly?" He snorts and then laughs. "That's cute. Really." He says the words, but I can hear his condescension in his tone. Can feel him thinking how ridiculous I was. "Cute but childish."

"Maybe," I murmur but smile to myself.

Did I just test him? Maybe subconsciously I did.

A small test to make sure what I already knew—that I made the right decision. That I picked the right man in the end.

Pick the man who says your ridiculous, whimsical dreams were awesome.

Not childish.

Not cute.

But awesome.

God, I can't wait to get home to him.

Chapter Forty-Nine

Blair

"**C**LOSE YOUR EYES."

"They're closed and you have a blindfold on me. That makes it kind of hard to see," I joke.

"Mmm," Lachlan murmurs from behind me as his lips kiss their way down the curve of my shoulder and fire every nerve he didn't already bring to life with the last kiss.

I can hear some rustling of paper. A weird noise that sounds like wheels. Wheels? I'm so confused. And then the sound of something—a box perhaps—being set down with a thump.

"What are you doing, Lachlan Evans?"

"You do know how much I want to show you off to the world as mine, right? How bad I want to utter the fucking words, *she's mine?*"

"No, but damn." His words make me stand taller and pull my shoulders back. "She's mine," I whisper.

"Exactly. I am so proud to call you mine. and I can't wait until all this bullshit is over so I can say it. I sign my contract in a few days. The gala will be over and will have been incredible. Then we can just kind of step into existence as us without having to so much as say a word."

"Promise?"

"God, Tink. I promise."

I smile. After so many years of being in the background, I can't wait to be front and center. To be . . . oh shit.

"What was that oof noise you just made?" he asks.

"I can be yours all I want but . . . *my job.*"

"Don't be mad, but I had my lawyer look into it. There's nowhere in any Formula 1 employees' contract that says that an employee can't date a driver on the circuit. Nowhere. There are rules on fraternization with bosses, etcetera, but not a driver. She's looked through many iterations of them over the years so if Paolo wants to make an issue of this, if his boss's boss wants to, then all he has to do is look at the incredible gala you're putting on tomorrow as proof that you can do your job and do a damn good job at it."

"But . . ." I open my mouth and close it. The last thing I want to do is ruin the mood by explaining that Paolo fears Monica is "helping" in return for a favor. And how weird it looks that all of a sudden, my boyfriend signs with the company she has huge influence with.

It all makes my brain hurt and is the most fucked up set of circumstances of coincidence I've ever been a part of.

I shake my head and chuckle. "It's a tad weird having this conversation while blindfolded."

"Took you long enough to ask." He chuckles. "Okay. You can open your eyes."

I slowly remove the blindfold, blink a few times to get used to the light in my place, and then do a double take when I see the rack of dresses in front of me. And not just any dresses. We're talking elaborate dresses with beading and sequins and gorgeous colors.

"Lachlan. What is—"

"I know it's late to the game and I'm lame for thinking of this so close to the gala, but I know you've been stressing over your dress and the tailor who is behind fitting it and . . . I should have had the forethought to think of this sooner. So I called a designer I've worked with in the past and she sent me over a rack of dresses in your size."

I stare at him and then move toward the dresses, running my hands over every single one of them. Dresses that are clearly designer *and* way out of my budget. "Thank you for your thoughtfulness but—"

"But you're not turning me down." He chuckles. "The bill has already been picked up so don't use that as an excuse." He leans in and brushes his lips over mine. "You're going to look incredible in all of them. Picking which one will be the hard part."

My hands go to his cheeks and hold him there. "You're the sweetest. I don't deserve you."

"Nah, it's me who doesn't deserve you." Then he points to the table. "And then there's those to choose from."

I take in the three clear cases of Christian Louboutin shoes with their gorgeous red soles and icepick heels. "Lach. I can't . . ." But my fingers itch to touch their gorgeousness.

He smirks. "Just think of them as a down payment."

"Them?"

"Yes, I took the pleasure of buying several different styles for you."

"Wait. A down payment?" I ask as I struggle with what to focus on— the dresses or the shoes.

"Mm-hmm."

"On what?" I ask.

He steps up behind me and wraps his hands around my waist and pulls me back against him. I can already feel his cock, hard and ready. My body reacts viscerally to the feeling. "On you being naked, sitting on my face, wearing only those."

"Oh." My voice cracks and body fires to attention. "In that case." I laugh as he spins me around, his hips pressing me against the table as his lips capture mine.

"That's what I thought," he says. And then when he kisses me again and I twist my fingers in the hair at the nape of his neck, his good deeds aren't forgotten . . . they're just overshadowed momentarily by the intoxication of his kiss. "Hey, Blair, I think you should try the shoes on. *Now.* The dresses can wait."

"Thought you'd never ask."

Chapter Fifty

Blair

THE AMPHITHEATER IS A MASS OF WHO'S WHO FROM HOLLYWOOD, from the racing world, and from the elite of the elite. For thirty-five thousand dollars a plate, the price tag to attend isn't for the faint of heart.

I look up from behind my mask and across the room and meet Lachlan's eyes. He hasn't been very far from me all night. Close enough to give me a look here and there. Near enough to walk behind me and brush a hand on my lower back. Always present with a quick text to tell me how beautiful I look.

I went with the red dress. It's floor-length with embellishments on the bodice, and I feel like a freaking queen in it. It hugs my curves but gives enough room to move freely without feeling confined. I'm a bigger girl and finding a dress I feel sexy and confident in that I don't worry all night what people look at me and see is an incredible feeling.

Especially on a night like tonight.

Only a few more hours and the stress will be gone. And my own personal victory celebration that I pulled this off will most definitely be on.

My head feels like it's on a constant swivel as I take in the crowd, the television crews, and Tori Michelle killing it on the stage.

"Blair?"

I turn to find Paolo. He's standing there in a tuxedo, his masquerade mask in his hand, and a drink that he's been nursing all night to appear to be drinking but not because he's technically still working.

I, on the other hand, haven't had a drink all night because I need to be in control of all of my faculties.

That, and Lachlan set out a very old, ridiculously expensive bottle of wine for us to celebrate back at the hotel room later.

I will be staying with him tonight. There is nothing that would prevent that.

It feels like everything is falling perfectly into place for us. His contract with Gravitas that will be signed soon. This gala—fingers crossed—going off without a hitch. The impending freedom for us to just be as a couple, whether that being is us out in public or tucked away at his condo. It doesn't matter. What matters is we don't have to care anymore.

And that is the absolute icing on the cake.

"It's going well," I state above the music.

"It is. Tori's fantastic," he says as she converses with the audience from the stage on the far side of the room. "Most performers who give their time for free, typically cut corners. It does not seem that she's done that."

"From what I can tell, she hasn't." The audience laughs at something she's said.

He studies me for a beat. "You did a great job, Blair. Incredible. You made us, our department, our cause . . . all of them look great. I see bright things in your future."

I nod and wish desperately for a drink about now to give me the liquid courage to say the things I want to say to him. To stand up for myself when I haven't been able to.

But the last thing I want to do is jinx this night. Jinx its success.

So I say a strangled, "Thank you," and then make my way toward the backstage area.

I'm stopped by a staff member and asked a question. Flagged down by another driver to tell me I did a good job. Stopped and met the stare of Rossi and gave the same soft smile back after he mouths "Good job," to me.

It feels like a full-circle moment, and I let it sink in.

"Blair?"

"Yes?" I look over to Kylie, one of the event assistants.

"We're having the staff round up the drivers right now for their introductions. We're telling them fifteen minutes."

"Great. Thank you."

"Tori is set up to call them up there. Just like we planned, they will each be handed envelopes with the top twenty contributors to tonight's event. One by one, the drivers will read their names off and thank them for being so charitable. We've made sure that the cameras are set up to show the driver's announcement as well as the donor in the crowd."

"God, the camera aspect just complicates everything."

"It does, but we've raked in so much more money this year because of it. I mean, triple from previous years." Kylie grins. "That has to at least net us all a raise and an extra week of vacation," she teases.

"I wouldn't hold my breath." I laugh. "But you do have my undying gratitude for all that you've done."

"That has to be enough. I mean . . . maybe a hot driver will fall for me as I hand them the envelope."

I snort and think of the peppermints sitting in my clutch right now. "Stranger things have happened."

Chapter Fifty-One

Lachlan

"**Y**OUR MOTHER KEEPS STARING AT US," I MUTTER TO ZOLA WHO'S standing beside me. I meet Blair's eyes and devour her with my stare. "Does it matter?" she whispers.

"*Carlos Bustos*," the emcee says on the stage beyond the curtain. The audience applauds as Carlos moves from stage left into the spotlight to highlight the sponsor inside his envelope.

"You have what you want—the contract you're signing tomorrow. I have what I want—another night of reprieve from Baron," she says. "And you're about to get your heart broken this week when I break up with you." She grins.

"*Hughes Laurent*," the emcee calls out and Laurent moves toward the stage to another round of applause.

"I didn't do this to gain favor for the contract, Zola. You know that. I did it because I was trying to help you."

"I know." She presses a kiss to my cheek. "And I'm forever grateful."

"Excuse me a moment," I say when I see Blair veer off into a small room off the side of the stage.

"You're the last to go. Don't be late," she says about the envelope in my hand.

"I won't." I scurry after Blair and close the door behind me as I step into the room. "God, you look so good I could eat you," I murmur and brush my lips over hers.

"Well, hello there," she purrs.

My cock's already hard. That's all it takes with her is one fucking kiss and I'm a goner.

"You've done an incredible job tonight. I'm so proud of you."

"Thank you."

"And, baby, I can't fucking wait to collect on that down payment later."

"Promise."

"You bet your arse I promise. Those red lips of yours. I want them wrapped around my—"

"I'm well aware where you want them wrapped." She pushes against my chest and wipes her thumb over my lips to presumably remove her lipstick. "You need to go. You're up soon."

"I know."

I brush my lips over hers one more time and then open the door to find Monica Chamalet reaching for its handle. There is a shocked look on her face. One that has me praying that fucking red lipstick isn't still on my lips.

Oh. Fuck.

"Monica," I say and offer a strained smile as she looks over my shoulder and no doubt sees Blair and her smeared lipstick.

"How dare you?" she spits out in a low even tone. "Zola. She's—you're—you're a cheating sack of shit. How dare you—"

"*Spencer Riggs,*" the emcee calls out.

"I can explain," I say calmly with my hands up. "It's not what you think."

"Not what I think?" Her eyes widen and her voice escalates.

I look around the room and Zola sees me the minute I see her. Her eyes are wide and dread etches in every line of her face. "Mother," she shouts as she scurries across the room.

"Blair? Where's Blair?" a shorter man asks, one of her assistants I believe.

"*Cruz Navarro,*" the emcee says.

"Here," she says, raising her hand and scurrying past me and out of the office toward him. Good. She needs to be gone right now. She's not a part of this scheme.

But as much as I know that and Zola knows it, the glare that Monica levels at Blair is brutal.

"Mum," Zola says. "It's not what you think. I promise. It's . . . we're not together. I needed a break from you and the Baron thing and so Lachlan agreed to help me. To pretend. To—"

"Use you to get to me," she says, not a single emotion on her face. But the ice in her tone says enough. In fact, it says it all.

"No. Never," I say resolutely.

"It wasn't like that, Mum. I promise. It was him being a good friend to me."

"Of course, he was." Her smile is tight.

"I assure you—"

"You just don't ever listen," Zola shouts at her mother.

"*Lachlan Evans*," the emcee calls. I stand there and stare at the two of them—mother and daughter—who are so alike but so very different.

"Lachlan," the stagehand calls over and beckons me toward her.

Everything is happening too fast. I need to right things with Monica. To explain. To convince her. To have Zola convince her.

"Lachlan," the stagehand repeats again as I look at both women and then move toward her.

"Lach," Zola calls out and grabs my arm. Flustered I shrug her off me. "Lachlan, I've got this. I'll handle her. Some woman is lucky enough that you love her. You need to stop hiding it and show her off to the world."

I stare at Zola. I hear her words as I'm all but pushed onstage. The next few moments are a blur.

You deceived Monica.

The lights from the stage.

You haven't stood up for the woman you love.

The applause from the audience.

You've hidden truths to protect your own career.

The reading of the name from my envelope.

This is not the man you are.

Blair is right in front of the stage, and I meet her eyes. She looks as concerned as I feel. But there's nothing I can do right now.

This is not the man Dad raised you to be.

Not a goddamn thing.

Blair deserves so much better than this.

"There's one more thing," I say into the mic when the applause has died down. "One very important person we need to thank."

I stand there looking at stage right where both Monica and Paolo stand. Her with her affluence and entitlement and him with his ridiculous parameters.

I shake my head as I look at them. Haven't I been all these things over the past few months? Not standing up for the woman I love? Hiding away from the world because I fear the fallout? Not believing in myself or my abilities nor the strength of what Blair and I have?

There is so much going on in my head. So many things I want to say but know I shouldn't. So many lines I'm about to cross and leap over them gladly.

"Blair Carmichael. Can you come up here?"

Blair eyes me dubiously from the audience but climbs the stairs cautiously until she's on the stage. Center spotlight to be exact. Right where she deserves to be.

"So small confession. I know Blair. Blair is . . ." I meet her eyes across the small space and see the tears welling in her eyes. "*She's incredible.* You see, Blair stepped up into this role when the prior coordinator left. An event this size, with so many facets, would take at least six months to put together. Blair did it in about three." The crowd cheers loudly, and I watch as Blair's cheeks flush. *God, she's beautiful.* "And I know this because I love this woman." More people cheer, probably not realizing what type of love I'm talking about here. "She's mine and I couldn't be prouder of her." Expressions begin to shift as the crowd realizes what I'm saying. "She's had to organize this whole, incredible event, while pretending she wasn't mine for fear she might be fired or accused of impropriety for simply loving who she loves. So I want to announce it here and now. This"—I hold out my hands to the entire room—"is all because of Blair's hard work. Her dedication. Her attention to detail."

The crowd erupts in applause. I can see Paolo looking on from stage right, and I meet his eyes. There might even be a little *try to fire her* in my look.

But even with everyone around us—a crowd, a telecast, everything—I feel like it's just Blair and me, like it's been for the past few months.

I'm sick of hiding. I'm sick of playing the game. She's risked it all for me, isn't it time I do the same for her?

"She got this position because she earned it. She nailed this gala tonight because that's what she does. It has nothing to do with dating me and everything to do with what an incredible person she is." I look over to her and her wide eyes and her nervous smile. "I love you, Blair, and I'm so very proud of you for this incredible event you put on tonight and for all the people you are helping with the charitable contributions raised because of it."

The crowd erupts again, and I walk off to the side of the stage to allow Blair the spotlight she deserves. To let her accept the praise she deserves. And my heart beats out of my chest with pride.

I wait for her backstage.

And when she walks off, I don't give a flying fuck who is back there—Monica, Paolo, Rossi, Zola—I wrap my arms around her and plant a huge kiss on those sexy red lips of hers.

This. This is what's been missing from tonight.

When I lean back and look at her, I know there's no one else for me. Ever. "You, Blair Carmichael, are fucking everything. The moon, the stars, and the goddamn sky. I might have overstepped by saying those things in front of all those people. Well, okay, in front of the whole world. Sorry, baby. But I'm so proud of you, of what you've achieved, and of the woman you are. I love you. Wholeheartedly. All of the above."

She leans her forehead against mine and simply smiles, her happiness palpable.

She's mine. And now, everyone knows it.

Chapter Fifty-Two

Blair

THE NIGHT IS A TOTAL BLUR.

Between congratulations and hugs from what feels like anyone and everyone to being able to stand beside Lachlan with my arm hooked through his or fingers linked with his and officially be his girlfriend . . . the entire night feels like a surreal dream that I was able to take part in, enjoy, and bask in the accolades.

And while I can still hear people partying out in the ballroom, I am done.

With my duties.

With the event.

With having to hide.

And it feels glorious.

Lachlan is getting the car while I collect my shoes—which have long since been off—and my clutch.

"Blair? Do you have a minute?"

I stutter at the sound of Paolo's voice. The last thing I want is my night ruined, but I stop and turn to face him. "Hmm?"

My lack of response must tell him all he needs to know because he approaches with his hands up in surrender. "I'm here to eat crow. That's all." He smiles genuinely. "I wanted to reiterate what an incredible job you did with the event. And I wanted to apologize for making you feel like you had to hide parts of who you were. I was wrong in doing that. What I should have done was let you be you, let your life be what it is, and if questions arose, gone to bat for you. But I didn't. I was too busy covering my own ass instead of realizing that you were just making it look better." He holds his hand out for me to take. "Apology accepted?"

Wow. Tonight is a night of revelations and I'm the benefactor of all of them.

"Apology accepted."

"Good." He nods his head definitively. "Now I can't wait to see what new idea you come up with next."

I stare at him. "What do you mean?"

"Well, you proved you could kick ass with an existing event. Now it's time for you to create one on your own. One that's one hundred percent your brainchild."

"Paolo . . ."

"You deserve the promotion. You really did a phenomenal job."

"Thank you."

"Now go and enjoy the rest of your night."

My grin is ear to ear as I head out to the valet just as Lachlan is pulling up in an obscenely sleek and sexy-looking car whose motor purrs.

He hops out, rounds the front of it, and before I can even step to the door, he's opening for me, he pulls me against him and kisses me in a soul-searing kiss.

My head dizzies and I forget where we are and who is watching.

But as it ends, as he looks at me with that gorgeous gleam in his eyes, I realize, I don't care who is watching.

We don't have to hide anymore.

"Lachlan Evans, you are incredible."

He quirks an eyebrow. "Now . . . what exactly do you think I could collect from you for a down payment on those Louboutin heels . . ."

I throw my head back and laugh before kissing him again. "How about all of the above?"

Chapter Fifty-Three

Blair

LACHLAN'S PLACE IS BRIGHT AND AIRY, AND IT FEELS SO GOOD TO BE here—to be somewhere else with him—than just hidden in my place.

"Tell me, Miss Carmichael, what would you like to do today?"

I glance up from my phone where I just might be scrolling all of the articles reviewing the event last night. The people squealing about Tori Michelle. The Formula 1 fans who are thrilled with seeing their driver cleaned up and wearing a tuxedo. And my personal favorite, the ones saying that the speech where my Lachlan Evans declared his love for me, was the best thing they've ever heard.

That it made them believe in the idea of love again.

That and the endless texts from Skylar saying how damn dreamy Lachlan seems and she must meet him STAT to verify that he is, in fact, good enough for me.

I glance around his bedroom, at the red soles thrown haphazardly on the floor, at the fancy dress left in a pile as we expressed our love for each other, and then back to the man I'm head over heels in love with.

"I can think of a hundred things to do with you." Walk the streets hand in hand with you. Kiss you in public. Never leave this bed or your incredible touch. "But the only thing that matters is I get to do it with you."

He crawls onto the bed and sits in front of me, his hands braced on either side of my hips. He dips his head down and teases my lips with a kiss so tender, so featherlight, that it sends chills over my skin. "How did you know that is exactly what I was thinking?"

"Kismet," I say.

"I can think of a lot of things you can kiss, Tink. So maybe we'll do that first and then we'll venture out."

"Yeah. I think we need to work up an appetite first."

He lifts a hand to his forehead and salutes. "Lachlan Evans, reporting for duty."

We collapse into a fit of laughter . . . that shortly thereafter slips into moans.

Chapter Fifty-Four

Lachlan

I'M FUCKING EXHAUSTED.

And exhilarated.

It's been an incredible few days. Days where I may have stressed over my speech at the masquerade ball while fielding apologetic calls from Zola. Apologies that I had to explain weren't hers to give since her mom's blow up wasn't her fault. Both felt insignificant though, because the best part about these few days is they've been eventless.

Eventless unless you consider I've fallen even more in love with Blair during the period—if that's even possible.

Is it bad when I gloated to my dad on the phone earlier about this? About how much I appreciated his advice on what to do, but didn't take it? I did what I needed to, I stayed true to who I was, and nothing bad happened. In fact, quite the opposite.

So I walk into Monza like a new man. Add to it, Blair's coming to town in a few days, and she actually gets to stand in the Apex garage as I take the track. No more peppermints left on her desk in clandestine operations. I finally get a good-luck kiss from her before I get into the car.

It's time for us to start our own pre-race tradition, and I can't wait to see what that becomes. The possibilities are endless.

The other incredible fucking news is the weight will finally be lifted off my shoulders. It should break in the media later today that I'm moving over to Gravitas. I signed the contract this morning. Once their powers that be sign it, it's a done deal. I'll switch my blue for orange. I'll race for a new team for the first time in my Formula 1 career.

God, I have a great feeling about this race. About fucking everything.

To new beginnings.

When I walk into the paddock, there's a crew of people surrounding Oliver Rossi. It looks like they're congratulating him.

He must have signed with Apex again.

Doesn't exactly make sense considering what he did to me, but with me about to sign with Gravitas, I can see why they're holding on to him. He's still one of the best drivers on the grid and Apex is due for a great season. Just hopefully not as good as Gravitas's.

I bypass the pseudo-celebration and head toward my side of the garage.

"Hey, Lach."

"Hey," I say to my jack man.

"Did you hear?"

"Hear what?" I ask.

"About Rossi."

"What about him?"

"He just signed a three-year deal with Gravitas racing."

My feet falter. My heart stops. My head whips over to where Rossi is standing, a grin on his face . . . and looking my way.

What the fuck?

"Rossi?" I ask but I'm not exactly sure what I'm asking. "How?"

I signed the fucking contract.

But they hadn't signed their part yet.

Monica.

It has to be fucking Monica.

"Apparently someone over there didn't like some game you played." He shrugs and grins. "Then again, all's fair in love and racing, right?"

What the actual fuck?

Epilogue

Lachlan
ONE YEAR LATER

"WHERE ARE YOU TAKING ME?"

I look over to Blair as I play with the wine cork in my pocket I'm saving for her. *She's going to want to keep this one.* She's across from me in the seat of the private jet, her face is pressed against the window as she looks out to the miles of ocean beneath us.

The crew has been informed not to tell her where we're going.

But after the past few months, this is what I needed. To do something for her. To show her how much she means to me. To let her know that I'm more than fine with losing the Gravitas contract because I lost it knowing what I did was right.

By not hiding.

Besides, they can have Rossi. For a man who swore up and down he'd never race for that team, it's amazing what desperation will lead you to do.

I was the only one Apex offered a contract to. I didn't know it at the time when I turned it down, though. The *three-year* deal they offered, along with the decision to switch engine manufacturers in the coming year, was a no-brainer. *That* I accepted.

Rossi can navigate the new waters. I'll stick with the ones that valued me even when I thought they didn't and proved it with the contract they offered in the end.

And as I watch her gaze out the window in wonder, I know it was all fucking worth it. Every agonizing minute of hiding. Every moment of feeling like an arsehole for not speaking up for us sooner.

It all led to right now and fuck if I couldn't be more right about anything in my life.

"Land. There's land," she shrieks as we begin to fly over some.

"Yes. There's land." I laugh and lean forward and press a kiss to her lips. "And pretty soon, you'll have to put the blindfold on so you don't ruin your surprise."

"I don't need a surprise, Lachlan Evans. I just need you." Another lingering kiss. "And you were the best surprise of all."

Epilogue Two

Blair

IT'S COLD.

I'll give him that. I don't need to lift this blindfold to know that much.

It's cold, despite the heavy jacket he put on me, and the terrain is uneven.

For the life of me I have absolutely no idea where we are.

But isn't that how this whole adventure has been with him? A random moment in time led us to this, right here, right now. To the contentment I feel deep in my bones and a happiness that seems so damn endless.

"I appreciate the fact that you want to surprise me, Lach, but this is getting a little ridiculous."

"Patience, Tink."

"Ha. I think I've given you plenty of patience," I tease, because I feel like I've been blindfolded forever.

I feel the warmth of Lachlan's body behind me as he wraps his arms around me and presses a kiss to the crown of my head. "Just one more minute," he says. "I want it to be perfect."

"I don't want perfect. I just want you."

"You remember that first night? I told you about the hummingbird and you told me you wanted to fly?"

"Yes?" I say slowly, trying to figure out what I'm missing. What he's doing.

"I can't give you the ability to fly, but I can give you this."

And with those words he lifts my blindfold off and I'm hit with the most incredible sight I've ever seen.

The sky around me, over me, before me, dances in green and blue and yellow lights. They are everywhere we look.

The northern lights.

I feel like I'm in a snow globe of never-ending amazement.

"Lachlan," I say, offering him a glance but afraid to take my eyes off the wonder all around.

"I know," he whispers. "It's incredible. It's better than I thought. It's . . ."

"*Everything*," I say. "You did this for me?"

"I wanted to give you part of your childhood dream." He links his hands with mine. "We can pretend we're flying though."

"I don't need to. This is enough. This is more than enough. This is—"

"Oh look, a shooting star."

"What? How? Where?" I spin to look where he's pointing, confused how there can be a shooting star with all this light—my head fuzzy with the incredulity of this moment. But it's my gasp I hear next.

"Right here," Lachlan says from where he's down on one knee with a diamond ring—his supposed shooting star—in his hand.

"Lachlan." His name comes out like a warning when I mean anything but.

"You asked me that night on the golf course what my wish was, and I said I couldn't tell you or it wouldn't come true." Tears well in his eyes. My heart has never been fuller. More complete. More anything in my entire life. "I'm so glad I didn't say anything. That I didn't tell you to try and win you over. There was no way I would spoil this wish, because this was the only one I ever wanted. *You.* You and all of the above with you were my wish, Blair. Screw the twenty-one days because I want a lifetime. Will you marry me?"

"Yes. A million times over, yes." I drop to my knees, put my hands to his cheeks, and kiss him.

The world dances on around us, the sky celebrating all that is good in it.

But all it takes is one look beneath those lights to know I got the best part of it.

I got him. Lachlan Evans.

And all of the above.

Did you enjoy Blair and Lachlan's story? Do you want to meet the rest of the drivers in the *Full Throttle* series?

Be ready for another lap around the circuit in these upcoming books, available for preorder now.

Off The Grid – For Spencer Riggs, his team owner's daughter is off-limits. But weren't limits made to be pushed? Available now.

On The Edge – Cruz Navarro needs to be on his best behavior to earn a lifetime branding deal and faking a relationship to the public is the best way to do that. Until faking it becomes making it. And this reformed playboy falls hard. Available now.

Out of Control – The bad boy of Formula 1, Oliver Rossi, is coming August 2024.

Looking for another sexy racecar driver to read until my next one comes out? Have you met Colton Donavan yet in **The Driven Series?** He's a reckless, bad boy with a good guy heart buried underneath. Available now.

About the Author

New York Times Bestselling author K. Bromberg writes contemporary romance novels that make you work to get your happily ever after. She likes to write strong heroines and damaged heroes, who we love to hate but can't help but love.

Since publishing her first book on a whim in 2013, Kristy has sold over two million copies of her books across twenty different countries and has landed on the New York Times, USA Today, and Wall Street Journal Bestsellers lists over thirty times. (*She still wakes up and asks herself how she got so lucky for all this to happen.*)

A mom of three, Kristy finds the only thing harder than finishing the book she's writing is navigating parenthood during the teenage years (send more wine!). She loves dogs, sports, a good book, and is an expert procrastinator. She lives in Southern California with her family.

Made in United States
Orlando, FL
17 June 2024

47985786R00152